In This Room...

a novel

Bradley Carter

This is a work of fiction.
The characters and events described herein are
imaginary and are not intended to refer to
specific places or to living persons alive or
dead.

No part of this publication may be reproduced,
distributed, or transmitted in any form or by
any means, including photocopying,
recording, or other electronic or mechanical
methods without the prior written permission
of the publisher except for brief quotations
embodied in critical reviews.

Facebook.com/**WrittenByBradleyCarter**

Instagram: **@WrittenByBradleyCarter**

Twitter: **@WrittenByBC**

www.theAcorporation.com

ACKNOWLEDGMENTS

Jaime Thorn…editor
Justin Bridges…editor
Amy Wilke, Troy Duran, Briana Cope,
Matthew O'Toole, Jennifer Mearling,
Mike Turpin, Christopher Wilke, Kat Zuhlke,
Greg Halter, Katie Gourley, Leslie Cornett,
Jessica Brown, Julie Ann Price, Jana Bridges,
William Renkosik, and the Booktastic Book Club

In memory of
Robb "Bulldog" Walter III
1979-2021

PREFACE

Here is my fair warning. This story may shock, frighten, and disturb you. At times, it can be brutal, horrifying, and unsettling. It might strike your nerves and punch you in the gut. You'll find it has its share of violence, sex, and death, and midway through this tale, you may likely ask how I can write such dreadful and horrible things. How can I put these characters through such torment? What kind of sick and twisted mind do I possess? Well, my friends, the answer is simple: I know how the story ends, and believe me when I tell you, nothing is as it seems.

Suppose you've read or listened to my previous novels; you should know by now, in my fictional universe, you can expect misdirection. After all, my entertainment comes from creating yours. I like to play around with all the buttons and switches when you allow me access to your mind. You may not notice my sliding hand or where I strategically place certain clues. You may not recognize the methods I use to make you second-guess yourself. But don't worry. At the end of this hell-bound rollercoaster ride, I promise to return you safely to the gate.

I've always had a thing for dark thrillers and not-so-happy-endings. When I was younger (around freshman year of high school), my grandmother introduced me to a woman named Ruby, who lived across the street from a Hardee's restaurant in my hometown of Evansville, Indiana. Ruby was a former ghostwriter for the original Twilight Zone series, a show I was, and still am, very much a fan of. Imagine my surprise when she showed me a certificate signed by Rod Serling and a few manuscripts she had written that later became televised episodes. More than anything, I wanted to be a storyteller in some shape or form, but throughout my youth, it just wasn't in the cards.

Fast forward to 2018, when I'm helping a recently divorced friend of mine move his belongings from his half-million-dollar home into a small apartment. While touring this beautiful house, I discovered each room had a story to tell, and not all of them were pleasant. Despite his losses, my friend's life had changed for the better, in that his past no longer plagued him. By then, I had written my first (or maybe second and third) book, and needless to say, on our ride back to the city, the premise and title for another popped into my head. I thought about it for days while working on whatever project I had going on at the time, and without an outline or structure, inevitably, "In This Room…" remained an idea I had to set on the back-burner.

As many people know, writing is not my only passion. Around the time I began this venture, I was also a paramedic responding to 9-1-1 calls on an ambulance. Not once have I entertained the idea of writing based on my career. With no offense to those who do, I personally feel basing a story on my experience at a job to be a crutch. Exploiting other people's misfortune doesn't sit right with me; however, it does tend to spawn new ideas. There's a popular phrase in my profession: "You can't make this shit up." Granted, I create fictional stories involving medics and EMTs, which I have done in the past, but only when it's beneficial to a more creative purpose. With that said, here's the part where I'm a hypocrite, but keep in mind, it's for a good reason.

My unit was called to a person suffering from a mental breakdown. When I arrived on the scene, I was greeted by police officers who told me they had responded to a domestic dispute. Inside this home, I found a young man (early twenties) on a rampage, shouting and screaming at his wife, members of the fire department, the police, and of course, at me. His gorgeous wife (also in her early twenties) stood in the kitchen, crying to us that she didn't have a clue what caused her husband's outbursts. She was more concerned about their son, a toddler, in his bedroom.

Everyone tried their best to talk this guy down to a calmer state of mind, but our efforts were useless, and he kicked us out, even the police, and told us to mind our own business. A little over an hour later, we were dispatched to return to the same address; only now, the incident had escalated to a hostage situation and a SWAT standoff with the police. The husband had his child in the home and refused to come outside. His wife had been trying to get in, but the doors and windows were locked.

The situation lasted a few hours and eventually ended with a peaceful surrender. Still, for some inexplicable reason, the entire event seemed to fit perfectly with my ideas for a novel about a house where good things go bad. At the time of writing this, that specific call is the only real-life experience I have used as inspiration.

So I had two (and a half) main characters to stir together in a dramatic story, but I needed a cause, a reason for someone to go crazy and drag his family on through his torment. Again, I had to let "In This Room…" simmer on the stove while I tended to other projects.

Hopscotch to 2019 and land on two other projects that made their way to the top of my list: Bodhi Crocodile and Anastasia Euthanasia. How it came about, I have no clue, but the idea of writing and releasing three standalone stories linked together had tickled my brain. Having each one connected by nothing more than a row of businesses on a downtown street in some big city seemed to be a challenge I was willing to accept. A diner, a massage parlor, and a hair salon, sharing the same block. Bodhi Crocodile would reference the restaurant, Anastasia Euthanasia would reference the massage parlor, but I needed a third to involve the hair salon. What better project to integrate than "In This Room..." for the hair salon?

Of course, what I didn't know at the time was that Bodhi Crocodile would take on a life of his own, and the other two projects would essentially have to wait until his story expanded into a three-part series. However, if you read or have read Bodhi, you can find the other businesses mentioned, as well as Addelyn Delacroix, a supporting character from "In This Room..."

Nearing completion of Bodhi Crocodile Part 3: Divinity, I began noting and drafting things for Anastasia, but I figured the Delacroix family had waited long enough. On the lookout for plausible reasons of insanity, I eventually discovered two more real-life events to inspire the book. Of course, I can't mention them here, because unfortunately, they can spoil the plot. Now, don't be a cheat. Don't go searching the back of this book for the answers. You'll have to wait until the end.

Meanwhile, I hope you enjoy this novel. I hope it tags you in all the right places at all the right times. If I had to choose a story of mine to become an episode of The Twilight Zone, this would be it.

—Bradley Carter

Inspired by four actual events.

"We are pleased to have helped you. Goodbye."

In This Room...

Did you know each time you recall a memory, the details stretch farther away from the truth? Time has a tendency to warp perception. That's what the doctor said. He said evocation is not static. People believe they know the specifics of how an event occurred, and they become so convinced, they are willing to bet their lives on it. This Ph.D. said recalling an event in precise detail is impossible. What you see comes from your impressions of hindsight, not from the original memory. The psychologist, or psychiatrist, said there are many reasons for this, though none are specific. Some people see what they want to see. Some remember the story the way they wish it happened, and when minor attributes escape, the gaps are filled with distorted reality. In all, this specialist, this whatever, said the brain is a big fat liar.

To uncover the truth, this doctor advised going a level deeper. Think back, think hard, not only about the big things but the little things about the little things—the smallest details of the smallest details. Go ahead. Give it a try. Take a trip down memory lane, and relive the worst moment of your life as though it were yesterday.

You remember a standoff, a serious and potentially deadly confrontation, an unwelcome invasion of sorts. You hear the sound of boots scurrying through the dew-covered grass in the middle of the night. Not cowboy or fashion boots, we're talking about tactical boots, the tight-laced footwear of soldiers, or, in this case, the SWAT team—specially trained police officers hustling through the backyard of your home. You hear the swishing of polyester uniforms and the soft clanking of bulky accessories as they hasten across the lawn. They move quickly but undetected since the motion-activated floodlights mounted beneath the gutters of your house remain unlit. These urban soldiers carry rifles loaded with deadly ammunition, and right now, they're taking their places behind tree trunks, bushes, and fences, anything they consider to be protective cover. Silence falls, and you listen closely. You hear a woman's muffled voice from a radio, like someone covering a speaker with their hand to limit the volume.

She says, "Northwest corner. To the front and to the left."

Your curiosity compels you to peek through the blinds, where you see squad cars blocking the streets. The surrounding residents have evacuated, and there's a strategically placed sniper crouching behind the chimney on your neighbor's rooftop, waiting to catch a glimpse of your head through the crosshairs of his scope, confident he can bring this lengthy standoff to an end.

Outside your front door, another cop fastens the straps of his respirator and prepares to launch a canister of tear gas through your window. Did you know tear gas smells acidic, like vinegar? Did you know it's not so much a gas but more of an aerosolized fine powder, irritable to the skin and mucous membranes? If it gets in here and fills this room, your eyes will flood like leaking faucets and burn as though you've doused them with mace. Your nose will gush like the busted levee of a seemingly endless reservoir of snot. Your lungs will burn, and you will choke and gasp for air like some form of asthmatic punishment.

You're getting anxious, so you should take a moment to

relax.

Take a deep breath and count backward from ten.

There's no reason to worry, right? You're safe inside this house, protected by layers of brick, wooden frames, and drywall. You know one thing is for sure: the cops can't shoot what they can't see. As long as you stay out of sight, everything will be okay. Unfortunately, safety is an illusion. It always has been. It turns out you're only as safe as your weakest barricade. The last thing standing between you and an intruder is a door. Some people feel by merely keeping it locked, the rest of the world stays contained outside, but a deadbolt means nothing when it comes to the pounding of a battering ram or the swift kick from a cop's boot to bust it open. As for the windows, they're nothing more than thin sheets of glass shielding you from nature's elements and weather, and the softest tap can break them into pieces.

You know there's a storm brewing, and right now, this moment is the calm beforehand. Those cops are becoming more impatient by the minute. They've been trying to get you to peacefully surrender for nearly five hours before they'll decide to use more invasive tactics. The negotiator calls your telephone. He's trying to get in touch with you to see if he can accommodate your demands, but you ignore him because you have no demands. Everything you care about is gone, and there's nothing anyone can do to bring them back. He wants to talk you down and offer you a chance to get out of this intense situation unharmed and alive, but what's the point? Why go on like this? Each time your phone rings, the harsh tones echo louder inside your head like an ascending alarm. An ache pulses in your temple. You cover your ears to deafen the shrill sound as it becomes more and more unbearable.

3

The main concern during any SWAT standoff is the safety of everyone involved, but in your mind, sooner or later, whoever is in charge of this shit-show will lose patience and attempt to bring you down no matter what's at stake. Eventually, they'll send in everything they've got at their disposal so they can finally dispose of you.

Don't worry, though. You're in control, remember? The army of police staged around your home doesn't have a leg up on you. You feel somewhat immortal and somehow doubt their fancy toys will affect you. You've come this far, evading capture, and you're too smart to fall for their silly tricks. Then again, the more you think about it, the more you realize the truth. The more you fear, after all, you may not have the upper hand. Those cops outside, they're not leaving until this situation gets resolved. They won't give up until you're in custody or worse…dead.

If only there were some way to make them understand you're not a monster. Not all of this is your fault, not exactly. You've made a few mistakes. You tried your best to handle your affairs but simply lost control. You let the worst get the best of you. With a bit of luck, people will empathize once they hear your side of the story. You should probably do the right thing and surrender. Toss in the towel and throw your hands in the air. Otherwise, it's highly probable you will lose this battle with a small infantry of officers who've taken an oath to protect society from people like you. Maybe you shouldn't have done what you did in the first place. It's too bad you can't change the outcome now that your future is grim with the inevitable. You realize this, and it's terrifying.

No matter how much you wish to go back, you can't. In a short amount of time, the one place you will be going is to prison for the rest of your life. Once they have you in handcuffs, the police will eventually find the dead bodies on your property. A judge and jury will declare you guilty of second-degree murder, and, given the nature of your crimes plus the number of victims, there's no doubt the prosecutor will seek the death penalty. Did you know this state enforces lethal injection? To you, however, capital punishment sounds like a blessing. To you, there comes an idea of something more horrific than dying.

The same attorney who failed at getting you off with a plea of insanity will fight to keep the needle out of your arm with recurring appeals, but how many nights can you sleep with one eye open? How many years will you spend looking over your shoulder? How many corners will you hesitate to turn, fearful of who waits for you on the other side? Once your fellow prisoners find out what you did, oh boy…who knows what creative and torturous methods of sanction they'll come up with? From keeping you starved by knocking your meal tray to the dining hall floor to daily beat-downs and gang-rapes in the shower, make no mistake, those inmates will deliver the living hell you deserve. From the second the bars slam shut to the moment you find eternal peace, you will fully understand what it's like to be the victim.

So, what do you plan to do about it? What's your next move? Sneak out the back and run away? The cops have your home surrounded. Even if you could escape, where would you go? How long will you survive on your own, off the grid, hiding your face from everyone who crosses your path? You know what you did. You understand the difference between right and wrong. More importantly, you know the past will eventually catch up with you. You can run from the law, but you can't hide from yourself.

There is one option you can choose to avoid spending the rest of your days in a concrete cell. There's one plan you can execute to prevent the life of suffering you face. That's right...the Colt .45 caliber revolver you have gripped in your hand, the gun loaded with six hollow-point bullets. Your thumb pulls back on the hammer, and you observe the cylinder rotate to the next loaded chamber. The clicking sound marks the split second you realize this shit just got real.

The anxiety nipping inside your chest won't go away. In fact, it's getting worse. Your hands feel clammy, and a thin layer of cold sweat glistens across your brow. Suddenly, you feel weightless but also heavy, like a criminal astronaut floating through the vacuum of space while at the same time getting sucked into a black hole. You shove the gun's barrel between your teeth, and the tip scrapes the roof of your mouth. The sharp pain makes your eyes water. Your heart pounds in the bottom of your throat. You can't swallow, and you can't stop shaking. Soon enough, the rest of your body goes numb because, like everyone else, it no longer wants anything to do with you.

Try to stay focused. Ask yourself simple questions. How did it come to this? What went wrong? Have you ever tasted metal before? Do you recognize the sensation of hard steel on your tongue? Is the idea of ending your own life anything like you imagined? All those trivial issues you faced before, all those times you thought you might be better off dead, they're laughable in the presence of this nightmare.

You wonder, but it's doubtful this will hurt. The tip of your index finger rests on the trigger, and if you squeeze it back any further, all of this goes away, fast, so quick, you won't even feel it. The brain can no longer interpret pain once it's been splattered across the wall. Your actions will be justified, and people will say you paid the price. They'll say you've squared your account with society. You've shed the blood of others, so it serves you right to shed your own. What other choice do you have? One way or another, you are going down. You know it, the police know it, everyone knows it, and there's no doubt about it; you've earned yourself a one-way ticket to hell. But wait a second. Take a moment to think this through.

Take a deep breath and count backward from ten.

Suicide is a permanent solution to a temporary problem. Most issues promise a resolution no matter how desperate the circumstances may seem. Then again, there's nothing temporary about the retribution those cops plan to give you, not after what you've done. There's nothing short-term about spending your remaining years on death row, begging for your final day to arrive so you can escape the torment you've set in place. You realize this may not be the best plan after all.

In the room where you stand, there's a grandfather clock near the wall, and it begins to chime, letting you know the hour has arrived. Through blurry tears, you see the face, and both the long and short hands point to the Roman numeral for twelve—XII—midnight. It's the dawn of a new day. A clean slate, but not in your case. You're not getting out that easily. It's time to make a decision. The longer you wait, the more nervous you become. With tears streaming down each cheek as you gag on a thick rod of metal, you wish someone had stopped you long before it came to this. You wish somebody had talked some sense into you, to convince you that what you did was wrong and what you are doing now is a very, *very* bad idea. What's left to say? There's no one else to blame for you landing yourself in this predicament. There's no one coming to the rescue. The people who loved you, who were there for you in stressful times, your friends and family, they're dead and gone. You know this because you killed them. You are the sole person responsible for their demise. More than anything, you want to go back in time and make different decisions, but guess what? We are way too late in the game for that.

As your surroundings become clear, you can't recall a time when reality has been so lucid. You anticipate the possibility that in a split second, the bullet will blast through your head and exit the back of your skull like a bloody, brainy bolt of electricity. With shaky hands, either you pull the trigger on purpose, or your trembling finger will accidentally do it for you. With sweaty palms, the gun might slip from your grasp, and then what? It might land on the floor hard enough to misfire and send a bullet whizzing through the ceiling. The cops might hear the shot and decide to move in. Then, you will have missed your chance to get out of this dire situation at your own will. The police will kick down the door and bust through the windows, and if you continue to pose a threat, they'll take you out faster than you can beg them not to.

Go ahead and close your eyes. Clear your mind. Don't think of anything. Let go of all you have ever lived for and squeeze the trigger. The bang is deafening. Your vision goes black. There's nothing, not anymore. No concept of time. No cognizance. No perception. You're dead, and you don't even know it.

Now, relax. Come back to life. Take the gun from your mouth and drop it to the floor. Forget the police. Pay no mind to the threat. Dismiss yourself of any anguish. If you're lucky, maybe this is all a scenario. Once you discover it may not be real, you'll sigh with relief. You might even laugh at yourself, knowing this horror never happened. You tell yourself it's all fake, something like a dream, something make-believe. You persuade yourself this is nothing more than some vivid hell-scape your imagination came up with, and it's not how your world truly comes crashing down...*or is it?*

Like the doctor said: time has a tendency to warp perception, evocation is not static, and the brain is a big fat liar. Take a look around. If these walls could talk, you know they'd speak the truth. Unfortunately, you're all alone, and there is no one here to substantiate fact from fiction, so you believe what you want to believe. Then, it becomes clear; you can't confide in anything because sometimes, yesterday can be as uncertain as tomorrow. Sometimes, retrospect can be deceitful. So, when the outcome of your future relies on the past, do you trust what you remember or what really happened?

Take a deep breath and count backward from ten.

On the Front Porch...

Whoever said money can't buy happiness sure as shit never lived here. It's a rarity when the police get called to this suburban area, much less the SWAT Team. No one who lives in this upper-class neighborhood would believe anything awful could happen. Wealthy families inhabit this utopia with blissful ignorance. Here, you'll find a lifestyle crime is too poor to afford, where the elite, so-called pillars of the community, pretend to live their perfect lives in a pleasant dream, safe from any nightmarish riffraff.

Some of these people share a false sense of entitlement. They swallow deception from social media posts, filtered photographs, scripted reality television, magazine covers, and stories of celebrity fame. As for their children, every girl wants to be a supermodel, every boy, a success, and they will be, as long as their parents continue fronting the bill. These families live in a place where someone always holds the door, where crowds of the less fortunate spread apart to make way for the prosperous and beautiful. These self-proclaimed stars lavish themselves with impeccable fashion, dress in expensive Gucci and Burberry outfits, and decorate their homes with exquisite art. They check the time on their Rolex watches, drive around town in luxury edition Mercedes-Benz and sporty Teslas. They socialize by hosting parties with friends and colleagues and maintain their social stature by showing off their expensive toys. Invite them to your birthday, your wedding, your kid's graduation party, and, heaven forbid they have to grace you with their presence; they'll arrive with fake smiles and pretend to give a crap about anyone but themselves.

Regardless of how much you may envy these residents, no matter how well they profess, on the surface, not everything is as real as one might think. What others don't realize is that many of these people have shamelessly exchanged their souls for supremacy. Even though their pieces may seem to fit effortlessly together, it's nothing for them to spend a few extra bucks to reshape whatever is out of place. They have the means of tightening themselves to look healthier, lifting their skin to appear younger, or augmenting their body parts to fill some empty void with vanity. However, amongst them hides a well-known truth; the perfect life comes at a price. It comes with strings attached. It arrives packaged in darkness and shipped from the depths of hell. Material possessions made by demons with brand names in a fairytale where some live *horribly* ever after.

With all this said, not everyone who resides here is pretentious. Some choose not to let their humble heads swell. They feel fortunate and blessed to have what they do. Some worked hard and suffered losses in order to gain their rewards. Others were taught to never want for anything and always to be grateful because, at any time, the pleasant world surrounding them can easily crumble.

Between the two and three-story houses spread long yards of grass divided by borders of small tree lines and fences. At the naive age of twenty-five, Calvin Delacroix believes he has everything figured out. Here at 2700 Ironsmith Court, he waits alone on his front porch for a guest to arrive. Even though this meeting is informal, Calvin strives to look his best with slim jeans, a loosely buttoned dress shirt, a bronze tan, and stylish, tawny-brown hair.

Along the sidewalk, a middle-aged couple, Mr. and Mrs.

Silver, come to a stop when the wife nudges her husband's arm and nods in Calvin's direction. Across the street, Mr. Lang fills his lawnmower with gasoline, and when he sees the Silvers with their pained expressions, with their backs are turned to Calvin to stay clear of the neighborhood misfit, Mr. Lang retreats to his garage, leaving his lawnmower unattended on the front lawn.

Their aversion goes unnoticed as Calvin is too busy thinking of how he got here. Not in a directional sense. He's not retracing the routes he took or the time wasted sitting in traffic. He's focused on the more significant questions. He thinks back, trying to recall what he's done throughout his life to achieve such failure. He thinks hard about what events led to his defeat. More importantly, he wonders where, oh, where did it all go wrong?

Daylight arches above this neighborhood as the wheels of a navy-blue Ford F-150 pickup truck come rolling into the driveway and squeal to a halt. A decal with the company name—*Graves' Northside Realty & Appraisal*—and a slogan beneath in smaller text—*'Moving you forward'* is printed on the side of the vehicle. The engine falls silent near a white, remodeled, Colonial-style two-story home. With a restored exterior, crystal clear windows, and newly painted black shutters, this original structure is surrounded by a yard of freshly cut grass. The interior has been modernized with the exception of its initial foundation.

Calvin waits for the driver to step out. Wayne Graves is wearing attire within the budget of his blue-collar profession. Jeans. Polo shirt. Work boots. His age salts his neatly-trimmed beard and hair. His appointment at the Delacroix house is his most important stop of the day, and with a *Crest*-white smile, he approaches with a single key in hand

and a clipboard tucked beneath his arm. Thick-framed reading glasses hang from a string around his neck, and he slides them to the bridge of his nose. He removes an ink pen from his breast pocket and scribbles on the sheet, but the pen needs a good shake before he can write 'Delacroix appraisal' at the top of the page.

"It's about time," he says. "Are you ready? I'm sure you have a million things you'd rather be doing, but time is of the essence."

Wayne peers over the top of his frames, across the street, and over two houses to where the nosey neighbors, Mr. and Mrs. Hill, watch from their window. When he waves hello, they scuffle to pull the curtains closed. He removes a packet of bubble gum from his pocket and tosses a piece in his mouth. He offers another to Calvin, who politely declines and hangs his head, spotting his dignity in the dirt.

With a hint of sarcasm, Wayne says, "They're saints, I'm sure. Don't mind them. Everyone has skeletons."

Calvin stands, brushes the judgment from his pants, and cranes his neck to see down the road.

"Shouldn't we wait for my family?"

Wayne pauses at the front door, and with a nervous slip of his fingers, the key falls and clangs near the doormat. He's quick to retrieve it and asks, "Are they coming?"

Squinting at the setting sun, Calvin hopes relief will come as a passenger in his wife's car once it turns the corner.

"Addelyn said she would meet us here."

Producing a cell phone from his pocket, he scrolls through his contacts and chooses Addelyn's name beside a heart-shaped emoji. He presses the call button, but the line goes straight to voicemail—"Leave a message after the beep."

"Addy, where are you? Wayne is ready to go inside. Can you…" He sighs. "Can you call me back?"

The tip of the key touches the lock when Wayne's eye catches the shimmer of something tiny and metal on the porch. With a swift but subtle motion, he kicks away a bullet's empty shell-casing before Calvin has a chance to see it. Chewing his gum, he says, "You know, I don't believe I've met your wife."

Calvin expresses sincere, unfeigned bewilderment. Strange, considering Addelyn is a busty, blonde bombshell who, for most men, is hard to forget. More, because Wayne is the same realtor who sold the Delacroix's this home last year.

"Of course, you've met her."

The sudden breeze carries a scent of his wife's perfume, a potent but sweet fragrance of Nashi pear, lotus flower, and balsa wood. Of all the senses, smell has the least resistant path to memory. Calvin's thoughts derail to an overwhelming interlude of déjà vu—a familiar reminiscence of where he stands now, and the same place he stood a year ago.

It was the same time last autumn when you first met with us to give us a tour of the new house. Addelyn always dreamed of living in a home away from the city lights so she could gaze at the stars. Her face beamed when you told her she could see the Milky Way on a clear night. She held our baby daughter, Maddie, who cackled with a slobbery finger pointed at your truck. You walked onto the porch and, before you opened the door, you said, "It's about time," and asked,

"Are you ready?"

First came the front foyer with a half-spiral staircase leading up toward the second floor. Spinning around like Julie Andrews on mountainous terrain, Addelyn marveled at how elegant the vestibule appeared with its shiny Carrara marble floors, raised ceiling, and glimmering chandelier. She mentioned how she loved the smell of fresh paint and polish. You were saving the best feature for last and knew it took me everything I had not to ruin the surprise.

You shot me a wink before leading us through the hallway and said, "First things first. Let me show you the basement, then we'll work our way upstairs."

You rounded the corner and we followed you down a carpeted stairwell. When Addelyn first set foot in the basement, she commented on the spacious area, saying, "You could fit our whole apartment down here."

We discussed furnishing the lower level with a bar, a backup refrigerator/freezer, and possibly a pool table. We decided on hardwood floors with area rugs, a recliner, and a sectional sofa. We imagined a high-resolution projector shining on the wall and a Dolby Digital surround sound system to make our own private movie theatre as a place to entertain guests or a second living space to spread out during the confinement of winter months.

You described the original floor plan as a single area and how your contractors built a divider to separate the basement into two rooms. The other half had fluorescent bulbs in the ceiling, mirrored walls, and plenty of space for a gym and tanning bed. In the corner, a wall section was left unfinished with exposed wooden beams, a stack of drywall, and a tub of paint.

Addelyn staggered and grabbed my arm when I told her,

"This is where the sauna will go."

"A sauna?"

I said, "That's right…a Clearlight corner sauna, the kind with an infrared heat supply and basswood finish."

Rather than return upstairs the same way we came, you showed us through the sliding patio door leading to the backyard and swimming pool. You pointed out the motion-activated floodlights mounted beneath the gutters. You showed us the picnic table left behind by the previous owners. Addelyn noticed a tree with a sturdy horizontal branch, the perfect height to hang a swing. Soon after, you walked us up the stone-edged path, around the side, to the driveway. You opened the two-car garage, and we entered the house through the laundry room and into the kitchen.

We explored the dining room, the living room, and you stated there was a half bath in the hallway in addition to a spare room we thought to be the ideal place for Maddie's nursery. You asked if we planned to have more children, and we teased the idea of creating our own Brady Bunch, and since we were already blessed with a girl, we pinned our hopes on having a boy next time. We enlightened you with our dreams of Maddie growing up to be as beautiful and intelligent as her mother and a son who would become someone important and well-respected. Regardless of their success, we expressed our firm belief, even as a wealthy family, our children would work hard so they wouldn't turn out to be spoiled brats. This reminded you of our recent tragedy and how I inherited my fortune, and you offered your condolences.

We returned to the foyer, and you continued the tour up the half-spiral staircase to the balcony on the second floor, where you revealed what you called a guest bedroom with a full guest bath across the hall. I noticed the panel on the ceiling, and you told me it had a sliding wooden ladder mounted to the inside in case I needed access to the attic. You showed us a smaller room I could use for a home office, and with Addelyn's attention astray, I expressed my excitement for the grand finale with a silly, cheesy grin. Maddie noticed me over her mother's shoulder and mimicked me by putting a finger to her lips to stay quiet. You stepped aside so I could lead us to the master bedroom, complete with its own full bath, and that's when Addelyn laughed and covered her mouth.

"Oh my God, a Jacuzzi!" She turned to me and said, "You did good, sweetheart." Then, she looked at you. "I've been wanting a hot tub since our prom in high school."

You questioned the relevance, and I replied, "It's a long story." Not really long, per se, but too lengthy to share at the time. I held the baby while Addelyn examined the tub, tracing her finger along the smooth, off-white, terrazzo marble surface. She discovered an exposed console near the wall with disconnected wires and an open toolbox someone left behind.

She asked, "Is it not hooked up?"

You explained, "While installing the tub, the contractor found a water leak coming from a rusted fitting. Don't worry; they're sending someone out to replace it. Unfortunately, we can't have the electricity connected until then. In the meantime, the standing shower works great."

Addelyn expressed her understanding of the delay but confessed to her lack of patience by saying, "We need to make it a top priority." Taking hold of Maddie, she grinned and said, "I can hardly wait."

I kissed her cheek and said, "Violet Fane."

She knew what it meant, but you didn't, and the only clarification I offered was by telling you it's something I learned from a very important person.

When the three (and a half) of us returned to the balcony and down the staircase, I asked Addelyn, in all, what she thought of the place.

She said, "It's perfect," and, "It takes my breath away."

She added, "I love you," and I replied with, "I love you," because we never say, "I love you *too*."

That's when you opened the front door, and the sunlight nearly blinded us.

———————————

Now, shadows cover the front porch. Wayne observes his client. With a raised brow above his narrowing eyes, he's not curious whether the story is true but rather astonished by how well Calvin recalls the events in precise detail.

"Are you sure?"

Calvin scoffs as if this guy might be kidding.

He asks, "Why wouldn't I be? I remember like it was yesterday. I can't believe *you* forgot."

As if he knows something Calvin doesn't, Wayne shrugs and makes cheap excuses to avert suspicion. He comes up with plausible reasons to explain his absentmindedness, such as, "It's been a long time," and "I've slept since then," as well as, "It's no surprise considering the number of clients I meet with on a daily basis."

His attempts to defer the topic succeed as Calvin stretches once more to look down the street at a familiar car heading in his direction. As the vehicle moves closer, he can tell it's not occupied by his wife and daughter, and his expectations untether.

"Thcy must be running late. Addelyn won't answer her phone while she's driving, especially with Maddie in the back seat."

The seconds of silence can be counted on one hand, broken by the sound of Wayne popping his gum and shoving the key into the lock. With the bolt unhinged, all it takes is a gentle push to enter the home, but he hesitates and focuses on his still fingers as they hover above the knob. He's choosing his words carefully because the wrong phrase may ignite a fire he won't be able to extinguish. He doesn't want to say anything to upset Calvin. Yet, he knows preventing his distress might be out of his control.

With a slow and steady sigh, he says, "We're not moving anything tonight. All we need to do is make a list of what goes and what stays."

Calvin hears this, but he's not listening. He's oblivious to Wayne's apprehension with a blank stare focused on a row of three bushes lining the rock bed to the right of the porch. Few flowers are left to wither away, and the petals, scattered along the grass, are crispy and frail. His head tilts to one side as though pulled by a bizarre observation, and he wonders if perhaps not every detail of his memory is accurate.

"These roses, they were white before. Now, they're red."

Wayne returns the key to his pocket. He doesn't turn around but stares ahead with his nose a few inches from the door like someone closed it in his face.

He lowers his chin, indifferent to Calvin's remark, and tells him, "They've always been red."

Birds chirp as seconds tick by. Already forgetting his regard for the rose bushes, Calvin checks the time on his

Jaeger LeCoultre wristwatch and peers at the base of the sun as it kisses the horizon.

"Addelyn, where are you?"

Strengthening his posture with his chest out and shoulders back, Wayne asks, "What do you say we get started?" He opens the door and steps aside so Calvin can lead the way. "Are you ready?"

In the Foyer...

It's difficult to define a beginning until it settles in the past. Once the start finds its place, the truth has nothing left to do but unravel.

Shards of broken glass crunch beneath Calvin's shoes as he makes his way inside the foyer, paying close attention to where he steps. The sidelight is busted, and a filthy pathway stretches across the Carrara marble floor from the hallway to the spiral staircase. He surveys smudges of dirt, tracks of mud, and traces of dried maroon, like someone used blood to finger-paint the walls. Above him hangs the chandelier with a layer of powder-like film covering its crystal prisms. A chunk of drywall is missing from the ceiling as if something the size of a bullet had embedded a crater into the surface.

Calvin says, "Oh, my God," while pacing slowly toward a grandfather clock that stands against the wall.

Its face is cracked and splattered with what appears to be chunks of bloody cranberry sauce. The pendulum no longer sways, and both the long and short hands are stuck on the Roman numeral for twelve—XII.

Popping his bubble gum, Wayne ignores the mess as if he's been expecting to find it.

He scribbles on his clipboard: Astoria Grandfather Clock—List value: $2,799.

He says, "I know a horologist who repairs these things like new. He might settle for a reasonable price if you're interested in selling it."

Calvin is too busy scanning the room, trying to make sense of the disaster.

He asks, "What the hell happened here?"

Wayne lowers the clipboard and mumbles softly, "Hell is right."

Without skipping a beat, Calvin steps toward the corner, eyeing a shattered photograph with a bent frame lying on the floor against the base of the staircase. A damaged family picture of Addelyn, Maddie, and himself. He runs his fingertips across the scratched faces as his saddened heart pumps questions to his brain. Who would do such a thing? Why destroy a family portrait unless the act has meaning? He looks over his shoulder and says, "This was the first thing we hung on the walls when we moved in."

Wayne taps his pen against his clipboard and says, "Things we hold high have a long way to fall."

Calvin continues to survey the room. It's a vestibule that's barely recognizable, completely unbelievable, and easily perceived as someone else's catastrophe.

"This place has been vandalized."

Lowering his chin, Wayne takes the frame from Calvin's hand to inspect it.

"Vandalism is an understatement."

"I'm calling the police."

He pulls out his cellphone, dials 9-1-1, and before his finger presses the call button, Wayne extends a hand to stop him and says, "I wouldn't," but it's too late.

Calvin tries to call, and the line buzzes with a busy signal. He redials, and the line buzzes again.

Wayne tells him, "It's for the best. The last people you want here are the police."

"Someone broke into my home and went on a rampage. I need to file a report."

"I don't recommend that either."

"Why not?" Calvin scoffs, trying not to laugh at

Wayne's carelessness. What is it with this guy? Has all logic gone out the window? He'd be doing the same thing if the tables were turned.

Wayne returns the broken picture frame to its place on the floor. He regrets his comment through a silent pause, feeling he may have backed himself into a corner but doesn't want to explain anything yet. He chews his gum and diverts with a more reasonable question. "From the time you woke up this morning until now, what do you remember?"

Calvin swears this isn't how he left home. As inappropriate as the inquiry seems, he takes a minute to recall a digital alarm clock blaring from the nightstand—8:00 A.M. Addelyn rolling over in bed. Maddie, babbling through the baby monitor. Warm shower. Hot shave. Ticking wristwatch—9:00 A.M. Comfortable clothing. Nordstrom cargo shorts and a cotton Guess t-shirt. A growling stomach. No breakfast. Good-bye kisses and I love yous—"Don't be late," before Addelyn's reply, "We'll meet you there."

The rest of the day is blank. The afternoon, the evening, everything up until the moment Wayne pulled his truck into the driveway is gone. Calvin fails to account for missing time, but one additional detail immerges.

"I had an appointment at noon."

Wayne blows a bubble and lets it pop.

"For what?"

Calvin is distracted by a fizzing sound, a hiss, like gas leaking from a compressed container. It's close but not coming from any definitive direction. It surrounds him, but the source is nowhere in sight. He breathes through his nose, and his lips curl and grimace to the bitter scent.

Sniffing the air, he asks, "What's that smell? It's acidic, like vinegar."

If he would look, he'd notice Wayne's blank stare combined with an unnatural silence, as though he's ignoring the question. If he could read his mind, he would know Wayne is concerned, not by Calvin's actions, but knowing the truth is beginning to unwind.

The hissing sound fades, and the strange odor dwindles. Calvin dismisses the brief, uncanny experience, almost like he's already forgotten.

He asks Wayne, "Why did you want to know about my day? What does it have to do with anything? You think I did this?"

With his hands spread apart to deflect accusation, Wayne says, "That's not what I'm implying. Though it is strange you don't remember, wouldn't you agree? It might help if you tried to retrace your steps. Somewhere hides an explanation."

With his phone in hand, Calvin selects his wife's name beside a heart-shaped emoji.

"Maybe Addelyn can fill me in."

He presses the call button, but once again, the line goes straight to voicemail—"Leave a message after the beep."

This time, he hangs up, curses, "Damn it," and wipes a palm across his face.

Wayne nods to the bottom of the staircase.

He says, "I know it's easier said than done, but you need to relax. Take a seat while I finish up."

"You can't be serious. Don't you think I have bigger things to deal with right now? Addelyn's going to flip when she sees this mess."

"There's no doubt this comes as a shock, but you need to take a break. Collect yourself."

Calvin's reluctant to do either and says, "I don't need a

break. I don't need to collect myself. What I do need is—"

Wayne cuts him off with, "Please, I insist."

As Calvin's mouth falls open, Wayne adds, "You're getting all worked up. Take a deep breath."

Calvin exhales through pursed lips like an untied balloon. He sits on the bottom step, bouncing his foot, anxious to see the rest of the house, and wondering when his family will arrive.

Wayne buries his face in his clipboard, writes something down, and blows a bubble. It cracks between his teeth before he says, "Tell me a story. You've known Addelyn your entire life, am I right?"

"Since we were kids."

"So, enlighten me. Tell me how you first met."

Most people enjoy sharing stories, especially when it involves someone or something they care about. Calvin sighs and rests his elbows on his knees. Discussing anything other than the situation at hand is not what he wants to do, but it doesn't take him long to step out of this disaster and into his childhood.

Love is not something to take for granted. Like wealth and fortune, either it's given to you, or you spend a lifetime trying to obtain it. The only love I ever knew was Addelyn. My heart has always belonged to her, and luckily, for me, she feels the same. What we share is the very definition of true love—an overwhelming and unconditional passion, equal and boundless, between two people who are meant for each other, as though the universe, indeed, has plans for them. The only question is what kind of plans, good or bad, does the universe have in mind?

We grew up in the same neighborhood, but we were in a park the first time I laid eyes on Addelyn. I hid behind bushes and watched her swaying alone on a swing set. Her violet sundress blew in the wind, as did her long, curly hair. Standing nervous in the sand, it took me a few minutes to work up the courage to introduce myself. We had to be eight or nine years old, likely both since I'm a year older. Most children aged in single digits worry little about making new friends. It comes naturally for them because they have yet to experience rejection. Somehow, I knew this girl would grow up to be the woman of my dreams, but I feared, at the time, I might not be good enough for her.

I made my way through the grass, where I picked a bundle of orange and violet pansy blossoms from the side of the trail. By the time I found the nerve to approach her, she had jumped from the swing and landed on her feet. She noticed me coming her way and waited, neither of us knowing our first moments would be the beginning of a fulfilling life together.

I held the flowers in my fist and said, "These are for you."

She smiled, lifting them to her nose.

"They're so pretty."

Shrugging, I said, "They're okay. I couldn't find anything as pretty as you."

She was at a loss for words, but her blushing cheeks spoke for her. My feet shuffled, and I couldn't help but rock my hips with a nervous rhythm. I tried to think of something else to say, but nothing came to mind. To avoid the awkward silence, I asked, "Would you like me to push you on the swing?"

Addelyn looked over her shoulder to the chains squeaking as the empty seat swayed in the breeze. She slid a strand of hair behind her ear and said, "I like to swing by myself. It's my happy place." At first, I took this as her way of telling me to get lost, but before I turned to leave, she leaned in and pecked the sweetest kiss on my cheek. "Thank you for the flowers."

Even though this story came at his request, Wayne doesn't appear to be listening. Regardless, Calvin feels even though a short amount of time has passed, given the situation, he's calmer and more collected than before. His feet no longer bounce, and the rattled nerves in his stomach have settled.

With a final glance, Wayne double-checks the foyer.

He aims his clipboard toward the hallway and says, "We should check out the living room."

Kicking away debris from his path, stopping near the wall, he turns back. Calvin stands at the front door, peeking through the torn curtains of the sidelights, wondering about Addelyn and Maddie.

Wayne pops his bubble gum.

"Calvin?"

"Huh?" He whips his head.

Wayne extends his arm as an invitation to follow him into the next room.

"Are you coming?"

In the Living Room...

Hell is what you create. Most people think of fire and brimstone, devils and demons, sinners bound in chains, infinite torture, and endless suffering. Yet, not all hell exists beneath the Earth's core. It's not always found in a blackened abyss. It's here on land, above the surface. Truth be told, purgatory is decorated how you see fit. It's adorned with ceramic sculptures and figurines, complemented by indoor potted plants and vase flowers, fragranced with scented candles, plug-in air fresheners, and potpourri. It's lit by energy-conserving lamps, furnished with throw rugs and window drapes, cushioned stools, beverage coasters, and magazine racks. It's surrounded by green lawns and a picket fence. It has a street address and a mailbox.

The devil can be found in a variety of sorts. Some people see it when they look in the mirror, style their hair, put on their makeup, shave their face, and dress themselves. Most fear, when they die, they may face eternal damnation; but for those who live, actual hell comes with the realization that you're already there, trapped within the walls you built, imprisoned behind the doors you sealed shut, born for no reason other than to pay bills and mortgages, and punished by your own version of misery.

Move-in day fell on a warm, sunny Saturday. I had enlisted the help of Addelyn's sister, Lillian, and her husband, Paul Campton. They arrived in the morning to unload the moving truck and finally see the new home. Lillian wore a beige camisole tank top with her flat stomach exposed over black draw-string stretched sweatpants that cut off at the ankles a few inches above her plain white sneakers.

Paul dressed lightly in beige cargo shorts, a faded *Metallica* concert t-shirt with the sleeves cut off, and his steel-toe work boots.

The two had met at a speed dating event, and uniquely enough, fell in love at first sight. Both felt it unnecessary to stay and meet other singles, so they left together and spent the next few hours conversing over bagels and coffee at a local deli. Paul made a respectable living as an electrical engineer, designing and maintaining radar equipment for airports across the country. A traveling job with a two-hundred-thousand-plus income. He owned his own large and lonely house, so Lillian broke the lease with her landlord and moved in six months later. They married the following spring, and in addition to Paul's sizable income, Lillian took a job as a regional manager for a respectable women's clothing store. If Paul had to leave town, it wasn't for more than a few days. Spending time apart proved to be beneficial to the Campton's marriage. Absence makes the heart grow fonder, so says the proverb.

Paul and I handled the heavy furniture while the women unpacked boxes and put away dishes and clothes. Amidst the commotion in the living room, Maddie sat quietly in her playpen, not so much entertained by her toys, instead, by watching the rest of us shuffle through the house.

As the sun rose higher in the sky, the summer heat began taking its toll. Paul's darkish hair dripped with sweat. He removed his shirt, exposing his toned chest, and used it to wipe his face. Lillian entered with a box of holiday decorations and set it down on the floor. Her sandy blonde streaks stuck to her neck and shoulders.

Pulling her hair into a ponytail and fanning her face with an open palm, she said, "This should be the last of it."

Addelyn came from the kitchen, carrying two glasses of iced lemonade. Handing them to Paul and Lillian, she sat down on the sofa and crossed her legs with a golden ankle bracelet glistening in the sunlight from the window. The sofa's black suede was soft to the touch, and with a fan oscillating from the corner, the breeze felt like heaven. Lillian sat beside her, sighing and cooling her forehead with her cold glass as I finished screwing the mount for the new television on the wall. Paul lifted the screen while I hurried to fasten the bolts in place. Stepping back, I took the remote control from the coffee table and pressed the power button. The screen lit up, displaying a repeat broadcast of the morning news.

"There," I said, with a relieving sigh, "Now we can watch the rest of the world be foolish."

Muting the volume, I fell to my knees and crawled to the playpen. Maddie giggled when I crossed my eyes and stuck out my tongue. I pressed my hand flat against the mesh, and she placed her tiny palm against mine.

"Enjoy it while it lasts, Princess. We'll put you to work too when you get bigger."

She grinned and cackled like she had called my bluff, as though she somehow knew I would never make my princess do manual labor. Paul took a drink and turned to his wife, clearing his throat as a reminder.

Exhausted but ecstatic, Lillian sat forward and said, "There is one more thing."

Paul confirmed with a nod and said, "Yes, we have one more item to bring inside."

Addelyn and I looked at each other, sharing the same bright-eyed and wondering expression. All of the heavy stuff was unloaded. The truck was empty. What else did we need to move?

With what little energy I had left, I stood to follow them, but Paul stopped me and said, "No, you stay here."

He and Lillian disappeared outside.

I looked at Maddie, pursed my lips, spread my hands apart, shrugged my shoulders, and asked, "What could it be, baby girl?" She giggled and mimicked my gesture, throwing her arms straight above her head. I picked her up, held her above me, exposing her belly, and asked again with a silly voice, "What could it be?" When I blew on her stomach, creating the sounds of flatulence, Maddie laughed hysterically. I did it again, and each time, she laughed harder. Addelyn joined in, watching the two of us play. Holding our daughter in my arms, I kissed her cheek and said, "Let's go find out." She pointed to Addelyn, and I said, "C'mon, mommy. Let's go see."

A minute later, the front door pushed open to a long cardboard box floating into the foyer. Paul set his end on the floor and rushed over to help Lillian with the rest. We met them by the staircase, curious to see what the box contained.

Paul said, "You have no idea how difficult it is to find the perfect housewarming gift for someone when they have everything they need."

Jokingly, I said, "We also accept things we don't need." Then, I made ridiculous guesses like, "It's a gun rack. No, a stripper pole. Oh, I know. A realistic sex doll. If so, Addelyn, you're sleeping on the couch tonight."

She laughed and nudged my arm. "Depends. Maybe it's a *male* sex doll."

Paul used his pocket knife to slice the taped edges and opened the flaps, revealing a brand-new grandfather clock with a polished oak frame and glass windows. Both the long and short hands pointed to the Roman Numeral for twelve noon—XII, and once they sat it upright, the long golden pendulum began to sway inside.

Addelyn gasped and covered her mouth as she did with any surprise.

"It's gorgeous!"

Impressed, I couldn't help but laugh and say, "This is better than a sex doll. Seriously, though. You didn't have to buy us anything."

Paul folded the cardboard pieces in half and rested them against the wall. Lillian said, "We figured a clock would be a nice sentiment for the time you spend in your new life together."

Overwhelmed with joy and fighting the urge to cry, Addelyn embraced her sister.

"You two are so sweet. Thank you."

Maddie must have approved because she pointed to the clock and said, "Caw."

"That's right, baby girl; it's a caw."

We returned to the living room when Addelyn took Maddie to the kitchen to fix a bottle. Paul wiped his hands on a cloth and stood over by the bookcase. He and I pondered the best place for it to go. Leaving it in one spot left another wall blank and empty.

Scratching his head, he stepped back to get a broader view and said, "You know what? You could use some artwork. Something to jazz this place up a bit. I have a friend who creates phenomenal paintings. I'm sure he can whip something up to compliment this living space."

Addelyn returned and said, "That would be wonderful."

Paul framed the sight of the wall with his hands, imagining colorful canvases to offset the bland, white tone.

"Once you settle in, Lillian and I will invite ourselves over for dinner, and I'll bring him along so you can meet him."

Addelyn and I agreed; dinner sounded like a fantastic idea. Being an amateur gourmet chef, I was intrigued but teasingly suggested they bring side dishes so I wouldn't have to slave over a hot stove. Addelyn rolled her eyes, chuckled, and winked.

Paul stepped closer to the bookcase and said, "First things first. Do you want to leave it centered like it is?"

Unsure, I turned to Addelyn and asked, "Honey, what do you think?"

With Maddie in her arms, sucking on a bottle, she considered for a moment, tilted her head, and suggested, "Maybe if we move it to the front, to the left."

———————————————

Wayne leads the way into the living room, and as Calvin enters, his first sight is the sectional sofa (what's left of it). The cushions have been torn apart and tossed to the floor. Black suede material has been ripped to shreds, exposing the white insulation as though a monster tore them with claws. The partly-mounted flatscreen television hangs cracked and crookedly from one side. In the center of the floor, a shattered glass coffee table, stained carpet, a path of bloody footprints leading from the kitchen to the hallway. Chunks of dark hair. Broken sections of a canvas painting—abstract artwork in orange-yellow and blue-violet with the artist's initials—VA—in the bottom right corner of the canvas. Maddie's tipped-over playpen. Scattered toys and soft baby blankets. Against the wall is an unharmed bookcase lined

33

with novels. Once again, Wayne comes across as oblivious to the mess and steps over to read a few of the titles.

'Family Matters' by Rohinton Mistry

'Remembrance of Things Past' by Marcel Proust

'Of Human Bondage' by W. Somerset Maugham

'Number the Stars' by Lois Lowry

'Things Fall Apart' by Chinua Achebe

'Line of Beauty' by Alan Hollinghurst

'East of Eden' by John Steinbeck

'Far From the Madding Crowd' by Thomas Hardy

'Tender is the Night' by Scott Fitzgerald

He inspects the shelves with his head tilted to the side and asks, "Do you plan to move this or sell it?"

Calvin stammers, "The bookcase? Uh, sell it."

Wayne clicks his tongue and continues chewing his gum. "A few hundred dollars is what I'm thinking." He lifts a pen to his clipboard and writes, 'Oak veneer bookcase—List value: $380.' He says, "Which brings us to $3,179."

Calvin sits on the arm of the couch, folding his arms and nibbling his thumbnail. Getting comfortable is out of the question. You're wasting time by sitting around. You need to see the rest of the house. Why is my family running late? His knees bounce, his hands shake, and he asks, "What is going on?"

Slightly annoyed by having to repeat himself, Wayne says, "Relax. Take a deep breath."

Calvin can see the appraiser has a wedding band on his left ring finger.

With a tight fist pressed against his face, holding back his frustration, he says, "You have a wife."

"Twenty-five years and counting."

"Do you tell her to relax when she's upset?"

Wayne chuckles and says, "Instant regret, every time."

As Calvin paces the floor, combing his fingers through his hair, his impatience begins to snowball.

"Comforting words only relieve tenuous situations. And this here..." He spreads his arms apart to showcase his surroundings. "This is too much for anyone to handle. What do you expect me to do when nothing makes sense?" He rushes into the foyer, pointing toward the front door, and shouting, "Addelyn and Maddie are supposed to be here!" Wayne chews his gum and removes his reading glasses, watching Calvin storm back into the living room. "And when I left this morning, the house wasn't in shambles!" Lowering his tone, he adds, "So please, do me a favor and stop telling me to relax."

Wayne tucks his pen back into his shirt pocket.

"What makes you so sure? This afternoon is blank to you, yes?"

Calvin surrenders to the question with a heavy sigh.

With his cell phone in hand, he dials 9-1-1 and says, "I'm calling the police."

Wayne secures his glasses to the bridge of his nose and turns his back.

Tracing his finger through a film of dust on the bookshelf, he speaks softly under his breath and says, "No, you're not."

When Calvin presses the call button, the line buzzes with a busy signal. He clenches both fists and falls to his knees. This is bullshit. Help should always be available. At the sight of blood-stained footprints, his thoughts spin, desperate to recall his most recent memories of being here. Then, it hits him. A puzzle solved.

"I get it now." He pauses and begins to laugh. "This is all a dream. It must be. It's the only logical explanation. When my alarm went off this morning, I must have hit the snooze button."

Wayne blows a bubble and bends over to retrieve Maddie's stuffed teddy bear that's been ripped in half up to its neck.

"When's the last time you had a dream and were able to acknowledge the events as they happened? When were you able to stop and tell yourself the experience wasn't real? Lucid dreams don't come along too often. Even so, why are you unable to recall the rest of your day? Addelyn smiling at you? Maddie babbling through the baby monitor? Warm shower? Hot shave? What you wore? Your growling stomach and no breakfast? If you fell back asleep, how would you know what came afterward? I wish I could give you answers, but one thing I can tell you is this is not a dream."

Calvin scoffs, sickened by the response. His stomach curdles with anxiety, and the bitter taste burns in his throat.

"A nightmare, then."

Wayne drops the bear to the floor. It's an act which could be perceived as ungracious if the child who loved it were here, disrespectful if the toy was able to be mended, but she's not, and it's not. He continues his exploration, speaking and chewing as he threads the room.

"Did you know when you dream, your brain enters a deep state? A REM cycle, they call it. However, sleep is required in order to reach this level. Trust me, you are wide awake."

Calvin scratches his chin.

"Your certainty baffles me."

Wayne says nothing but snickers and kicks aside the remains of the smashed painting. Once more, Calvin scrolls through his contacts, selects Addelyn's name beside the heart-shaped emoji, presses the call button, and the line goes straight to voicemail. "Leave a message after the beep."

What a joke.

"For fuck's sake, Addy, I need you to call me back right away… It's an emergency."

The living room's triple-pane window displays an isolated tree in the backyard. Two ropes hang from a thick, horizontal branch, leading down to a wooden plank—a swing. Calvin moves closer and envisions Addelyn sitting alone, at peace, wearing a sundress and a white, wide-brim beach hat. He can hear Wayne's muffled voice as though it comes from underwater.

"There's no point in trying to understand the present without a clear recollection of the past."

Calvin watches his wife's legs straighten and bend to create momentum. Her toenails are painted with a light shade of lavender. She's all alone in her happy place, and in this reminiscence, her life couldn't be more perfect.

Instantly, Wayne's voice clears as he says, "I'm sorry."

Calvin whips his head. "For what?"

"I realize how obnoxious it can be when I say it, but it's important you stay calm and focused. Tell me more about you and Addelyn."

Looking back, the swing is empty and swaying in the breeze as though someone recently hopped from it. The tree branches are bare from fallen leaves. The sunset casts an abstract orange-yellow and blue-violet hue across the sky.

Calvin hangs his head and whispers, "Please. Why?"

Wayne adds other items to his list.

"I'm trying to exercise that brain of yours to help jog your memory. Besides, there's more in here to catalog, and your story keeps me entertained."

Calvin's eyes close and he shivers. Not from a cold, but rather a chill shooting through his spine.

Wayne adds, "Go on. You met as kids and then what?"

The night Addelyn and I shared our first kiss is a night I will never forget. One summer, her parents asked mine if they could send the two of us for a week at junior high camp. We reached the point in our lives when it was easy to fall in love, but because we had become such close friends, our emotions were somewhat confusing. We didn't speak of it, but we knew we were too young to be in a serious relationship, while at the same time, curious to see what love was like and too afraid to find out from anyone else.

When the sun went down and the moon came out, after the campers and staff finished dinner in the cafeteria, we gathered to play a game of capture the flag. The best part of playing this game was the dark. The blackness added excitement to the quest. It's hard to tell what lies ahead, where someone is hiding or when they plan to jump out. The extensive woods stretched for miles around the campsite and offered the perfect space for people to scatter. The counselors split the group into two opposing teams. Addelyn had to carry a red bandana, and I had to carry a blue. The red team was given a head start so they could find places to hide before my group began the hunt. The game's object was to collectively work together to retrieve the other team's flag while individually tagging each other out. The more kids removed, the weaker their team, and the fewer people they would have to protect their flag.

I snuck off to the side between trees and brush along the beaten path, hoping I could avoid patches of poison ivy. I did my best not to make noise, and anytime I heard a commotion, I froze and ducked behind whatever I could find. I saw flashlights up ahead, combing through the woods, crowding together around a cabin. I assumed this is where the red team kept their flag, and I knew they would be on the lookout for anyone approaching. I had no idea where Addelyn had run off to, but I liked to pretend she was with me. In her absence, I imagined myself leading the two of us on an adventure. My reality set in when I felt a tap on my shoulder and spun around to find her standing with a flashlight shining upward on her face like she's telling a ghost story.

She said, "Boo! I got you."

She laughed, chasing me. I ran as fast as I could, but at the same time, letting her gain on me. You would have thought we were the last two players in the game, running through the woods, careless of being discovered by the other campers, careless of what colors divided us. We stopped far enough away to no longer see any flashlights but still in the vicinity of hearing the others scream and shout. Out of breath, I gave up and found a tree to lean against.

Addelyn said, "Oh, come on. You're giving up?"

Panting my words, I replied, "You're too fast. I'm out. You tagged me already."

"I didn't say you were out."

"It's okay. I'll let you win."

She raised her head to the sky, pointing her finger at the heavens, and said, "Look! You can see the Milky Way!"

With my sight adjusted to the night, I could see the known universe and the faint orange hue which housed all the planets and stars.

She told me, "When I grow up, I want to live someplace away from the city so I can see the Milky Way at night."

Huffing my breath, I told her, "You can have it all, I promise."

She stood in front of me with her hands behind her back, swaying like she had something she wanted to say or do but was too shy to follow through.

She asked me, "Have you ever French-kissed before?"

"Random, but no, I haven't."

"Do you want to try it?"

I can't recall a time I'd felt so nervous.

I said, "I'm not sure. Do you?"

Smiling with tight lips, she nodded. We inched closer to each other, and I checked around for anyone who might be watching. I told her I didn't know what to do, and she said her sister, Lillian, said we're supposed to touch tongues. It's strange to think, at the time, the idea didn't seem as gross as I would have expected.

Addelyn tapped her foot and said, "Kiss me, already."

So, I did, but only a peck on the lips, which felt magical enough to send the stars above in a spin. My mother was the only girl I had kissed before, but in no way was this the same. Addelyn's kiss unleashed a warm, fuzzy feeling in my stomach.

She giggled and said, "Okay, now do it again, but this time, do it longer."

After a brief moment of working up the courage, I swallowed, held my breath (for some reason), and did as she instructed. We pressed our lips together, and eventually, hers spread apart, which made mine open, and I felt her soft, warm tongue slip into my mouth. Even today, I can't think of words to describe the sensation. My eyes closed, and our jaws moved together in sync, like feet against bicycle pedals. The urge to stop became too overwhelming, but each time we started to pull away, we went back for another round. My heart was like a sponge, swelling with a newfound love for her. Even though I'd never kissed anyone this way, what I considered to be my natural instincts kicked in, and without any thought, my hand caressed the side of her face. I grazed my fingers through her hair and held her close, wishing I could stay in the moment for the rest of my life.

In the distance, a group of voices shouted, "Get the flag!"

An army of flashlights rushed together, and the crowd cheered. Addelyn's team had won, but she missed it for a good reason. She took me by the hand and ran, pulling me behind.

Later, the camp gathered around a large campfire, roasting s'mores and hotdogs. A counselor played *"Yellow"* by *Coldplay* on his acoustic guitar while everyone sang the lyrics. You should have seen the way the fire made Addelyn's face glow, the way it made her eyes sparkle. I wanted to kiss her again, but there were too many people. I didn't know what to think, what to do. Even though we were not officially boyfriend and girlfriend, she had stolen my heart. It must have been an even exchange because I felt her soft fingers slip between mine, and we held hands beneath a blanket we shared to keep warm from the brisk night air.

A horrific vision interrupts Calvin's enchanted memory. Flashes of bloody feet, running down the staircase, through the foyer. Panicked breaths, hissing through clenched teeth. Droplets of spit. Pounding thuds. Ripped material. A spinning mobile above a crib, and its chiming lullaby slowing to a stop. The blade of a large meat cleaver penetrating the wall. A woman's voice calls out, "Northwest corner. To the front. To the left. That's where you'll find it!"

Wayne's bubblegum pops, and asks, "Find what?"

Calvin's eyes spring open with a batter of blinks. He knew what he saw and heard a second ago, but the meaning slips away like waking from a bad dream.

Yet, a dream it's not.

In the Kitchen...

Everything in our new home had been adequately placed and decorated, except for the blank spaces on the living room walls. Lillian and Paul planned on stopping by for dinner, along with Paul's artist friend. Baby Maddie sat on a blanket spread over the rug in my view from the kitchen stove. She drooled and chewed on a plastic toy staring endlessly at the motions of the television screen. The news spoke tragically of a young boy shot at the mall by a runaway gunman. As horrific as it sounded, the news merely made background noise, and since I didn't know the victim's family, it didn't concern me. The rest of the world, being foolish.

In our wrap-around kitchen, the walls were patterned with black onyx tile. Addelyn had decided to go with a Mosaic-style backsplash, sterile white-shaker-style cabinetry, mahogany granite countertops, and an Island black stainless steel refrigerator. A stainless steel pot sat in the kitchen stove with billows of steam leaking from the edges of the lid. I swiped away the top of a cutting board with the back of my hand and produced the first knife I could grab from the drawer—a meat cleaver.

Next to me, I opened the flaps of a cardboard box on the countertop and reached inside, removing a live lobster with its pinchers bound by thick rubber bands. I raised the ugly-faced beast in front of me and slid the blade underneath the bands, snapping them free. The claws stretched and pinched in the air, but by holding the lobster by its shell, my fingers remained free of harm.

I spoke to it, saying, "Don't get snooty with me. It's not

my fault you got caught." I sat the lobster flat on the cutting board and slid the tip of a blade over the hard shell near its head. "If it's any consolation, my friend. My tastebuds will thank you later."

The steel pierced its brain with a downward slice, causing it the most instant and humane death. Immediately, I lifted the pot's lid and tossed in the dead creature to cook.

The garage door opened, and soon entered Addelyn, carrying bags of groceries. She kicked the door closed with her foot and hustled to set the bags on the counter.

Eyeing the box of remaining lobsters, she grimaced and said, "Oh, I came in too early. Watching you kill them is the worst part for me."

"They don't mind." I turned and pecked a kiss on her lips. "Believe me, I asked."

Addelyn snickered and opened the refrigerator.

"You got their permission?"

I removed another lobster from the box and cut its pinchers free.

Holding it at eye level, I asked, "Do you fellas mind if we have you for dinner?" Obviously, the lobster didn't respond. "See? They don't mind."

I placed it on the board, stabbed its brain, and tossed it in the boiling pot with the other. Addelyn laughed while stocking the refrigerator.

She said, "You're so weird, sweetheart, but that's why I love you."

I turned and said, "I love you."

We never say I love you *too*.

Even though we had moved from our apartment, despite the extra distance, Addelyn favored a salon near downtown, next door to a massage parlor and diner. As she put dry goods on the counter, I noticed her hair. I told her she looked nice. She opened the freezer, stuffing it with groceries. She groaned, rubbed her neck, and said she forgot to buy cream. I thought she meant cream for the sauce, but we had some already.

Before I mentioned this, she said, "I met this adorable old woman named Irene. Sweet lady. So friendly. She told me all about her husband, Willian (with an N), and their son, but I can't remember his name. Oh, but to hear her talk about them was so inspiring." A light fog rolled from the freezer, and my sight set on the inside of the small compartment. Addelyn turned around. "My poor stylist, bless her heart, accidentally burned my—"

"Ouch!"

My wrist felt as though someone had pinched it with heat, and I dropped the lid of the boiling pot to the floor, wincing with pain.

She rushed to my aid and asked, "Are you okay?"

I held my forearm underneath a cooling stream of water from the faucet, and said, "I should have been paying attention."

I looked over to Maddie, still sitting in front of the television, drooling on her toy. Addelyn examined my wrist. It was red but not blistered.

She snickered and said, "Lobster's revenge. Serves you right."

———————————

Standing behind Calvin, who is lost in a daze, Wayne chews with his mouth closed and says, "It's getting darker," before blowing a bubble.

The pop snaps Calvin back to the here and now. His furrowed eyebrows release, and he pauses to examine the room.

"How did we get down here?"

With a slack expression and a slight head shake, Wayne appears to be stumped by the question.

"Down from where?"

Calvin looks in every direction and feels as though the floor is falling from beneath him.

"From the master bedroom. We were in there a second ago."

Pulling his head to the side, Wayne squints, and says, "No, we haven't made it upstairs yet. First things first. We still have the rest of the ground floor to cover."

Calvin sighs and says, "I'm losing my mind."

Wayne resumes chewing his gum and replies, "Doubtful. I think you were lost in telling me about the dinner," yet, he's ignored as Calvin wanders into the next room.

Once he makes his first step inside, he stops, sighs, and his chin falls to his chest. He says, "So much work went into creating the perfect kitchen. Addelyn chose the design and decor. She selected the appliances. She'll likely break down and cry when she sees the damage."

The pattern tile with dried blood stains and chunks of hair. The backsplash with missing tiles. Cabinetry with doors hanging by the hinges. Sheets of dust cover the once-clean countertops. The refrigerator is unplugged. The top part, the freezer, has loose bands of crime-scene tape and residue. Wayne hurries to pull the ribbon and stuffs it in his pocket before it's noticed.

Approaching the refrigerator, Calvin prepares himself for what's inside. He yanks open the freezer door to find nothing. The once collected frost is now gone. It's warm and smells of lingering mold and rotten food.

"We haven't been robbed because nothing is missing, but why would someone break in here and tear it apart if they didn't take anything?"

Wayne jots down notes on his clipboard and says, "You tell me. "What do you think happened?""

"If I knew…" Releasing a short bit of rage, Calvin slams the freezer closed and shouts, "I wouldn't be asking!"

Wayne stops writing and lifts his head.

Chewing his gum, scanning the cupboards, he murmurs to himself, "Clues are everywhere." He moves closer to open the cabinets and examine what's inside—expensive dinnerware, left in pristine condition. "I can get you a pretty penny for stuff like this. That is, of course, if you want to sell."

He writes, 'Christofle silverware—$1,615'

Calvin runs his fingers through his sweaty hair. He turns to the living room, with the same line of sight from where he once watched Maddie on the floor. Only now, she's not there.

Wayne scribbles some more, writing, 'Glancy Fawcett porcelain dishes—$1,299.'

He says, "Pay closer attention. This doesn't work unless you stay focused."

"What doesn't work?"

Knowing he can't give him the answers he needs, Wayne responds with a diverting request, "You and Addelyn were high school sweethearts. Am I right?"

Calvin ends his nod with a stare at the floor.

Wayne blows another bubble and says, "So, tell me about it. How did you two come to be?"

The only thing more important than love itself is the person you love knowing how you feel about them. Over the years, my friendship with Addelyn sprouted. She and I shared a connection like no other. In addition to our first kiss, we experienced countless moments together. Our parents took us to the zoo, amusement parks, and vacations. We attended each other's family gatherings and holidays. Everyone else knew before we did; Addelyn and I were destined to be together, but it wasn't until sophomore year when she almost slipped away.

She grew to be a beautiful young woman, and because of this, I learned, always being in the spotlight, she was sure to attract attention from other boys, especially those with newly-developed hormones. As shallow and senseless as it may seem, I spent a lot of time worrying about someone else taking her virginity. I wanted to be her first. I wanted to be her everything. I feared another guy would come along, and for some strange reason, the idea of her with this faceless stranger felt like my world would explode. I wasn't thinking about sex in the way most guys my age thought about it. My parents raised me to believe sex was a gift shared between two people who were truly in love, and I wanted nothing more than to share my gift with her. Of course, other girls flirted with me. They whispered my name on the bus and in the locker room. I'll admit, the offers were tempting, but I knew they would never work because my heart belonged to Addelyn.

When she became head cheerleader, I attended the football games, not in school spirit, but for her support. I watched her jump and flip. I felt her energy extend through the roaring crowds. Each time she smiled, I felt my heart skip a beat.

Of all the husky football jocks, one, in particular, caught Addelyn's attention. A good friend of mine at the time. A guy named Vance Allen. A child of divorce. A wanna-be hipster who kept his shoulder-length hair pulled back in a trendy man-bun, the type of guy who wore hemp bracelets and ate nothing but organic foods. He often flirted with her, and his attempts at getting a date gave me a palpable sensation of desperation in my chest. As I said, her happiness made my heart skip, but seeing her with Vance made me wish it would stop beating altogether.

His slavish approach entertained Addelyn in certain ways. When he complimented her long hair and compared it to the golden sun, she would smile and giggle at him for being so cliché. If he commented on her eyes, saying they were as blue as the ocean, she would roll them like the tide, unimpressed by his lack of originality. But I knew how playful Addelyn could be. I knew her all too well. She didn't verbalize her emotions, but her body language and mannerisms spoke volumes. A light brush of the arm. A gentle touch on the shoulder. Her blushing cheeks and fluttering eyelashes.

For the first time in my life, I felt as though she didn't love me. I figured a relationship with Vance became her backup plan since I had yet to step in. It left me empty inside, desperate to go back and say something sooner. Addelyn would have been his perfect match. I hated him for this reason, but in all honesty, he was kind and humble. Like I said, a good friend who didn't know us well enough to recognize his intrusion. Other girls liked him, and I could see why Addelyn did too. Still, I feared it would only be a matter of time before I missed my opportunity forever. The time came to make a decision. I needed to make my move. I couldn't stand the idea of not being with her. The mere thought of her in someone else's arms felt like a punch to my gut and made me sick to my stomach.

Finally, I found the nerve to confront her. No matter what, I wanted an answer. It was time to step out on the plank and dive into the shark-infested water. It happened after the last game of the season. I told Addelyn beforehand that meeting me under the bleachers afterward was important. She waited for me with her back against a post, holding her pompoms with her ponytail dangling over the small of her back, dressed in her short, mid-thigh skirt and sleeveless top. A smile on her face like Cinderella waiting to try on a properly fitted slipper. I focused on the ground, with both sweaty palms in my pockets. I kicked a rock, brushed the dirt with my shoe, and spoke a nervous mutter.

"I want to, no, I *need* to ask you something. You can say no. I mean, I don't want you to say no, but you can because it's your decision. If you say no, that's fine."

Entertained by my bashfulness, Addelyn giggled but tried to contain her laughter.

I said, "I care about you more than anyone in the world, including myself. Nothing would make me happier than to be with you, the girl I've always loved. I want you to be my girlfriend."

Corny, I know, but it's not how I practiced beforehand. My nerves were shot. Addelyn chuckled, but could soon tell I meant business when I stared directly into her eyes with a serious expression on my face. Her smile went flat. I took a brief pause to reset my words with a heavy sigh.

"Part of me wants you to say no. At least then I can accept it and move on because wondering every day if we can be together is *killing* me."

She smiled again, this time as if she'd been waiting for me to ask. She looked back through the beams to Vance, who stood on the field alone, searching around for her, holding his football helmet. He seemed lost, but rather than run to him, Addelyn said, "Well if you insist," and wrapped me in her arms.

She pushed her lips against mine. We nearly lost our balance but indeed, fell madly in love. The heavy burden lifted freely. We couldn't stop kissing. Her face, her skin, close to mine, the warmth of her body. She felt like, well, home. Like opposite ends of a magnet coming together. A force of nature.

As I caressed her cheek, she smiled and said, "I love you," and I replied with, "I love you."

Not once, in all the years together, have we ever said, "I love you, *too*."

Wayne tells Calvin, "Think back, think hard," and asks, "Are you one-hundred-percent?"

Curious, he turns and asks, "About what?"

"After the football game, under the bleachers."

"It was ten years ago and a milestone in the relationship with my current wife. I think I'd remember."

With his clipboard in hand, Wayne rests his fists on his hips and takes a final glance around the kitchen.

"The only thing left are bits and pieces of things we can't salvage. I'm worried the same goes for your memory."

Calvin moves toward him with authoritative steps, barking, "Yes. I am one-hundred-percent certain, without a shadow of a doubt, that my wife and I began dating our sophomore year."

"Are you sure it wasn't Vance who met her beneath the bleachers, holding and kissing her after she said yes to him?"

"What the f—?"

"You said she saw Vance standing on the field alone and lost. Are you sure it wasn't you?"

"What's wrong with you? Why would you ask—"

Calvin's eyes close and flashing images return. He sees things from opposite points of view. From the football field, searching around for Addelyn until his eyes land on movement of two people hiding beneath the stands. His vision scoots close enough to see her wrapped in Vance's arms, dropping her pompoms to the ground, slipping her tongue in his mouth. Everything fades to red, then more images flicker. Ripping duct tape. Muffled screams. A slamming door. Pitch black darkness. The unfamiliar woman's voice comes clear, but not heard by ears, rather an audible thought from inside his head, shouting, "To the front! To the left! That's where you'll find it!"

Startled, Calvin clutches a fist to his chest. He returns to find himself in the present, in the kitchen, with Wayne standing by his side, who says, "Bits and pieces," and writes something on his clipboard, circling it twice.

Total so far—$6093.

Acting as if he didn't bring Calvin to his knees with gut-wrenching suggestions, Wayne blows another bubble and says, "Let's see what we find in the dining room." Leading the way, he adds, "So you had everyone over for dinner. Then what happened?"

BRADLEY CARTER

In the Dining Room...

Paul and Lillian arrived moments before dinner was ready to be served. They brought their own side dishes, along with their guest, a local artist with long hair rolled into a bun. He wore a men's linen henley long-sleeved cotton beach yoga shirt. His pants were rugged and worn, with frays hanging loose above his sneakers. Despite his appearance, he was clean and trimmed and smelled of expensive cologne.

The first thing to distract me was Lillian's sundress and how it was thin enough to see the outline of her undergarments. Her hair hung down over the thin straps of her dress, supported by her soft, smooth, tan shoulders. I've always thought of her as a very attractive young woman, but it made me curious why she would show off so much. Who was she trying to impress?

Addelyn stood next to me, and Paul placed his hand on his friend's back, guiding him over to introduce us.

"Meet the artist I told you about. This is—"

Addelyn interrupted, "Oh my God! Vance!"

I noticed her eagerness to welcome him with a hug and subtle cues, simple things like her pushing a strand of hair behind her ear, the blush rising from her cheeks, the length of their embrace, her flirtatious smile. More importantly, her failure to acknowledge her own husband.

Paul asked, "You two know each other?"

"We're old friends."

Noticing the awkwardness of a missing introduction, Paul pointed at me and said, "This is her husband, Calvin."

"We've met." I stepped forward, extending my hand.

Vance blinked a few times as though his gazing daydreams had been interrupted. He shook with a good, sturdy grip. He said, "It's been a while," and returned his attention to Addelyn. "Thank you for inviting me to your home."

Paul showed him the living room, gesturing at the bare walls. Vance observed, admiring the spacious room.

He rubbed his chin, nodding, and said, "I have some ideas."

I couldn't put my finger on it, but there was something about Vance that felt off. Last I recalled, we were in good standing. True, our friendship faded after high school, but still, there was something strange about him, like a forgotten memory, something I didn't want to resurface. Then, it clicked. College. Spring break. How could I forget?

In the kitchen, I observed Lillian opening the refrigerator to retrieve a bottle of wine and turn, closing the door with her back. She asked me, "Where did you decide to stock the wine glasses?"

I raised my hand to point, but for a second, I couldn't remember. Where did we put them? On the tip of my tongue, a simple answer, unable to be retrieved. Lillian could see right through me. She stepped forward and pressed her palm against my chest. Her lashes fluttered and she leaned close to whisper, "Relax. Take a deep breath."

I couldn't help but wonder, is she coming onto me? Seriously? Or is this some sort of distraction?

She said, "I know you're not thrilled with Vance, but I assure you, everything is fine."

My head flinched back slightly and I asked, "Why would I be worried? That was a long time ago, and by the way, the wine glasses are in the cupboard above the stove, the row in the front, to the left."

Turning away, I headed into the dining room. Lillian followed, carrying crystal glasses and sat them next to each porcelain plate. She filled them to the brim with white wine. The table looked like something you'd find in an issue of Bon Appétit Magazine. A serving platter of lobster tail with individual cups of melted butter. Twice-baked mashed potatoes. Tomato and cucumber salad. Crispy asparagus. I took a seat next to Maddie's high chair so I could feed her small spoonfuls of baby food. Everyone at the table was awed by how cute she looked in her bib that read, 'Daddy's Little Angel.'

Vance stood behind a chair, overlooking the food, and said, "Everything looks wonderful." He added, "A far cry from the Ramen Noodle meals we had in college."

Addelyn giggled, but I didn't. His comment carried no humor.

We all sat down, and with a mocking tone, Vance asked, "So, Calvin. I hear you have a job at *The A Corporation*. What is it you do there?"

Without giving away too much detail, I explained how *The A Corporation* had recently constructed a new team to develop artificial intelligence technology. My job was simple: keep the stockholders informed of progress and manage their investments accordingly.

"Logistics?"

"Sort of, but not."

I knew what he was thinking. How can a six-figure income afford a spacious home like this? If he didn't already know what led to my inheritance, I wasn't about to bring it up.

Lillian took a bite of lobster, leaned her head back, and

moaned as the orgasmic flavor burst inside her mouth. Covering her lips with a napkin, she said, "Wow, this tastes incredible."

Addelyn smiled and sipped her wine.

"All thanks to Calvin who suffered a small injury to fix it for us."

Examining my wrist, I noticed the redness had shrunk to a tiny dot, the same as if someone had poked me with a needle. Strange, I thought. I figured those pinchers would have caused more damage.

"It's nothing. Those little gremlins had it worse."

Swallowing his food, Paul spoke up, saying, "I read somewhere lobster is one of many foods that serve as an aphrodisiac."

Addelyn replied, "Don't talk like that in front of Maddie," giving him a stern but friendly glare. "A baby's brain soaks up all kinds of information."

Maddie waved both arms and held her mouth open for another bite.

I dipped the tiny spoon into the jar and said, "Somehow, I doubt 'aphrodisiac' will be her first word." I used my index finger to pretend and tickle her bib, making silly faces. "Can you say that big word? Can you say 'aphrodisiac?'"

"Calvin," Addelyn chuckled.

"What about, 'libido?'"

"Stop it," she laughed.

Maddie cackled and squealed. Lillian stabbed another piece of lobster with her fork and dipped it in the butter sauce. She said, "Give my sister a break. It's her first child. She worries about everything."

Addelyn said, "I do not," but her voice sounded cloudy to me as though she were speaking far away from another room. The conversation between the others soon faded to an inaudible rumble, and I stared off into space through my full and untouched wine glass. I can't tell you what caused this, but time seemed to pass into hours.

Then, suddenly, like air returning into a vacuum, the sound came back in seconds to break my daze. The only one who noticed my brief mental absence was Lillian. She swirled her glass and smirked with a mischievous grin.

Addelyn moved the discussion to another topic.

She asked, "So, Vance, do you paint for a living?"

Wiping his mouth, he replied, "More of a hobby. I paint to keep my personal and professional lives separate. It's all about balance."

"What's your profession?"

"Neurology."

Addelyn said, "Oh, I remember. You majored in neurology with a minor in art."

Nodding, he grinned as though excited to gloat about his achievements.

"What about you? Did you follow through with your dream of becoming a psychologist?"

For ten seconds, I sat there, seemingly absentminded. Vance noticed my awkward silence and lowered his napkin to his lap.

Addelyn answered by saying, "With the new house and the baby, it takes time to settle so things can fall into place. Calvin makes enough money for the both of us."

"Congratulations," he added. "You two seem happy together. Love like yours is rare these days. Most people now are so terrified of—"

I interrupted with a stern, "Thank you."

Vance froze and moved his eyes to Addelyn, then back

to me before finishing his sentence. "—monogamy." To avoid embarrassment by ignoring me, he continued. "Together since high school. That's a long time."

I sensed a hint of unmasked criticism in his voice. With her smile fading straight, Addelyn cleared her throat. She glanced at Paul, at Lillian, who shrugged the minor episode off as no big deal. Perhaps, I had been chewing my food. Perhaps, I didn't hear Vance at first. Maybe I was too focused on feeding Maddie, and it didn't occur to me right away how I should respond. All these possibilities allowed me a free pass from my unintentional interlude. Yet, none of these explanations were correct. Like the last snowflake landing on a mountain, this minor slip in my mind threatened to initiate an avalanche of jealousy. I still remembered what happened *after* high school, and if things had turned out differently, Vance would be sitting at the head of the table, living in this house, raising a daughter, sleeping next to the woman who would have been my wife each night. So, I began chugging my wine to extinguish these burning thoughts.

Lillian turned a suspicious glare to Paul, and judging from the scolded puppy look and the frustrating way he stabbed his salad with his fork, the palpable tension in the room must have been relative to something she believed he had done. She narrowed her eyes and swallowed a generous gulp of wine.

Reaching for a new bottle, she said, "It's human nature, I guess. People are drawn to cemeteries."

The cork popped, and I coughed, briefly choking.

"Drawn to what?"

She filled her glass and replied, "Symmetry. It's what attracts people in terms of physical attributes."

"I thought you said, 'cemeteries.'"

Shaking her head with half a grin, Lillian winked and filled my glass as well.

"No, dear. Pay closer attention."

Vance's interest floated to Addelyn, and it appeared he spoke directly to her, saying, "It's true. Symmetry is what gives us beauty." I kept quiet, focusing on the subtle interaction between wife and guest, waiting to hear what he had to say next, which was, "Da Vinci used the Divine Proportion in his work, as do I. It's found everywhere in nature, even in mathematics. It's what makes things the most pleasing to the eye."

Fucking gag me with Maddie's baby spoon. Her tiny hands reached for it, but I had it gripped in a white-knuckled fist. If someone had questioned my anger, I would have denied it. No sense in rehashing the past. Everything turned out in my favor anyway, so there was no reason to bring it up. It's a shame. At first, I still liked the guy, but all it took was him reentering my life and turning on his *Fabio* charm to remind me why our friendship fell apart.

Addelyn asked, "What about you, Vance? Any lucky lady on your arm?"

"Not at the moment, no. I've been keeping busy with work and art."

"Speaking of which. You said you have some ideas for our home?"

Nodding, he said, "I have a few tricks up my sleeve."

Tricks? Old habits must truly die hard. I can't wait to see what mangled rabbit you pull out of your hat this time.

A clink of Maddie's baby spoon landing on the floor drew everyone's attention to me. My empty hand hovered in front of her high chair.

"Sorry," I said, "Butterfingers." The perfect excuse with a lobster dinner. I leaned under the table and noticed Vance and Addelyn's feet were inches apart. My stomach squirmed and nausea began churning inside me. Rising, I set the spoon on the table and pushed back in my chair. "Excuse me. I'll be right back." I rushed out of the room, down the hall, toward the half bathroom.

Wayne pops a bubble and slams a hand on the wooden surface.

"What are your plans for this table?" He pushes down to check its sturdiness. "Is this oak?"

Observing the shredded painting on the walls, Calvin surveys the room with a face shrouded by disbelief.

"Yes. It's heavy too."

"If you want, we can pay someone to move it for you."

"What does it matter at this point?"

Before the tip of Wayne's pen touches paper, he lifts his head.

"I get it. It's hard to part ways with things that remind you of good times, but unfortunately, this is necessary."

"Good times?"

"I'm sure you recall pleasant times with you and your family before—"

"Before what?"

Wayne chews his gum and scribbles on his clipboard, 'Hargrove table and chairs —$1,499.'

Even though he wonders what happened with Vance in college, he says, "You mentioned your high school prom before. Tell me about it. I assume you and Addelyn went together, correct?"

"Why are you so fascinated by our relationship?"

"Passing time. I'm intrigued. Tell me."

Squatting over a chair with his arms hugging the back, Calvin sighs and presses his forehead against the wooden finish.

By the time we reached our senior year of high school, it had become well known amongst the student body, teachers, and parents that we were inseparable. Vance had moved on to other relationships. I can't say whether he wanted to find love or play the field. All I know is he claimed to respect Addelyn's decision to be with me. No one else bothered asking her to prom, and the other girls held no expectations of going with me. The two of us together were untouchable, as sure as the air we breathed.

Each head turned when Addelyn entered the school's gym. Her classmates had never seen her dressed up, so beautiful, and glowing with her arm linked with mine. As we danced, she noticed Vance standing alone in the corner. "Poor guy," she said, spinning with me so I could see him too. "He looks so sad."

In all honesty, I couldn't have cared less.

Toward the end of the event, our fellow peers included us in group photos and invited us to after-parties. However, I had more romantic plans in mind. Like most teenagers after prom, we spent the night together. Our parents approved, knowing, if we hadn't already, there was nothing we would do in a hotel room we wouldn't do eventually. My father had rented us a hotel room and paid the staff to pre-arrange with candles, rose petals on the bed, soft adult contemporary music from a radio set at low volume. That's the night Addelyn first wore a new perfume, the sweet fragrance of Nashi pear, lotus flower, and balsa wood. The night we didn't *lose* our virginities, rather exchanged them. Centered in the room, she marveled at the king-size bed, silk sheets, pillowcases, curtains, lighting, and overall cleanliness as if we were the first guests to stay there.

"If we get married, I insist we buy a house as nice as this." She turned to an open shower room and gawked at the sight of a hot tub. "And I insist we buy a Jacuzzi."

I hugged her from behind, pressing my cheek against hers. I said, "Not *if*, but *when*...you can have anything you want. Perhaps we can start with this."

I produced a small jewelry box tied with a violet ribbon from my pocket. Addelyn grinned and opened the gift to reveal a gold ankle bracelet. She gasped, covered her mouth, turned around, and smiled.

She asked me, "What's the occasion?"

Lost in her eyes, I replied, "You. Every day, it's you."

My words took her breath away. Our first kiss at summer camp was undoubtedly the best, but the kiss we shared on this night was tough competition. Like a pair of stars floating in the Milky Way, properly aligned, we became the only two people in the world, in the universe.

With a prom dress spread across the bed and a tuxedo hanging from a closet doorknob, Addelyn and I soaked in steaming, bubbling waves. She leaned her back against my chest as I massaged her shoulders, with her foot resting on the edge of the tub showing off the glistening gift around her ankle. We talked about the other students at the dance, what they wore, how handsome and beautiful they looked compared to how they appeared in class.

She said, "Poor Vance. He could have any girl he wanted, and there were plenty to choose from."

I kissed her cheek and said, "No one is as gorgeous as you."

She turned to me and said, "I hope our lives stay this perfect."

I kissed her shoulder, tasting her skin with the tip of my tongue. Addelyn's eyes rolled back before they closed, and I whispered, "I promise."

For the first time, we made love surrounded by rose petals. Naked, together, between thick blankets and clean sheets. Like many firsts, the event came with a stomach full of butterflies, and for Addelyn, a slight pain. She winced, and I caressed her chin.

I asked, "Should we stop? I don't want to hurt you."

She smiled and shook her head.

"It's okay."

Her friends had warned her what sex would be like for the first time. I told her I'd rather die than do anything to make her uncomfortable, but soon enough, the discomfort unlocked an indescribable pleasure. I'd never heard her moan as she did. I'd never felt her fingernails dig into my back. I'd never experienced such an overwhelming sensation, both physically and from the heart. Afterward, we held each other and gazed into each other's eyes.

She said, "I love you," and I replied with, "I love you," because we never say, "I love you *too*."

Calvin can tell Wayne is unsure of the details from the

gloom expression on his face.

"What?! You don't believe me?"

Wayne smacks his gum and says, "It's not a matter of whether *I* believe you. The question is, do *you* believe you?"

What's this guy's deal? What kind of an asshole disputes the stories he wants to hear?

Calvin takes a breath and asks, "Do you want to explain to me what goal you're trying to reach? I was there! I lived it! Which part do you think I have wrong?"

Wayne stands next to the cupboard. The door is open, and he inspects a set of crystal wine glasses. He writes on his clipboard, 'Baccarat glassware—$600.' Other dishes remain on the shelves, shattered to pieces. "Unfortunately," he says, "without the entire set, I don't think we can get much for these."

"Answer my question."

Swishing his gum inside his mouth, Wayne turns around. "The mind denies what it cannot recall, even if it is the truth. I want you to be right, Calvin. I do, but you need to be certain someone else wasn't wearing your shoes."

Calvin scoff transitions to laughter. "You can't be serious. Are you suggesting Vance took Addelyn to the prom?"

"Amongst other things."

He stomps toward Wayne with a fist waving in the airs and shouts, "You need to stop this right now before I—"

The faint scent of chlorine finds its way in through Calvin's nose, and more images flash like a camera in a blackened room. The sight of Vance dancing with Addelyn, viewed from the side of the gym. Vance holding Addelyn in the hottub. The two of them together in bed. Their faces mashed together. Their bodies wrestling beneath the sheets.

Them whispering 'I love you' to each other.

The visions switch and cause Calvin to wheeze a gasp into his lungs. The house. Splashing water. Wet skin. Lights, activated by motion detectors, going dim. The sound of laughter. The whip of a rope. A mouth, screaming underwater, "Northwest corner!" Bubbles, rising to the surface, unleashing a woman's voice, "To the front, to the left."

Calvin's heart pounds from his chest to his throat. Sweat pours a pale tint over his face. His hands tremble, and his knees wobble. A bitter taste makes his mouth salivate.

"I can't..."

Wayne watches him, concerned, but still chewing his gum.

"You can't what?"

"Excuse me. I'll be right back."

Calvin rushes from the dining room, and a few seconds later, the slam of a door echoes from the hallway—the door to the half bathroom, followed by the sound of heaving vomit.

Wayne shakes his head and circles a number on his page: Total so far—$8192.

In the Half Bath...

Lobster's revenge. Serves you right. This is what I was thinking while hunched over the toilet bowl, trying not to lose my dinner.

Addelyn scooted back and stood from the dining room table, laying a napkin on her empty plate.

She said, "The wine is getting to me," even though everyone reasoned her statement as an excuse to check on me.

She left Lillian and Paul to babysit little Maddie and entertain their guest, Vance, in her absence.

Addelyn rounded the corner into the hallway, knocked twice on the bathroom door, and whispered, "Are you okay?"

I murmured from the other side, "I'm fine. Just a little queasy."

She tried turning the knob, but it rattled from being locked. I flushed the toilet and washed my hands and face. I gulped a swig of mouthwash and spat it down the drain. When I opened the door, Addelyn blocked my exit. She stepped inside, wrapped her arms around me, and hugged me close.

"Did you get sick?"

Shaking my head, I replied, "No. Too much wine, I guess."

She pushed her fingernails up under my shirt and dragged them down my stomach. She kissed me, shoved her hands beneath my belt, down my pants, and whispered, "Good."

I watched the mirror as she lifted on her toes to kiss the

side of my neck. I gripped her arms and held her face-to-face. The sharp jolt startled her and doused her with a subtle fear, but realizing my intensity came from passion, we smashed our lips together again, and her fear transformed to hunger. At first, I questioned her cravings, wondering what set her off. It could be the seafood aphrodisiac. It could be genuine affection for her husband. It could be taking her lust for Vance out on me. I didn't dwell on this too much, as soon I forgot my suspicions when Addelyn pushed me back against the sink as though the world would end at any minute, and her last dying wish was to make love once more.

She unfastened my pants and pulled them to my ankles. I spun her around to face the mirror, bent her forward, and pulled up the back of her dress. I unsnapped her bra and loosed it enough to slide my hands underneath and squeeze her breasts, all while panting and licking her neck and shoulder. She moaned and pulled her panties down to her knees. To prevent anyone from hearing her, I covered her mouth. With a single thrust, my jaw fell open, and she groaned, muffled by my palm. She gripped my wrist and pulled my hand away. Licking my fingertips, she whispered, "I love you."

Gnashing my teeth, I told her to "Shut up."

Any other time, Addelyn would have been concerned by my response, but it came more as a turn-on in the heated moment. Fighting the urge to sound off with blaring orgasms, we both finished quickly as if our building aggression stemmed from decades without sex. Addelyn smacked her hand against the mirror, sliding her palm down and leaving streaks on the glass.

I held her close, hugging her from behind, trying to catch my breath. I backed away and lifted my pants, and fastened my belt. Addelyn stared at my reflection with a satisfied grin while she fixed her appearance. She fluffed her hair and said, "I hope that's baby number two."

My chuckle came with a reply, "So do I."

I returned to the dining room first to avoid the obvious and potential embarrassment. Lillian noticed the sweat on my brow and smirked. A moment later, Addelyn entered with flushed cheeks, acting her best not to let on she had finished having incredible sex. Paul grinned with half a smile, entertained by our inability to hide what we had done. Maddie babbled silly sounds from her chair. The only straight face in the bunch belonged to Vance. I like to think the reality of never filling my shoes hit him hard in the gut the same way I like to envision kicking him in the groin.

Calvin leans his back against the bathroom door as it closes, huffing, puffing, and covering his face with sweaty palms. He flips on the light, exposing the sink, toilet, and crumpled hand towels on the rack. Shreds of dark hair scatter the floor. He lifts his boot and discovers the pattern on the bottom matches dirty prints on the floor. In an instant, his empty stomach sinks and the room threatens to spin.

Oh, shit. Why are your shoe prints here? You haven't been in here until now. Did you do this? C'mon, you don't own the only pair of these boots. Could have been anyone. Calvin thinks these things, but his attempts at consoling himself do little to alleviate his fear.

Wayne holds his gum in his cheek, and his voice precedes a knock at the door.

"Are you okay in there?"

Startled, Calvin turns, pressing his hand against the frame to keep him from coming in.

"I'm fine. I need to splash some water on my face."

He crawls to the sink and spins the knobs, but nothing comes from the faucet except an eerie growl.

With a sympathetic tone, Wayne says, "The water is off."

"So I've noticed. Give me a minute, please."

Calvin listens to Wayne's footsteps as they fade away toward the other room. He tries to calm himself, staring endlessly at his reflection that's been smeared by a bloody handprint. Too large for a child, too small for a man. The central point of what seems to be a blunt impact has caused the glass to crack in all directions. He trails his fingers over the sharp ridges, and a ridged edge cuts his skin. A trickle of blood oozes down his knuckle, and he sucks it clean.

Behind closed eyes, Calvin sees chunks of hair floating like feathers. Some land in the sink, others fall to the floor. He runs his hand across his head and feels a smooth, bald scalp. Something buzzes. Red lines decorate his head from the blades of an electric razor. In his reflection, he's skinny and frail with dark circles beneath his eyes. No sleep, not in weeks.

Another knock at the door startles him back into the moment, to the sight of a full head of hair. The dark circles are gone. He spins around toward the door.

Wayne presses his ear against the surface and asks, "You okay in there, boss?"

Confused and filled with anxiety, Calvin chokes on his response.

"I...I'll be out in a second."

Confirming he's not dreaming, he pats the top of his

head, gripping his hair and tugging at it to ensure the follicles don't come loose. He wipes his chin with his sleeve and surveys the room.

Once the door is unlocked, Wayne steps in and says, "You look like you saw a ghost." He peeks around the corner. Nothing he sees comes as a shock nor of value. Calvin suspects he knows of the disaster, and likely, the events which took place to create it. Wayne says, "Why don't you take a seat. Collect yourself."

Calvin lowers the lid to the toilet and rests. Leaning against the wall, Wayne holds his clipboard with folded arms. Clearly, something is bothering his client more than the catastrophe that is his home. He glances at his watch and sees it's time to dive into the meat and potatoes of Calvin's past.

"What did you study in college?"

"Communications and finance. Why?"

"I'm curious. Did you and Addelyn attend the same university?"

"I should check outside to see if she's here."

Calvin pushes by and heads down the hallway, but Wayne's voice stops his journey to the foyer.

"The front door is unlocked. I'm sure she knows her way inside. Tell me about college. Tell me more about this Vance guy. What was so devastating about spring break?"

With a subtle groan and a hefty dose of resentment, Calvin slides his back down the wall and sits on the carpet.

My father, Brent Delacroix, was an executive board member, shareholder, and one of several attorneys for *The A*

Corporation, a worldwide communications company, also known from entry-level employee training videos and paycheck stubs as *Abigail Corporate*. Following in his footsteps, I decided to major in communication engineering, hoping to land a job with a potential six-figure income. My minor went to finance since stock investments played a significant role in my family's wealth. My mother, Elaine, indulged in the housewife lifestyle, free to do whatever she pleased throughout each day. It seemed like an easy life, and I hoped to one day support Addelyn so she could have the same freedom.

Compared to high school, college shared more similarities to real life. More people, more strangers, but all students who faced daily struggles to succeed academically. Instead of hall monitors, the campus police kept things in order. Instead of earning a living, we strived to earn good grades. Everyone focused on the same light at the end of the same tunnel, preparing to transition into the world. Whatever we wanted to possess later, we learned how to get it then, or not at all.

Addelyn and I graduated high school with honors as the children of wealthy parents, which gave us free passes to our chosen university. She majored in psychology with a minor degree in fine arts. Aside from classes, there was never an event we didn't participate in together. We made straight As, associated with the best people, attended parties, and rarely left each other's side. Whatever we did, we wanted to do together so we would treasure the memories in the future.

Before Spring break, another student approached Addelyn on campus—Vance Allen, with more muscle mass since she last saw him in high school. She greeted him with a hug.

He kissed her cheek and, not mentioning me, he asked, "How is everything?"

"Things are great! I didn't know you were a student here."

"Sure am. You and I are taking the same art class, but I have Professor Bridges in the afternoon." Skipping right to the point, he asked, "Do you have plans for Spring Break?"

"No, not really. Visiting home."

"A group from my art class rented a house in Destin, Florida, but one girl backed out, and now we have an open spot. The ticket is already paid for. I thought you might be interested."

"Sounds like fun. Calvin will be thrilled."

Up until this point, I'm sure Vance assumed Addelyn was single, or at the very least, didn't give a shit. His enthusiasm lessened to disappointment when he said, "I didn't know you two were still together."

"We are. In fact, he's around here somewhere. I know he'll be excited to hear—"

"Honestly," he interrupted with a final attempt at getting her to accept, "we don't have the room, and the flight is already booked. He's welcome to join if he can find his own way."

Not the best idea. Addelyn knew me well but felt bad for saying no without considering the invitation first. She always wanted to visit Florida, and in her mind, she thought it would be a nice vacation for us both.

She said, "Hold the spot for me; I'll talk to him."

Vance took her hand and wrote his phone number on her palm. He smiled, winked, and said, "Great. Let me know something soon," while squeezing before letting go. "It's good to see you, babe."

Addelyn and I stopped by a local burger joint on the way home from class. She mentioned Florida over a basket of French fries.

"Vance? Vance Allen? From high school?"

"A few of his friends are taking a trip to Florida for spring break, and he asked us to come along."

"Both of us?"

"Well, sort of."

Addelyn explained the situation, and I could barely believe what I was hearing because my thoughts went to trying to understand how Vance knew she took the same art class and more, how he knew her schedule. He's been attending school here this whole time? In secret? And why pop out of the blue so instantaneously to offer a free trip across the country? I was suspicious, to say the least.

"Who else is going? Anyone we know?"

Clearly, I wasn't too thrilled with the arrangements (two couples and a fifth wheel), so I told Addelyn, "We should go by ourselves."

She threw in a rebuttal, "But he's already paid for the plane ticket."

Sounds like *his* problem. Then, it hit me. It's spring break. Every college kid in the country has a ticket and hotel reservation.

"Do you have any idea how difficult it is right now to book a trip to Florida? Besides, my father isn't doing too well. Mother said he's been acting strange, angry, not himself. He forgets things and gets frustrated when he can't remember. It's not how I planned to spend my vacation, but I can't be hours away while worrying about him." As much as I knew I would regret it later, I said, "You go. Have a good time."

Addelyn hung her head and picked at her fingernails.

"That's unlikely if you're not coming with me."

"It's fine. At least one of us will have fun. You should go. I trust you."

Famous last words.

"Why wouldn't you?"

She was right. Why wouldn't I trust her? Vance is who I didn't trust, but no need to make a big deal of it. Addelyn loved me wholeheartedly. Nothing could come between us.

The evening came when she set off to Florida with her friends. She called me before leaving for the airport, told me she already missed me, and said she'd bring back a souvenir. A five-hour flight, overnight, and she'd call me the following day once she arrived and settled in. I joined my parents at home for dinner, scraping my plate and rearranging the food instead of eating. My stomach felt heavy and full. Nauseated. My father sat at the opposite end from my mother, who seemed to be withdrawn from the conversation and keeping to herself.

Dad asked me, "How's school coming?"

Little appetite. Short answers.

"Fine."

Mom said, "Sit up straight, Calvin. Don't slouch."

Even as an adult, I wasn't allowed to express my sadness. Dad gave her an evil glare, cleared his throat, and said, "My colleague in the communications department said to tell you he's waiting for you to call him when you graduate. *The A Corporation* is in the process of selecting members for a team to develop their artificial intelligence technology."

IN THIS ROOM...

For a second, I forgot about my worries. "Seriously? That's great, but what do I know about programming?"

Dad said, "Programmers make shit. No, you'll likely be in charge of keeping the stockholders informed of progress and managing their investments accordingly."

"What, like logistics?"

"Sort of, but not."

He gripped my shoulder and tried shaking the doubt from me. "It's a six-figure income, and it's waiting for you to pluck from the trees. It's a headstart, and the only way to go is up."

Oddly enough, my mother didn't appear to be so thrilled, but I doubt she was in a good mood to begin with. My first instinct was to call Addelyn with the good news. With a secured future and a good job, we could talk about marriage and buying a home. Oh, that's right. She's on an airplane. No phone service. Not for hours.

The telephone rang from the kitchen. My father removed a napkin from his lap.

"I'll get it."

Mom dropped her fork and said, "I can get it."

Dad slammed a fist on the table. The silverware and centerpiece rattled. A short silence caked the tension before the phone rang again.

Red-faced and chewing his food, Dad said, "I will get it."

He stormed from the table and answered the phone, speaking with inaudible dialogue from where I sat. Mom avoided eye contact with me and took a sip of wine.

"See what I mean?"

"How long has he been acting like this?"

She shrugged and said, "Ever since the new neighbors

76

moved in next door. A younger couple. Todd, the husband, recently divorced and married a younger, pretty wife, Selina, after his son left for college. I wouldn't be surprised if your father has a new girlfriend."

Shaking my head, I told her, "You know as much as I do, Dad would never do something like that. Maybe he's stressed from work."

"Don't make excuses for your father. You haven't been here to see how he acts around them. I doubt you want to hear this, but they moved in last month, and we haven't been intimate since. Every night we go to bed, I try, but he claims he has a headache and falls asleep. Men don't care if they have a migraine when it comes to sex. Having a headache is the woman's excuse."

After a heavy sigh, I poked at my food some more. I told her, "I've never seen a happier couple than you and Dad. In fact, I've never seen you argue about anything, ever. You've always been perfect for each other."

She said, "Not everything is peaches and cream. It may seem that way on the surface, but there's something else going on."

The phone slammed the receiver, and my father returned with an eager smile on his face.

Mom refilled her glass and asked, "Who was that?"

"Selina, from next door."

He sat down and resumed his meal. Mom raised a stiff eyebrow.

"What did she want?"

With a mouth full of food, Dad replied, "Hmm? Oh, uh, she and Todd invited us to attend a party at the *Blue Hills Country Club* this weekend."

Mom smacked her lips and finished her drink in one

gulp. Unmasking her sarcasm, she said, "Sounds like fun."

According to the clock beside my bed, Addelyn had three more hours remaining on her flight. No matter how hard I tried, no matter what I did to entertain myself, painful thoughts toyed with my emotions. I couldn't help but picture Addelyn sitting next to Vance on the airplane, holding hands, leaning on each other, and desperately waiting to land so they could spend private time together. I envisioned the airplane restroom, with Addelyn pinned against the wall, with Vance between her legs, gaining their membership into the mile-high club.

Wincing the thought away, I sat up, turned off my light, and turned on the television. Each flicker of the screen flashed images of wheels of an airplane landing on the runway. Suitcases circling the carousel. A cab ride to a hotel. The door closes and the first thing Addelyn does is fall back onto a bed, pulling Vance on top of her. Clothes getting tossed on the floor. Pillows pushed aside. Blankets rolling off the mattress. Zooming into wrestling tongues. Heavy breathing. Addelyn, gasping, moaning. Closeups of her sweat, her fingernails, digging into Vance's ass cheeks, pulling him inside her with violent motions like she can't stand to wait another second without it. Licking her lips. Laughing. An entire week of this, miles away from getting caught, and not a person with them who would tell me about it.

I stood from my bed and paced the room. Two hours remained on her flight. Given the long drive home, I was exhausted. Despite my tiredness, there was no way I could sleep. I heard my parent's bedroom door close and my father's footsteps thumping downstairs. I hurried to the window and peeked outside. Across the lawn, across the fence, the neighbor's bedroom light glowed. The neighbor, Selina, undressed in front of an open window. Her seductive eyes gazed outside as though putting on a private show for someone watching from ground level.

From my room, I heard the front door open. My father's voice, mumbling. Then, the door closed. Smaller footsteps made their way toward my bedroom. A knock. Two knocks. So, I opened the door.

There stood Addelyn with tears trailing down each cheek, holding her suitcase. She dropped it to the floor and buried her weeping face in her hands.

"I couldn't go."

I imagined the ocean waves of Destin, Florida washing over me with relief.

"Why? What happened?"

"I couldn't shake this feeling like something bad might happen."

She didn't need to say it. Vance's intentions went far beyond simply filling an empty seat. He would have had Addelyn all to himself for a week. Yet, I couldn't shake my curiosity of what she meant by 'something bad might happen.' Neither of us were big on precognition or superstition. She had no way of knowing if the plane would crash, or if she'd get kidnapped by some Colombian drug cartel, or whatever. Vance didn't seem like the kind of guy who would force himself on women. So, I came to the conclusion through mere common sense; Addelyn didn't trust herself around him. She feared she might have done something bad, something she would later regret.

She hugged me tighter than ever before, sobbing against my chest.

I combed my fingers through her hair and said, "It's okay. I'm glad you're here. I don't know why I thought I could make it so long without you. I would have lost my mind." Kissing her forehead, I added, "I would have gone crazy."

Calvin returns to the present with a touch on his shoulder from Wayne.

"How are you feeling now?"

"As well as can be expected." Lifting his head, he senses Wayne has something to ask but doubts the appropriate time. "Don't say it. Don't even go there."

Wayne moves toward the door and says, "People believe what they want to believe, regardless of the truth."

"Well, I'm not *those* people."

Wayne turns around and asks, "Did Vance truly invite Addelyn to Destin, or was it you?"

Calvin snickers, hangs his head, and softly says, "You are a piece of shit," His voice grows louder, "for even suggesting such a thing. How else would I be able to recall the precise details?"

"Calm down. I'm simply asking a question."

"What am I, your lab rat?"

Calvin's mind races through other possibilities. Is this some television show with hidden cameras, and any minute, a celebrity host will pop in to reveal it's all a prank, like *MTV's Punk'd*, or *Candid Camera*? Or, is this some government conspiracy? Some mind control experiment? Am I lost in *The Twilight Zone?* He sighs and tells himself to get real. There has to be a logical explanation.

Wayne blows and pops a bubble. He says, "My intentions are to help you."

"Help me with what?"

Wayne checks his watch and, ignoring the question, says, "C'mon. It's time to go downstairs."

In the Gym...

Up until this point, speculation was the only thing itching inside my head. There was no reason to accuse Addelyn of being unfaithful as she made her loyalty quite obvious by not traveling with Vance. Yet somehow, I felt as though Vance didn't lose the game, but like resuming an aged game of chess, came back to take another turn. As time went on, subtle things about Addelyn's demeanor began to feed the idea.

The contractor left minutes after putting the finishing touches on our sauna. I expressed to him how my wife was anxious to try the new Jacuzzi in our master bath, but it wasn't connected because of a leaking water pipe. He checked his worksheet and told me the job wasn't on his list, but he would contact his office and make it a priority. He gave me a business card with a number to call if I didn't hear anything over the next few days.

In the gym half of the basement, lying on my back, on the bench press, I gripped the bar and prepared myself for an intense workout. I've always enjoyed staying fit, not buff, but toned. A tight chest, washboard abs, rock-hard leg muscles. By this time, I had worked my way up to lifting two hundred pounds from the one hundred I could do in high school. Tightening my lips, I pushed hard, exhaled, and lowered the heavy weight to my chest. My muscles burned, pushing away with each breath. Addelyn's voice echoed from the stairwell, growing louder with each step.

She called out, "Sweetheart?"

I set the bar back on the rack and sat up. I turned to my beautiful wife as she hopped from the last step, dressed in a sports bra and tight shorts. She asked, "Do you mind if I join you?"

I used a towel to wipe a glaze of sweat from my forehead and said, "Of course."

I found it rather curious how she suddenly sparked an interest in working out since she didn't before. The majority of her exercise came from evening walks around the neighborhood or swinging in the backyard. She didn't lift weights. She didn't do cardio. She didn't need to. Addelyn was blessed with a high metabolism and flawless skin.

She came close and pecked a kiss on my lips, telling me, "I need to get back in shape."

Back? In shape? I touched her arm, caressing one long stroke down to her wrist, and said, "You're perfect the way you are."

She smiled and replied, "I haven't worked out since Maddie was born. I need to tighten back up."

Since Maddie was born? I couldn't recall a time Addelyn cared about her appearance. That level of confidence comes from someone with a natural beauty. I watched her hop onto the treadmill and press the start button. It beeped, and the belt beneath her feet began to turn.

"Baby fat," she said, hustling to keep up with the speed. "I want to look sexy for you, sweetheart."

Lying back down, I gripped the bar again.

"You've always been sexy to me. Seriously, there's not an ounce of baby fat on you. Not even a stretch mark."

Addelyn increased the machine's speed and jogged faster.

"I'm fortunate, but I feel like I need to stay active. I'm gonna need it."

"For what, babe?"

"To stay healthy, what else?"

I continued pushing the weight and then pulling it back, over and over, focusing on my breathing. For ten reps, my arms felt more and more like Jell-O, and toward the end, I could barely return the bar to the rack. The metal clanked, and the tension vanished.

"Any time I can spend with my love is cherished; you know that."

I sat up, catching my breath and sipping from my plastic water bottle.

Addelyn continued running in place.

She said, "I love you," and I replied with, "I love you," because we never say, "I love you *too*."

I moved over to a raised bar for pull-ups. Wrapping my fingers around the padded handles, I lifted myself from the floor, folding my heels together and stretching my chin to the bar. Addelyn pressed the stop button and hopped from the treadmill.

"See? I can tell I'm out of shape by how short of breath I am already."

Struggling to lift myself once more, I grunted.

"It won't be long before your body regains its stamina."

Addelyn laid on a mat, positioning herself with her knees bent and cupping her neck with her hands.

"I hope so." She sat up, crunching her stomach. I let go, landing on my feet. She did another situp. I took a break and watched her. My heart pounded even harder than it did through the workout. Continuing, Addelyn responded, "Sex with Vance hasn't been this good for a long time."

In the process of wiping my face, I dropped my towel, shot her a look with my stinging eyes.

"What did you say?"

She pushed herself to tighten her abs and touched her elbows to her knees. Her skin glistened with sweat. Wet strands of her hair dangled in front of her face. Her mouth fell open, panting heavy breaths as her body rocked.

"Addelyn!"

"Huh?" She stopped.

"What did you say?"

Rolling onto her knees and fanning herself with her hand, she repeated, "Exercise hasn't been this intense for a long time."

Wayne says, "You oughta get your hearing checked," to which Calvin replies, "There's nothing wrong with it."

The gym is located downstairs on one side of the basement, and inside, mirrors are mounted on the walls. Calvin fears what they will reflect, but he takes the first step and walks inside. Wayne inspects the room and says, "Expensive equipment," as he begins listing the machines on his clipboard. Treadmill—$3,995.

He glances down at his stomach and then over to Calvin's toned arms.

"Did you know the first treadmill was developed to reform convicts while simultaneously crushing grain? Abuse for the greater good. But I guess it's worth it."

Calvin snickers and asks, "Was it?"

"We torture ourselves to look better. After all, symmetry is what gives us beauty."

Calvin pauses with separated lips and asks, "Why would you say that?"

"It's a fact. You've never heard it before?"

"I have."

Chewing his gum, Wayne continues examining and documenting each piece of gym equipment.

Resistance body climber—$4,590.

"Why? Isn't that how it works?"

Calvin tilts his head and grits his teeth. His eyes, welling up with tears. He doesn't know what to say.

Wayne clicks the button on his ink-pen and continues to write. Rowing machine—$1,900. He can sense something is wrong, but his concern is minimal.

He says, "Talk it out, Calvin. This is your gig. Only you have the answers. You're the star of your own show and the member of your own audience. I can't tell you what's going on inside that head of yours. It's up to you to fill in the blanks."

Exercise bike—$1,795.

Calvin lowers himself to his knees. He tries to collect his thoughts. There's someone else. Someone came between us. Addelyn rarely exercised. I should have suspected when she wanted to improve her looks. I should have recognized the timing. She didn't start until Vance came around.

Wayne adds another item, 'Squat stand—$725.'

"You think your wife is cheating on you with another man? A far fetch, my friend."

"Are you reading my mind?"

Wayne chuckles and says, "Please." He blows a bubble and adds, "I was your age once. I know how it goes. You're wondering if she's with another man and maybe that's why she's not here. Besides, you look like you're about to puke again." Listing the mirrors on his clipboard, he says, "$895 each, times four walls."

Calvin clenches his fist, punches a mirror, and the glass shatters to the floor.

Wayne scribbles over his recent entry, writing beneath it, and says, "Times three."

He lifts a twenty-pound dumbbell from the rack and sets it back down, jotting another note on paper and ignoring Calvin's distress. Complete dumbbell weight rack—$965.

"Tell me about the wedding."

Calvin sniffs and sways his head before he throws it back.

"Jesus, Wayne. What for?"

"We've come this far, and have a ways to go. Fond memories tend to dilute sour thoughts."

The weekend at the *Blue Hills Country Club,* my mother approached the bar, upset for reasons I had yet to learn. She told the bartender, "I need a drink. Not wine, something stronger."

She always drank wine because the taste of hard liquor made her sick. Her request was how I could tell something serious was going on. So, I asked, "Mom, what's the matter?"

I followed her glare across the room to my father clinking wine glasses with the neighbor, Selina.

My mother said, "Look at him. He's a snake."

Turning her away, I replied, "I'm sure there's a reasonable explanation. Let me talk to him."

Mom scoffed and said, "Stand up straight, Calvin. Don't slouch. The room is watching."

Not surprised by her statement, I shook it off. For a

second, I thought, "No wonder dad is acting this way," but I didn't want to cloud my impression of my parents being anything other than perfect. Determined to get to the base of the situation, I let it slide.

Addelyn approached me, took my arm, and said, "Dance with me."

Even though I was hesitant to leave my worrying mother alone to get drunk, she told me to go ahead.

She said, "I'll be fine."

I kissed her cheek and assured her everything would be okay.

Then, I smiled and answered Addelyn, "Of course."

Instrumental music played as we danced in the center of the room, surrounded by other rich people—lawyers, doctors, bankers. To them, we were two more bodies in a crowd, but to us, we were alone, like the time we danced at our prom. Addelyn held my hand close to her chest as we swayed to the rhythm. She said, "This reminds me of high school."

I chuckled and said, "Sure does. I was thinking the same thing, except there's not a recognizable face among us."

Over my shoulder, she could see my mother chugging a glass of whiskey like she had to put out a blazing fire.

She asked, "Why is your mom upset?"

I told her it's nothing. "I'm sure a lot of her problems are in her head. She's always been a pessimist who won't listen to reason."

My mood was something I didn't want to allow my parent's issues to ruin. I noticed other men, young and old, turning their heads to Addelyn. That's when I grinned and touched her face.

"There's something I want to ask you. You can say no. I mean, I don't want you to say no, but you can because it's your decision. If you say no, that's fine."

She giggled, having heard this same line before.

"What do you want to ask me?"

The room seemed to slow down. The commotion settled. The music stopped. Addelyn's smile fell straight, and she covered her mouth as I bent down on one knee, still holding her other hand.

"You will never know in this lifetime or the next how much I adore you. I love you with every breath I take, and without you, I can't think of a reason to go on living." She teared up when I asked, "Addelyn Cope, will you be my wife?"

Everyone in the room inhaled the anticipation of her answer. A joyful tear trickled down her cheek.

She laughed and said, "Well, if you insist."

She pulled me to my feet, and we kissed. The music resumed, and the crowd cheered. My father applauded from the corner. My mother, however, smiled with a half-ass grin and clapped slowly. She always saw the glass half-empty and had a way of pissing on parades. If someone gave her a diamond, she would try to find its imperfections. She looked at my dad and then at me, and her smiling lips vanished into her drink.

Fast forward to after college when Addelyn and I rented a small one-bedroom apartment in the heart of downtown. A spacious loft with hardwood floors on the third floor, overlooking the busy streets and tall buildings. My friends used to jokingly say, "There's no faster way to ruin a relationship than to move in together." But the statement didn't apply to us. It's what we'd been waiting for, to finally share our lives.

The day of our wedding arrived, we held our service at the *Our Lady of Sorrows Parish Catholic Church*. Anyone who has ever attended a Catholic wedding knows it's a big deal. The priest tends to go on for hours before and after bonding a couple in holy matrimony, but there was only one single moment I looked forward to.

I dressed in my tuxedo in the men's room. My hands shook to fasten each cufflink. My father entered and popped the tab of a soda can. He tossed a pill into his mouth and chased it with a chug, swallowing like he had a purpose.

I asked his reflection, "What's that?" trying to adjust my tie.

He approached from behind and assisted me in fixing the bow.

"Pain medication."

"For what?"

"Migraines. I've been under a lot of stress lately."

"Sorry, Dad. We could have waited to do this."

Gently smacking my arm, he said, "No. Don't ever apologize for something like this. Your happiness is *not* an inconvenience. I've been anxious to see my only son get married. The rest of the world could come crashing down for all I care. This is *your* day."

He spun me around to face him. Picking up a lint-roller, he dragged the sticky cylinder along the fabric. I told him I wanted to ask him something without getting him upset.

He said, "Anything, always."

"What's the deal with you and mom?"

"What do you mean?"

"She's not here. We're alone. Whatever it is, you can tell

me."

"Nothing for you to worry about, son. Your mother is the happiest today than I've seen her in years, even on our wedding day."

I decided to skip through the bullshit and ask him bluntly, "Are you cheating on her with the neighbor?"

My father stopped and scoffed.

"The neighbor? Selina? Absolutely not. How did you come up with such a ridiculous theory?"

"It's mother's idea, not mine."

"She said that to you? She thinks I'm being unfaithful? I love your mother more than she knows, more than she will ever know. I've worked hard to provide a decent life for her, for you. I would never, in a million years, jeopardize our marriage."

While he adjusted my sleeves and cuffs, I said, "You need to talk to her."

"I will, but not today. Now, forget all this foolishness."

He stood back, soaking the image of me, his pride and joy on my big day, into his memory. The hug he gave me was the most powerful embrace between a loving father and son, as if it was our first and possibly our last. Of course, I thought nothing of it at the time. I could see in his eyes; he wanted to cry.

He cupped his hand on my cheek and said, "Now, you get out there and marry that gorgeous girl."

God, you should have seen Addelyn walking through the entrance of the cathedral, passing into a new world where all her family and peers waited patiently, excited to see her face, stoked to see her walk by wearing her Alexander McQueen wedding dress by design. The mere sight of her took everyone's breath away, including mine. I stood at the podium next to the priest and my fellow friends. Never had I seen Addelyn more beautiful, and never had I felt so lucky to call her my bride. When I saw her smile, my heart did the thing where it skipped a beat. Had it stopped altogether, I would have died a happy man.

As we took each other's hands, we lost ourselves in each other's eyes. The priest recited the standard vows of marriage. Something like, "I take thee to be my spouse, to have and to hold, to love and to cherish, from this day forward, for richer or poorer, in sickness and in health, for better or worse..."

So engulfed by her elegance, I repeated these words, but before he pronounced us man and wife, I unfolded a small sheet of paper from my breast pocket and presented Addelyn with my own vows. I told her, "It's difficult to define a beginning until it settles in the past. Looking back, I realize the day we met was the day I was forever changed. The only way my heart can express its feelings is through my words. So pay attention. Listen closely. To love you, to adore you, is my purpose. To protect you, to care for you, to provide for you, is my mission. To make you happy to the fullest extent is my promise. Never forget our hearts beat together. To break yours is to break mine. Therefore, I swear I will never cause you tears. I love you, Addelyn. You are my everything."

Her eyes welled with tears, and when she smiled, one trickled down her cheek. With my thumb, I wiped it away, and our kiss silenced the room.

With chairs full of friends and family of both the bride and the groom, the reception came with many congratulations and gifts. Addelyn and I fed each other pieces of cake and chased them with champagne. We danced our first dance to *"Love at First Sight"* by *Jordan Mackampa* while the crowd watched from their tables. She rested her chin on my shoulder and said, "I love you," and I replied with, "I love you," because we never say, "I love you *too*."

As the song came to an end, everyone applauded. Then, it happened. My happiest moments came to a halt. My smile fell straight when I saw my parent's neighbor, Todd, standing beside my mother near the refreshments. He whispered something in her ear and squeezed her butt cheek. I expected her to swing around and smack him across the face, but she wasn't offended. She didn't push him away. Instead, she grinned, licked her index finger, and tapped his nose, all while my father stood ignorant to the situation, clapping his hands with the rest of the crowd.

I told myself this would be nothing like my parent's marriage. Addelyn and I will find the perfect home where we can start a family and live a life of love and laughter, without secrets, without betrayal...'Til death do us part.

Calvin notices Wayne still chewing his gum and asks, "Is that the same piece you've had this whole time?"

He nods, blowing a bubble, and replies, "The taste lasts longer than boring old chewing gum. You want a piece?"

"No, thank you."

Wayne adds another item. Adjustable bench press— $950. He sifts through plausible reactions if he were to ask questions like, "Are you sure Vance didn't marry Addelyn?"

Calvin would likely lose his shit and become even angrier. Or if he asks, "Are you sure Vance's father didn't work for *The A Corporation?*" Calvin might blow a gasket and go berserk. Instead, Wayne remains quiet. Now is not the time. This young man, this kid, seems to find comfort revisiting his proudest achievements, whether or not they truly belong to him.

Wayne tosses his head to the side and says, "Let's take a look at the sauna."

In the Sauna...

My new job at *The A Corporation* was no big secret.
Everyone knew I had been sling-shot to the position because
of my father and his associate. Still, I sensed some
resentment from the other employees. The younger Ivy
league guys in their impeccable suits, the men slightly above
my age, they could see right through me and within my
transparency, could tell I was scared shitless.

A secretary led me to my new office on the fifth floor of
the building, through a prison wing of cubicles where data
analysts and advisors worked their magic. I overheard a
small trio of programmers and engineers whispering from
their seats. One had been talking non-stop before I came in,
droning on about what I could only assume was me. The
chatter transitioned to a slight mutter when I walked by.
They called each other by their last names, and if I remember
correctly, the blabber mouth's last name was Harrison.

He mumbled statements like, "He better not let this job
go to his head," and "I give him a year before he fucks it
up," and "You should see his wife." From the corner of my
eye, I saw him cup his hands to his chest, insinuating he had
seen Addelyn's voluptuous breasts before. "Hottie," he
whispered.

A second guy from the threesome said in a low voice,
"He's not so tough. He looks like he could trip over a fart."

The third lowered his head and used his hand to shield
his face.

He asked, "Are you crazy?" He smacked the second
guy's shoulder and said, "Even Harrison knows when to shut
up. That guy's father is a member of the board, and all it

takes is a call to daddy to have you canned faster than tuna."

For a moment, I considered ways to earn their respect. I pictured myself as one of them, out in the nightclubs until the morning hours, drinking from five-hundred-dollar bottles of liquor, snorting cocaine off beautiful women's tits, howling at the moon. I could pay for it all, my treat. I could indulge in the stereotype, go sailing on boats to visit private islands. I could give up everything easily and stay numb all the time at the expense of my bottomless bank account, but why risk it? I had a wife who loved me, and a respectable apartment overlooking downtown. Addelyn and I were planning to start a family, so why let it spiral down the drain?

Regardless of my intentions, I felt out of place, wondering how long it would take before I caved under pressure. Yet, by afternoon on my first day, someone helped me feel right at home.

My father had scheduled me for lunch with the CEO, Quincy Mayfield, who founded *The A Corporation* in the 1970s. Despite his challenges, he became one of the richest men in the world, but you would never know it. He didn't prize himself above anyone. He dressed for comfort, not style, in all black pants and shirts and white sneakers. We sat alone in the cafeteria with everyone else passing by as though he was one of them. Nervously, I ordered what he ordered. A caesar salad, avocado toast on wheat, and bottled water. He insisted I call him Quincy and not Mr. Mayfield or Sir. He told me he wakes up in bed, takes a shower, dresses himself, and comes to work like everyone else. The only difference is his position at the company.

He said, "Empty people define themselves by their career."

Quincy gave me a brief rundown on the history of his business and how he named it after his mother Abigail who he never had a chance to meet.

He said, "Many times, the perfect life comes at a price." He explained when he was a baby, his older brother murdered his family and set his crib on fire, leaving Quincy with a burned scar over half his face. His older sister survived as well, and raised him to become the man he was. He struggled for years to overcome his fear of being in public, worrying how others saw him, but in the end, things worked out fine.

Quincy reminded me the best place to be is in the present, focus on the future and not dwell on the past. He told me what a tremendous asset my father was to his company and how excited he felt for the next generation coming through. He asked, not interrogated, about my life and plans. I told him about my wife and our recent marriage. He asked if we wanted children and I shrugged, saying, "We're planning on it."

He mentioned his daughter, a police officer named Avery Mayfield. He told me she was a handful growing up, but despite his wealth and success, he raised her to be humble and not a spoiled brat.

He said, "Children are the real treasure. The best way to keep them on the right path is to not only protect them, but also express how much you love them, even if they don't understand the magnitude."

In closing, as we returned our empty trays to the dishwashing station, a lady approached and apologized for interrupting. She handed Quincy a note and said something about a journalist from *The New York Times* wanting to write an article about his life and how he revolutionized modern-day technology.

He said, "Violet Fane."

The lady smiled and walked away, seeming to understand the message. Quincy noticed the puzzled look on my face. He laid his hand on my shoulder and informed me Violet Fane authored a poem which coined the phrase, "Good things come to those who wait."

An unsettled dread plagues Calvin's conscience. To remember bad memories is to relive them as new experiences, each leaving behind more questions without answers.

Wayne itemizes the next thing in sight and says, "I'm twice your age and don't have toys like this." He writes down: Tanning bed—$2,999. "How does a twenty-five-year-old kid make this kind of a living?"

"You know this already. Don't you remember? When you sold us this house, you mentioned my tragedy and offered your condolences."

Wayne leans against the wall with his clipboard folded in his arms. "You're right. I'm sorry." He continues chewing his gum and tucks his pen away to his pocket. He asks, "Why are you so afraid to be happy?"

Calvin tilts his head. "I'm not afraid of being happy."

Wayne takes a lap around the room while he says, "They have a name for it, you know? Acrophobia is the fear of heights. Basiphobia is the fear of falling. There's also Cherophobia, the fear of happiness eventually being destroyed by misfortune. People say it all the time: if something is too good to be true, it probably is."

"Can you blame them? Life has no guarantees."

"A lesson you learned the hard way." The room fills with a temporary silence, punctuated with the pop of Wayne's bubblegum. He adds, "In this day and age, stress has become part of society. Anxiety used to be abnormal, but now, it's hard to find anyone who doesn't panic over petty circumstances. However, fear has to sprout from a seed, and to grow, a seed needs to be planted." He pauses and asks, "For what tragedy did I offer my condolences?"

Calvin sits on the edge of the tanning bed with his head between his knees, knowing of all the joyful memories Wayne has asked him to recollect, a hapless incident would inevitably arise.

Many parents say the best day of their life is the day their child is born. When Maddie came into our lives, mine changed for better *and* for worse. Addelyn and I loved our daughter without even knowing her, before she was conceived, loving the idea of her existence. And when she finally arrived, we couldn't have been happier. Some people warn how much of a burden raising children can be. I couldn't think of anything more special, nor could I recall a time my life had ever felt so complete. Maddie gripped her tiny hands around my finger. The doctor, the pediatrician, said this was a natural, involuntary reflex. Yet, I knew her grasp to be a bond. I promised her she could depend on me to always protect her, and this connection we shared, would never break.

Addelyn's eyes drew to mine, and we kissed before I said, "I love you," and she replied with, "I love you."

We never say, "I love you *too*." Adding the word 'too' in response to our affection seemed more like reassurance or a bland acknowledgment. For both of us to simply say, 'I love you,' felt more authentic, more meaningful.

While Maddie slept, Addelyn expressed her hunger since she had nothing to eat during her ten hours of labor. I offered to run and get her something to eat from a nearby restaurant, rather than the boring hospital food from the cafeteria. When I returned, my father's secretary called to inform me he was also in the hospital. One minute, working in his office, and the next, in the snap of a finger, began seizing and fell into a coma.

I left Addelyn in her room with the baby and took the elevator to the intensive care unit, where I found my mother sitting in a chair at his bedside. She said she had to go home, that the day's events were too much for her to handle, so I stayed up all night, splitting time between my new family and my father. He had a fever, and nothing the doctors gave him could control it. They said he suffered from an undiagnosed brain tumor and told me he would never wake up.

New parents are exempt from limited visiting hours, and the hospital staff was friendly enough to extend this courtesy so I could bring Maddie along to see my dad. I like to think he somehow opened his eyes, even a glimpse, to see his granddaughter. I don't care about the truth; it's what I wanted to believe. I couldn't accept it otherwise. For the nine months leading to her birth, my father could barely contain his excitement. He spent a fortune on baby clothes and furniture. The most expensive things were still not enough for his new angel. He bought her a teddy bear and kept it waiting on a blanket in her crib. He purchased a playpen and other toys as well as a spinning mobile that played a music box of lullabies.

That night, my body ran on caffeinated soft drinks from a vending machine. My mind, on the other hand, was fueled by thoughts of a hopeful future and devastating grief. The next morning, I waited for my mother to return so I could go home and freshen up. I planned to bring some things back for Addelyn and, fingers crossed, eventually take a nap. She felt dirty lying around in a hospital gown and asked me to return with some clean clothes. Mom, however, didn't show up.

Around noon, I stopped by her house, and that's when I found them.

My mother's moaning, "Fuck me," over and over again, kept her from hearing my entrance. I opened her bedroom door and found her naked, straddled on the neighbor Todd like a bull rider in my father's bed, shouting, "Fuck me like my husband is watching."

I froze. I couldn't move. I stood there, feeling my blood boil inside me. Since my father wasn't home, I took the brunt of her betrayal. It's as though she betrayed me too. The whole time, she'd been lying, casting the blame on my dad. And the phrase she used to excite her treachery, how despicable, as if the thought of my father's suffering had become her fetish.

She and the neighbor stopped when they noticed me. Rather than dive under the covers, my mother lit a joint and told me to stand up straight and stop slouching before instructing me to close the door. I didn't know she smoked marijuana, but some secrets require others to stay hidden. Anything to mask the guilt, I guess.

Later, she tried justifying her actions by telling me my

father had been cheating on her with the neighbor's wife, Selina. When she found out, she said she didn't think it was fair if he had all the fun. Doing the same thing behind his back made her feel better about it. Revenge, she said, but I refused to believe her, not after what my dad told me on my wedding day. From then on, I was afraid that if the people I trusted could be so heartless, who's to say I could trust anyone?

My father died the next day. I don't know if my mother believed it could happen. I don't think she expected his illness to be real. When Addelyn and Maddie were discharged, I called my mother, feeling shitty enough as it was, thinking a feud with her only worsened our loss. Even though I felt she didn't deserve it, I thought maybe she would like to see her granddaughter. However, each time I dialed the number, her phone continued to ring. Eventually, I drove to her house, fearful of what I might discover. Again, I found her naked in her bedroom, only this time, she was dead, lying on top of the sheets with an empty bottle of my father's prescription pain pills and a depleted bottle of wine.

As I suspected, as it turned out, my father was never unfaithful. He had no affair with Selina. My cheating mother had been sleeping around behind his back ever since the neighbors moved in. Dad knew it. That's why he was so upset and under so much stress. That's why he insisted on answering the phone and why he spoke with Selina at the Country Club. The two shared common ground. I learned this from my mother's confession to me, the suicide note she left on the nightstand. It said she couldn't face me again, not after what she had done. Still, to this day, I think guilt is what killed her. I'll never forget the look on her face. The empty, cold stare into nothing. It doesn't matter how rich or how poor they are—everyone dies with the same lifeless expression.

What they say is true: when you die, your possessions don't come with you. The only thing more disturbing than one funeral is having another at the same time. My mother and father were both displayed in separate coffins placed head-to-head, surrounded by flowers and heart-shaped balloons. To those blind to the situation, they had been put to rest as two lovers who lived and ultimately died together. I'm not sure why, but I didn't shed a tear throughout the entire service, not even afterward. If I had to guess, I'd say because the shock had yet to settle in.

Many of my father's acquaintances approached me with unfamiliar faces. People he worked with, people from his golf club. All their outfits were the same. Suits and ties. Shiny loafers. Each smelled of similar expensive cologne. They shook my hand with firm grips and offered their condolences. Their nameless wives wore fancy dresses and hats with lace, see-through shrouds hanging over their faces. They used their husband's handkerchiefs to wipe away fake tears from intoxicated eyes covered by black sunglasses. These women came to Addelyn and gawked at our new baby and told her what a shame it was we had to suffer through this misfortune. These heartless adversaries were numb because they could afford to be. They had become soulless, careless, and their attendance was nothing more than a show. They told me things I knew already, like "Your father was a good man," and "Your mother was so beautiful." With a dry mouth, it became hard to speak, hard to respond to them, to thank them for their kind words, and after a while, I stopped trying altogether. It became clear these people were not there to express their sympathy, rather to squeeze in a little for themselves. My parent's funeral had become a business meeting, a gossip column filled with people organizing to fulfill some sort of social obligation. The men conversed about merger proposals, client lists, and profitable accounts. The women rapped about people they hadn't seen in a long time. Some congratulated me on my success, my position at *The A Corporation*, and those who heard of my newly inherited prosperity, invited me to take my father's place in their social circle.

I promised Addelyn we would have a perfect life, but not how these people saw fit. My goal was to provide for my family the best way I knew how without falling heir to my parents imperfections. Addelyn saw the strength in me. She assured me if we could make it through this, we could make it through anything.

The day after the funeral, I met with the family attorney to discuss my options. One, I could keep my parent's property, their vehicles, their house, anything and everything that once belonged to them. However, with all the stale memories attached, I had to let go. There's no way I could visit their home without expecting them to greet me when I walked in. I'd have to keep reminding myself they're gone, and if that's the case, all their stuff should go with them. So, the attorney and I settled for the second option, to sell everything and save the money in the bank. Their cars, I traded in for different models. I gave one to Addelyn and kept the other for myself. Most of their furniture was sold to friends or consignment shops, however, their bed (mattress, frame, and sheets included), I dragged into their backyard, doused it with gasoline, and tossed a match. As the flames feasted on the symbol of my mother's sins, I threw her suicide note in as well. Later, their house went up for auction.

My father left everything to me, the sole beneficiary of his estate, his seven-figure bank account, more money than I knew what to do with, yet no amount could fill the void he and my mother left behind. Through their deaths, they ordained me into this lifestyle, but I couldn't have cared less for all the money if it couldn't bring them back. That's when I finally broke down. That night, I cried harder than I ever had before. Addelyn stayed up late, lying next to me, holding me, comforting me. I couldn't stand the thought of my parents never getting to know their granddaughter. I couldn't handle the idea that I would never be able to tell my father how much I loved him. Worst of all, my mother would never know I forgave her.

Addelyn said something to put my mind at ease. She told me my parents left their possessions as a means of passing along a torch, so I wouldn't need or want for anything, and when our time comes, we'll pass them along to our children. As long as their names are mentioned, their memory will never fade.

Wayne paces with slow steps, inspecting the rest of the room.

He asks, "Did you know our brains predict the outcomes of our actions based on our experiences, not what is likely to be true. This leaves us with a less accurate view of the world, shaping our reality into what we already expect or believe."

Calvin wipes his nose, sniffles, and asks, "Why do you talk like you're at a seminar?"

Wayne pauses, and says, "Seems to me your fear of

happiness comes from what you encountered with your parents."

For whatever reason, Calvin doesn't want to admit his agreement, even though, to him, it makes perfect sense.

Then, Wayne asks, "Did you know the average length of time couples spend having sex, without the foreplay, is only five to seven minutes?"

Calvin stands motionless, unaware of what to do or what to say.

"I'm speechless, to say the least. I finish telling you about my parent's death and you respond with a random tidbit of information about sex?"

Wayne moves toward the sauna, to the undamaged compartment encased with glass.

He smacks his gum and says, "My words are like pencils; they all have a point."

Calvin rolls his eyes.

"Great, now we're using puns."

"You should appreciate my weak attempt to lighten your mood." Adding another item to his list, he whispers to himself, "God knows you're gonna need it." Clearlight infrared sauna—$8,299. "As I was saying, "No matter how many years you spend building relationships, a life, a family, a few minutes is all it takes to pull the rug out from underneath."

As Calvin steps out of the way, the basswood finish sparks a vision of thick steam rising and revealing handprints on the glass. A closeup of Addelyn's wet mouth. Beads of sweat trailing down her back. Someone's shirtless body wrapped in her arms with their face buried between her breasts. The diamond on her wedding band glimmers in the light. Her sparkling ankle bracelet. Her curling toes. A man's

BRADLEY CARTER

fist, gripping and pulling her hair. Their interlaced fingers. Her lips panting heated breaths in his ear. Their entangled body parts, rocking against each other. Addelyn, acting as though she's found a new love. Vance, snickering while he uses her body as an accomplishment, an achievement.

Snapping back, Calvin's pain is comparable to a horse kicking him in the chest. Wayne notices his colorless face and queasy expression.

"Do you know what provokes the heartache you feel? Do you understand what drives you insane? It helps to know the cause and effect of your emotions, the origin from which they bloom."

Attempting not to whimper, Calvin says, "I love her."

"Is it love, though? Try biology. It's a blessing and a curse. Say you weren't in love with Addelyn. Say you saw her passing by in the street with another man. Would you be this miserable?" Wayne blows a bubble and it pops, leaving a sticky residue on his lips. He uses the entire piece to dab away the excess and puts it back in his mouth. He continues by saying, "We all strive for perfection, but no matter what, there's always someone else better looking, more attractive, healthier, stronger, sexier, more successful, better in bed. These are the rules of nature, and it's our own nature working against us. Tormenting us." He digs in his pocket and removes a small calculator. Resting it on his clipboard, he punches numbers and buttons while he says, "People consider sex as taboo, but on the contrary, it's our basic animal instinct, necessary for the survival of our species. There's no denying it; sex feels good. We crave it. We yearn for it. We indulge in it recreationally. That's the point. I'm not saying our goal is to go out and make a bunch of babies, but at the core of this lustful gift, the sole purpose of sex is

107

reproduction, and reproducing keeps the species intact. If we didn't love it, we wouldn't do it, and eventually go extinct." Wayne grunts at his calculator like he's made a mistake. He clears the screen and reenters the numbers. He asks, "Have you ever wondered why the same people who shame sex celebrate pregnancy or the birth of a child? I'll tell you why. It's because they're all a bunch of hypocrites. It's not their fault. We're animals." He taps more buttons and chews his gum. "It's in our nature to hunt, to reproduce, and to kill. Because we have a conscience, because we've become *trained* animals, we set rules in place to protect the herd. We create standards, categorizing them by what offends us, what threatens us. We reward good behavior and set consequences for those who don't follow along. Unfortunately, more often than not, some people don't abide by the rules. They forget about the animal inside until it takes control, and when it happens, when the dust settles, they wonder what went wrong."

Calvin is listening, but the more Wayne lectures, the more confused he becomes. Not from the information, but trying to find the tip of the hypothetical pencil. His face scrunches, watching Wayne carry on as he says, "The resentment toward a cheating spouse is involuntary. Look at it from a perspective of evolution. Some people argue jealousy comes when someone you care for finds pleasure from another partner when, in fact, it's a trait designed to protect one's bloodline. Mating occurs when two parties bond together. Their features attract one another, which tells the parties involved how healthy their offspring will become. Ever notice how wealthy people seem to have better genes? There's a reason for this. The rich want nothing but the best. The better the symmetry, the better the outcome."

Calvin lowers his head more with each sway and says, "Forgive me for being so blunt, but what the fuck is your point?"

Wayne continues chewing his gum while adding on his tiny machine. He explains how a spouse showing signs of interest in another potential mate sends a signal that he or she has chosen to reproduce with someone else. He says, "The jealousy becomes physical. Someone else has entered the picture. Someone else your wife wants to have sex with. And when the person you love betrays your trust, the anger comes from the threat against your bloodline. They don't want you anymore; they want someone else, someone better." He pauses to press the total button and bounces his head. "Quite often, the more you tend to believe something, the more you realize it's possible. The mind has the horrific power to turn against itself. With your world crashing down while rising at the same time, you feel your sanity slipping away while becoming so transparent. You can't deny the possibility that jealousy began to sprout when your mother engaged with another man right underneath your father's dying nose, but what you should be asking yourself is; did it really happen?"

Calvin throws his hands aside and begins to shout, "Are you—," but Wayne holds a finger out to hush him.

"Hear me out. I'm not saying I'm right. I'm not saying you're wrong. The point is for you to second-guess yourself, to find the facts beyond doubt. Consider the possibility you may have become so envious of Vance's perfect life that your mind slipped you into his reality. Is what you remember a glimpse of your obsessions? Are you experiencing Vance's reality? Did he experience these horrific things? And if so, why are *you* the one paying the price?"

This endless jargon dizzies Calvin as it spins in a whirlwind with him in the center. He grabs the top of his head and his knees weaken beneath him.

Enraged, he shouts, "Stop!"

Wayne does so.

He takes a step back, lowering his clipboard, and says, "Take a deep breath. I'm sorry. Perhaps I've gone about this the wrong way. You're right, everything you remember throughout your earlier life is true. Meeting Addelyn in the park. Summer camp. The football game. The prom. The wedding. All of it." He chews a few times, allowing a brief moment to pass for Calvin to calm down. Then, he adds, "The reason I ask these things is because I believe it's the only way for you to understand what happened here today."

The spinning stops and Calvin rolls over on the floor.

"How?" He covers his face with his hands. "How does it help me understand?"

Wayne uses the empty wrapper from his pocket to dispose of his gum.

He says, "By training your brain to see both sides, how things were, and how different things could have been. By enabling your ability to question everything. Think about it. What you remember in clarity takes place before you bought this house. Once you moved in, things began turning sideways, and eventually, accumulated to the point where your memories became entangled with, for lack of a better word, the truth."

Wayne writes the total amount accumulated so far— $37,095, before flipping to the next blank piece of paper.

He removes his glasses, and asks, "After all, Calvin, isn't that when you started hearing voices?"

Northwest corner. To the front. To the left.
That's where you'll find it.

In the Clubhouse...

Wayne unwraps a fresh piece of bubblegum, noting Calvin's embarrassment for having a potential psychiatric condition.

He says, "What you went through with your parents is enough to make anyone nuts, but don't worry..." He tosses the gum in his mouth and trails his finger down a list of items on his clipboard, then begins chewing while he scribbles Basement entertainment room, and continues by saying, "...Their death has nothing to do with the voices."

Quizzically speaking, Calvin asks, "How do you know?"

Blowing a bubble, Wayne holds it long enough to deflect one question with another. The bubble pops and he asks, "Do you know what else can drive someone insane?"

Calvin waits quietly for an answer.

Wayne says, "Perfection is a mirage. It's a rainbow in your backyard. The closer you get, the farther it moves away. It's something you can chase but not acquire. The problem is the pot of gold doesn't exist. Everyone has flaws, especially these conceited people at your parent's funeral. Do you remember your neighbors from earlier? Remember when I showed up, when you saw Mr. and Mrs. Silver walking along the sidewalk?"

Calvin bobs his head, anticipating an explanation.

Wayne says, "Dark secrets fault everyone." Before leaving the gym and sauna, he turns off the light. "If not for their pride, the Silvers could have been walking their baby grandson in a stroller. Instead, upon learning their daughter, Olivia, was pregnant at the age of sixteen, they forced her to get an abortion. God forbid human nature tarnished their reputation. The Silvers tried to hide their secret so they could sustain a good standing reputation with the members of their church since premarital sex is frowned upon. If anyone found out, they vindicated their actions by lying and telling them their daughter was raped."

Wayne kicks pieces of a broken mirror out of their path as he and Calvin walk together.

"Remember Mr. Lang refusing to mow his lawn in your presence? Last summer, he was bragging to his colleagues about the success of his yacht business. To keep his stomach settled from the threat of filing bankruptcy, he's been chewing through handfuls of antacids each day. His boating company is sinking, and to keep his trophy wife from filing for divorce, he plans to evade paying taxes over the next year, which will inevitably leave him with nothing but a hefty jail sentence."

Calvin snickers and says, "You're kidding me."

"And remember Mr. and Mrs. Hill across the road, closing their curtains when you caught them spying on you? Behind those drapes hides a life they don't want you to see. Mrs. Hill has her nose stuck so high in the air, she gets nose bleeds from the altitude. All her lavishing acquaintances, the members of her social circle, those so-called friends she meets with for brunch, they'd be disgusted to learn her dirty little secret. Really, those nosebleeds come from hepatitis. When Mr. Hill comes home late from work, he eats leftovers for dinner. Though she ignores it, his wife has known about his habitual conference calls with a prostitute at a shit-hole motel. For the sake of their two children, to uphold the oath of 'for better or for worse,' she pretends to believe his excuses. Right now, as she's warming his plate in the microwave, she's trying to find a delicate way to break the news that, through his deception, he's infected her with the disease, and if word gets out, the news will undoubtedly taint their eminence.

For the first time today, Calvin laughs at someone else's expense, but Wayne pauses to face him until his smile falls straight.

He says, "You have secrets, too."

Calvin leans against the wall, clutching a fist to his chest. He struggles to stand from the weight of his guilt, having yet to discover the cause.

Wayne is completely still except for the motions of his chewing jaw.

He asks, "What happened between you and Addelyn?"

Shaking his head, trying not to throw up, Calvin says he doesn't know.

Wayne tells him to stop trying to think of everything at once. "Retrace your steps along the timeline."

Ending a series of panting breaths, Calvin inhales, holds it, and lets it out slowly.

Addelyn's parents showed up to take the baby for the weekend. She and I answered the front door and Maddie began crying from the living room. The four of us returned to find her standing up, supported by the rails of her playpen. I rushed to her aid, leaning over and holding my arms apart to pick her up, but the closer I came, the louder she fussed. Her screams escalated to a wretched shriek.

Addelyn's father said, "Babies cry to communicate discomfort, like a wet diaper, an empty stomach, or because they're sleepy. When infants have cheeks drenched with tears, it's a sure sign of pain or fear."

Puzzled, I asked, "What's the matter, sweetheart?" I lifted her and tried soothing her by bouncing her in my arms, but she squirmed and kicked, desperate to break free, reaching for her mother. The split-second Addelyn took her away from me, Maddie instantly calmed down as though nothing had happened. Confused, I scratched my chin and said, "I guess she wanted her mommy."

Both her parents gave me this suspicious look, not as if I had done anything wrong, but that I might sometime in the future. They didn't say another thing to me, even when they left.

Shortly after, Addelyn peeked into the living room, where she found me lying on the sofa with a wet washcloth folded over my forehead. The television was on, but muted. For some reason, my vision became blurry while trying to watch the football game, and the sound of the announcers gave me a headache. Addelyn laid beside me and caressed my face.

"Poor baby. How are you feeling?"

"Better, now that you're here."

She kissed my cheek and asked, "Do you think you might feel like going out later?"

"I don't see why not. Ibuprofen should be working by then."

"Good. I need a break. All work and no play," she said, rolling off the couch. She sprung to her feet and headed to the kitchen to retrieve her cellphone. "We need to liven things up a bit."

I said, "I couldn't agree more," and asked, "What did you have in mind?" but she had left the room already.

The headache went away, and before heading to the nightclub, I doubled up on Ibuprofen in case it returned. We arrived to find a string of patrons stretched around the block. Some danced to the muffled thumping of house music from inside. A steady four-four bass drum and electronic baseline. Each time someone entered the building, a sample of techno bliss leaked out in clear harmony. Several patrons wore short skirts and pleather pants, halter tops and baggy shirts. Addelyn wore a flashy red tank top and black jean shorts, with her belly button exposed and decorated with a golden hoop. She pushed her back against my chest and wrapped herself in my arms and made small dancing motions. Behind us, Paul and Lillian were holding hands with their fingers interlocked. The fifth wheel of their group, Vance, who I wasn't told had been invited, stood with them, glancing around the other patrons as everyone slowly moved toward the entrance. Above, the marquee read: The Clubhouse welcomes world-renowned DJ *Bad Boy Bill.*

Inside, a repetitive bassline in A-minor, but more so than not, a heavy drum with a recorded sample of a man's voice repeating, "Let me work that." The music vibrated the hairs on my arms. Strobes captured still images of silhouettes against a white glowing fog. Green laser beams dazzled over the crowd. Multicolored smart-lights bounced across the room, chasing the music. The bass from the speakers drowned the eardrums of the partygoers and tickled their bodies.

The DJ, dressed in a Fortune t-shirt, black G Star jeans, a Chrome Hearts hat, and black Jordan One high-top shoes, hugged one side of his headphones between his ear and shoulder, matching the beat, so a new song could segue seamlessly from the previous track. His fingers pinched and twisted knobs on the illuminated mixer-board between two sets of Pioneer decks. He did all of this as though it came as second nature, as if he'd done so for decades, fine-tuning the audio and blending the previous track to the original mix of *'For President'* by *Deorro,* to seem like a single, endless and uninterrupted song. A sample of a woman moaning from sex, along with the humidity in the room causing sweat to form on the exposed skin of bodies in motion, gave the club a orgy-like atmosphere. The beat stopped, and a melodic, rising tone drove the crowd wild. They shouted and screamed. They raised their hands in the air. The DJ put his fingers on a record and began making scratching sounds, like vinyl whips.

In a single breath, Addelyn exhaled a life of stress into a rolling fog from the machines on stage. I hugged her close and ran my fingers across her sweaty stomach. G-major piano chords and a synthesized ambient sound built to a peak, and right as the tune rolled over the top, the chunky bass riff grew faster, escalating alongside a progressive snare drum, building higher and higher until the bassline dropped as though it fell off a cliff. At the bottom of a musical canyon, the kick drum returned with a pounding force of 128 beats per minute, sending spectators into a frenzy.

With the music so loud, verbal communication became impossible. To shout in someone's ear, the listener would have to pretend and nod if they understood, even though most of the time, nothing could be heard. An excited Addelyn led me to the dance floor by pulling one hand behind her. Paul and Lillian bounced to the beat. They screamed and whistled as the song transitioned. Vance was nowhere to be found. Perhaps, he mingled around the venue or made his way closer to the stage to observe the intriguing works of the DJ. By pointing my thumb over my shoulder, I motioned to my wife the need to get something to drink from the bar. She kissed my cheek and pointed to the ground, gesturing she would wait for me in the same spot.

Passing by a police officer at the door, a woman with a jet-black ponytail and a sleeve of tattoos decorating her left arm, I asked directions to the bar.

She shouted, "Northwest corner. To the front. To the left. That's where you'll find it."

Her voice seemed to come from inside my head rather than an external source, clear and distinct enough to hear over the amplified music. I thanked her and walked away, but when I looked back, the officer was gone.

The line to the bar seemed endless despite its short length and visibility of the bartenders pouring drinks and collecting cash. I waited patiently with my debit card in hand, taking slow but progressive steps closer each time another customer left with their drinks. When it came time for me to place my order, I leaned over to shout for a whiskey and coke, as well as a vodka cranberry for my wife. The bartender nodded and began fixing the drinks. During that time, I browsed the sight of the club. I observed the magnificent sanctuary of people, all shapes, sizes, and colors, coming together under one roof in celebration. Each stranger, for whatever reasons, letting loose and taking a break from the stresses of life.

That's when I noticed a couple near the wall beside the stage. From the distance and the darkness, their identity seemed distorted, but I would swear the man was Paul with his face smashing together with another girl that was *not* Lillian. People passed by, blocking my view, and each time I saw them again, my assumptions became more and more clear. Then, a tap on my shoulder distracted me.

The bartender shouted, "Twelve dollars!"

I handed her my card and looked back. This time, the couple was gone. Almost as though I'd imagined them, I glanced around in search of Paul and his mistress, but my curiosity vanished like steam above the crowd. With drinks in hand, I walked over to a nearby stairway leading up toward a VIP area on a balcony. Across the way, I noticed a Hispanic young man, close to my age, surrounded by beautiful women, snorting lines of cocaine from a glass table through a hundred-dollar bill. The UV lights made his white suit reflect a hue of purple. Overall, a glimpse of what my life could be like had I chosen a different path. A security guard stopped me and asked to see my pass, but I told him I didn't have one. I explained I was searching for my brother-in-law, but he said if I didn't have a pass, I needed to stay downstairs.

I made my way back to where I left Addelyn, lifting the beverages to avoid being spilled by patrons as they bumped into me. One of the many lights on the ceiling moved quickly across the crowd, and a bright beam flashed in my eyes. Like a fuse to a firecracker, the pain in my temple started to ignite. With both my hands full, I wasn't able to rub the pain away. Confusion set in. Each direction seemed the same. My vision went blurry, like the room was spinning around me. The view of people laughing, dancing, screaming, played over and over like a short piece of film stuck to a reel. The music, blasting as one solid noise, rose in volume. As I stumbled closer to the center of the dance floor, the crowd spread apart to let me through. Glancing around, I realized Addelyn was gone and so were Paul and Lillian. My heart raced. I feared a panic attack amongst strangers, not knowing anyone who could help me. I tried to breathe but struggled to fill my lungs with air. The glaze of sweat on my palms made holding the drinks more difficult. My ears rang, and soon enough, everything went silent. The dancers appeared to move in slow motion. The DJ pounded his fist in the air at a slow pace. My eyes drew toward the front, against the railing beneath the stage. They focused as each flashing strobe illuminated a split-second frame of the action, like a camera capturing single insights into each passing moment. I saw Addelyn facing my way with her back against Vance and his hand reaching down the front of her pants, and the other wrapped tight around her neck. She rocked her hips as though she was grinding her ass against his crotch. With her head tilted back against his shoulder, his lips investigated her earlobe and his tongue tasted her skin.

In the same slow motion, both drinks slipped from my fingers. Liquid spilled from the rims as each glass tumbled, tossing ice cubes, and eventually shattering across the floor. The sight of Addelyn with another man was devastating, killing me, and all I wanted to do was run and find a secluded place to die alone. Then, out of nowhere, Lillian's hand touched my shoulder. Sound returned, everything resumed to normal speed, and the people continued dancing.

"Calvin!"

I shot her a look and then another back toward the stage. Addelyn and Vance were gone. Were they there to begin with? Did I imagine them?

I leaned closer to Lillian and shouted, "Where is Addelyn?"

She pointed at the exit, and I swear I heard her say, "She's giving him head in the car."

"What?"

She put her mouth closer to my ear and yelled, "She's heading to the car."

Checking the time on my watch, I discovered the minutes had passed into hours, and the club was about to close.

Lillian took me by the hand and said, "Come on; we're leaving!"

In the Basement…

Wayne paces toward the other half of the open basement with hardwood floors and throw rugs. Each smack of his gum matches his steps. He flips a switch on the wall, and individual bulbs fade to a warm glow from their filaments. Scratching his head, he scans around. He puts on his glasses and examines an array of liquor bottles, some empty, some half-full, some broken, and all scattered across the bar. The floor is soggy from a pile of moldy towels and swimsuits Calvin swears were not there before.

He says, "I didn't leave this mess."

Wayne prepares to list more items on a new page and asks, "Are you sure?" Not hearing a reply, he looks to Calvin with a blank expression, shaking his head. Wayne pops his gum and says, "Don't worry. This isn't so bad. You haven't seen the worst of it."

Calvin turns and, with a flat, suspicious tone, asks, "How do you know?"

Has Wayne been in here before? Has he already seen the disastrous house in its entirety?

Wayne doesn't say a thing.

Instead, he pops his gum a second time and asks, "Is this where you entertained your guests?"

Calvin pushes an empty bottle of wine across the counter and comes to a stop beside a tipped-over stool. There's an untouched dartboard hanging from a wall with all the projectiles piercing the bullseye. Wayne steps over to survey the game and logs it in his notes.

Price—$449.

He spins around to a blue-top pool table. The balls hide

in each pocket and a dozen pool sticks rest on a mounted rack.

Price—$3,899.

As he continues to catalog each salvageable item, he makes his way near more furniture.

Harris suede recliner—$1,999.

Calvin kneels and lifts a small vanity mirror from the carpet. Its surface is cracked, and he swipes his finger along a white residue. His eyes close, and he drops to the floor, clenching his fists. He tries to recall the last time he hosted guests, but everything is black.

Wayne clicks his teeth, chews his gum, and searches for anything else he might be able to sell.

Alesund modular sectional sofa—$4,079.

"You're trying to retrieve too much information at once." He opens the door to a mini-fridge behind the bar. There's nothing inside, so he closes it and writes it down. Price: $789. A cabinet above a small sink houses several drinking glasses for martinis, whiskey, and wine. He opens another and finds bins of ground coffee, a large package of sugar, and bottles of creamer. He asks, "Have you eaten lately?"

Calvin scratches his forehead and paces the center of the room.

His stomach growls, and he replies, "Not since breakfast."

Wayne slides open a drawer of plastic silverware, drinking straws, a corkscrew, and a stack of bar napkins.

"I wonder why."

Calvin clenches his stomach, and it growls again.

"Dinner wasn't in the plans."

Wayne turns to face him from behind the bar.

"You can't remember anything after you left this morning, but you know you didn't plan to eat afterward? There must be a reason."

Sighing, Calvin throws his head back and rests his hands on each hip.

He says, "I have no idea."

Wayne finds a pair of scissors lying out of place.

Chewing, he says, "When people fall under a lot of stress, their emotions can suppress hunger." He pinches the handle and lifts the scissors closer to inspect the clean blades, then sets them down.

Calvin spins around and says, "I wasn't hungry until you…" His eyebrows rise, and his mouth hangs open. "…brought it up."

Wayne says, "Good," hunching over to snatch a small, empty plastic bag from the floor. "This is working."

The inside is coated with the same residue as the mirror. He wipes his finger inside and takes a closer look at his fingertip.

Calvin asks, "*What* is working?"

Ignoring the question, Wayne tastes the powder. It numbs his lips.

Snickering, he says, "You must have held quite a party."

"It wasn't a party." A lightbulb flickers twice in the ceiling, and Calvin begins to remember. "Only a few…people."

The ride home from the club was anything but quiet. It seemed as though the rest of the group didn't witness my brief episode on the dance floor but continued to relive the experience through conversation, recalling funny and entertaining times in the preceding hours. No one questioned my silence or sensed that I was upset. My headache had gone, but I couldn't shake the image of Addelyn and Vance together near the stage.

Driving farther from the city, heading through backroads through tree lines and toward the suburbs, my mind was foggy, like the passing haze above the empty fields lit by the beams of headlights. Paul sat in the passenger seat, turning around to speak to the three in the back: Lillian, Vance, and Addelyn. I adjusted the rearview mirror, but I couldn't see beyond their faces. Who knows if Addelyn and Vance were secretly holding hands? Perhaps, one hand down the other's pants, like before. They wouldn't be stupid enough to show affection, not with her sister and brother-in-law in sight. Then again, if it came down to it, Lillian would take Addelyn's side, no matter what. She wouldn't say anything to me, whether or not she agreed with her actions. And Paul? He wouldn't say anything either, not at the risk of being scolded by his wife.

As unlikely the scenario, my knuckles turned white as I gripped the steering wheel. My thigh muscles tightened. My foot pressed harder on the gas pedal. No one realized the increase in speed, not even me. With a straight face, I stared at the road ahead, lost in passing lines of white and yellow. A cloud of haze began glowing brighter from ahead. I couldn't help but envision Addelyn and Vance playing footsie. When Paul and Lillian laughed, I thought they were laughing at me for not knowing, for playing the fool, and for celebrating my wife's secret new relationship with an old flame. With a sharp turn approaching, I imagined these things. The haze grew brighter, revealing a truck's headlights in the near distance. I continued straight, crossing the yellow line, careless of the potential danger. I used to wonder what it was like not to give a shit about anything, and through my depression, I discovered apathy. I kept my sight fixed between the lights as they grew closer. The driver blasted his horn, and my passengers shouted for me to look out, to pull over, to correct the situation. How cute, these people who banished me from their secrets, now depending on me to save their lives. There I was playing chicken with oncoming traffic. I wondered, but it's doubtful it would have hurt. With my hands on the steering wheel, if I held my path any longer, the car would smash into the truck's front end, and all of this would go away, fast, so quick, I wouldn't feel it. The brain can no longer interpret pain once it's been splattered across the pavement. The truck came dangerously close, but at the last second, I jerked, skidding the car back into my lane. The truck blasted its horn again, and the sound faded behind us. Everyone sat frozen, speechless, tense, except for me. I can't tell you why, but all I could do was laugh.

Back home, in the basement, a variety of liquors sat neatly lined on the bar. A row of drinking glasses glistened from the lights above. It appeared as though the rest of the group had forgotten their near-death experience, but Addelyn wasted no time rushing over to fix herself a beverage.

She tapped the caps of each bottle, deciding which one to select, and spoke the same words my mother said at the *Blue Hills Country Club*.

"I need a drink. Not wine, something stronger."

Addelyn snagged an unopened bottle of Fireball and

twisted the cap. I turned on the projector, but rather than put on a movie, the wall shined from the evening news, the ending of a brief update on the story of the continued search for the gunman involved in a shopping mall massacre.

Turning down the volume of the Dolby Digital surround sound, I said, "There goes the rest of the world being foolish."

Addelyn stood beside me with her cinnamon-flavored drink in hand. The scent caught my attention, and I watched her take a healthy chug as though washing an unpleasant taste from her mouth.

She said, "I don't get it. People complain about video games, movies, and books containing too much violence. There's nothing more disturbing than the news. And it's real life, not fiction, which makes it even more horrific."

She sipped another drink and exhaled once it went down her throat.

With a smirk, I said, "Better be careful. You'll be drunk before you know it."

Playfully, she smacked my arm, showed me the glass, and told me, "It's not a lot, but enough to take the edge off."

At first, I thought the edge was Addelyn's newfound stress from being separated from our daughter. The signs were there. Her nervous demeanor, slightly shaking hands, her inability to stand still. She finished her drink and hurried to refill the glass. Standing behind the bar, I found no reason to say anything about the pain in my head. No need to be a party pooper. I withheld mentioning what I thought I saw and heard at the club.

When Vance stepped over, I tried not to make my insecurity too inconspicuous and asked him, "Can I get you something?"

He said, "Beer, if you got it," and asked, "Do you mind if I use your bathroom?"

"Of course." I pointed at the steps and said, "Upstairs in the—"

Addelyn interrupted me with, "I'll show you," and took Vance by the arm.

My wife had changed to a giddy child, excited to give the company a tour. With a nod, Vance followed her upstairs. I stepped behind the bar to grab a cold brew from the mini-fridge. Lillian took a seat on the stool and smacked her hands on the counter.

"Is Calvin playing bartender tonight? Alright, I'll have a dirty martini, extra olives, please."

Snickering, I sat the beer can down and flipped over a martini glass.

"Don't expect me to serve all night; I plan to have a few myself."

Lillian winked, grinning, and quickly puckered her lips as if simulating a kiss. Strange, I thought, looking at Paul, who took a seat on a section of the couch with his back turned, saying, "I'll have whatever she's having."

Shaking my head, I poured vodka and vermouth into a shaker and replied, "Coming right up."

Drops of condensation slid down the outside of Vance's unopened beer can. Everyone had a drink, including me—a tall glass of straight Kentucky whiskey. I noticed Lillian sitting across from Paul at opposite ends of the room. To a stranger seeing how they avoided conversation, it would have appeared they barely knew each other. Does she know about Paul and the girl at the club? Speaking of which, does anyone know why Vance and Addelyn have been gone so long? I didn't check to see what time they left, but it seems like forever ago. Noting their absence, I nibbled my bottom lip and stared at the floor. The ache in my head threatened to worsen. I remember leaving the ibuprofen upstairs in the half bathroom. There's a perfect excuse to investigate their whereabouts, but do you really want to see what they're up to? Could you handle it?

Heading up the carpeted steps, I tried to make little sound so I could listen as I approached the ground floor. The house seemed empty, vacant, silent. I made my way down the hall, where I found the half bathroom door wide open with the lights off. No Vance. No Addelyn. I checked the living room, the kitchen, and the dining room. No one. I checked the nursery, the garage, and the front porch. Not a soul. Only one place they could be. Standing in the center of the marble-floored foyer, I sent my eyes trailing up the half-staircase to the second floor. Creeping with each step, I listened for any peep, any sound, but nothing came. The lights to both bedrooms and my home office were off. I searched each room, expecting to find my wife and our guest somewhere doing something that would likely destroy me, but it had to be done. Much to my relief and confusion, all the rooms were empty.

Back on the ground floor, laughter and commotion echoed from the basement. I returned by stomping down the steps to announce my presence, but of course, it went unnoticed. Vance sat at the bar, sipping his beer next to Addelyn. From outside looking in, it appeared they were a couple drinking and conversing with another couple, Paul and Lillian. Vance was no longer the fifth wheel, and somehow I had taken his place on the sidelines.

Standing quietly at the base of the steps, I asked, "Where were you?"

The four went silent and turned their faces toward me.

Tilting her head side-to-side, Addelyn asked, "What do you mean?"

"I went upstairs to get ibuprofen thinking you and Vance were still there."

She chuckled.

"Oh, no. I was giving him the grand tour. I showed him the gym and sauna. We must have missed you in passing, babe."

Vance smiled, raising his beer, and said, "It's a gorgeous house, Calvin."

We made eye contact, but I said nothing out loud. What I did say was to myself, in my head.

I don't need some spineless prick's approval. I know the house is gorgeous because I live in it with my *wife*.

I assume my blank stare made things awkward, judging from the lengthy silence.

Resting her drink on the bar, Lillian cleared the air by shouting, "Paul. Did you bring the, you know, stuff?"

Nodding, he chuckled and asked, "Are you sure it's cool?"

Lillian swiped a lock of hair behind her ear and lifted her martini to her lips.

"Of course, it's cool. They're family."

Family? You're right. Everyone except Vance.

Paul reached into his left pocket and removed a small plastic bag of white powder, massaging it with his fingers.

"Addelyn, do you have a small mirror?"

I leaned in to get a closer look and asked, "Is that cocaine?"

Hoping for a positive response, Paul asked, "You don't mind, do you?"

"I don't mind. I've never done it before."

Addelyn stepped closer to the bar, pausing to examine the bag.

"Neither have I."

Vance straddled a stool and threw in his opinion, not like anyone asked him to.

He said, "Oh, you'll love it. It makes you feel... I don't know...alive."

How strange, a neurologist indulging in the sinful life of drugs. What a bad example he must set for the healthcare community. Unless, of course, he too has something to hide.

Sipping and then sloshing my drink in my wife's direction, I asked, "So, honey? Do you have a small mirror?"

Addelyn detected something different in my tone, as if I was being sarcastic or snippy, or even better that I didn't have a care in the world. Perhaps she thought the liquor had lowered my inhibitions, but she would have noticed my first glass was still full had she been paying attention.

She muttered, "I, uh...I think there's one upstairs."

Watching her leave up the steps, I shot a glare to Vance, who stood in front of me, looking like an idiot, trying to decide if he should go with her or sit back down. Needless to say, he chose the latter, and to conceal my anger, I faked a smile and asked, "So, Vance. How's the painting coming along?"

My stern voice had drawn quizzical expressions on everyone's faces.

Clearing my throat, I added, "I'm sorry. It's just that *my wife* and I have been looking forward to seeing your work."

Vance nervously bounced his head.

"They're coming along fine. I'm excited to show—"

Addelyn shouted, "I don't know about this," as she hopped down the stairs. She came back with a vanity mirror in hand. "I'm nervous."

Keeping my eyes locked on Vance, I sensed the relief washing over him.

I said, "Of course, you are," returning my gaze toward her. "It's your first time doing someone, I mean, something new."

Addelyn froze when she heard me say '*someone* new,' but she figured she must have misunderstood since the others had no reaction and continued to gather around the countertop.

Paul poured the powder onto the mirror and whipped out a *Capital One* credit card from his wallet.

"Don't leave home without it."

Lillian rolled her eyes, swirling her finger in her drink.

"That's *American Express*, dummy."

Pulling open a cabinet, he asked, "Does anyone have a straw?"

I stepped over to the sink, slid open a drawer, and removed a plastic drinking straw and a pair of scissors. He cut the straw in half with a snap, long enough to use for snorting.

I wasn't about to experiment with the others. As the sober person of the group, who knows what I would have said or done under the influence of a drug I'd never taken before? With my drink, I strolled over to the couch, where I took a seat in the recliner.

Lillian noticed and tilted her head to me.

"Calvin, don't you want some?"

Ignoring her, I glared at the screen on the wall, watching

images of some late-night talk show, waiting for Addelyn to say something, to acknowledge my aggravation, to acknowledge me at all. Lillian was the only person who noticed. Her eyes floated from me to Addelyn, Vance, and Paul, and then she took a sip.

Vance instructed Addelyn on how to snort cocaine properly. He held her hair back while she leaned over, holding the tip of the straw in her nose, and covering one nostril. She sniffed hard and followed the vanishing line of powder across the mirror. She stood up and gasped, and after a short moment, she felt a wave of euphoria. Smiling, she handed the straw to Vance, nudging his chest with her elbow.

She said, "You're right. It *is* amazing."

A sharp pain splintered my temple, and my vision blurred. I overcame the discomfort by biting the inside of my lip. The bitter taste of blood seeped inside my mouth, and I washed it down with a swish of whiskey. From the corner of my eye, Paul stood with his back facing me, and Lillian waited beside him, for her turn.

Empty bottles of vodka and beer cans sat on the counter. The residue of powder remained on the mirror. The lights had long been turned off, leaving the room in the subtle glow of the projector and muted sound system. On the screen flashed an infomercial for beauty cream, the kind you can buy at any store, but on sale with an exclusive offer. I leaned back in my recliner with my elbow on the armrest. Lillian sat a seat away from me, sniffing and sipping a half-empty bottle of wine, shaking her head at Paul, who was stretched out on the rest of the curved sofa, gazing up at the ceiling in some sort of trance.

On the floor beneath him, Addelyn and Vance sat side-by-side, leaning their backs against the couch. She listened as he babbled something about his parents and how they divorced a year ago.

He said, "My dad bought a new house on the northwest side with his new girlfriend. She's closer to my age which makes things a bit strange, but she's nice."

I lost track of how long the two had been involved in their own private chitchat. Vance explained his artwork, which Addelyn seemed interested to hear. He told her about the basic complimentary color theory—two colors opposing the other, like each side of the same story.

Addelyn said, "I was thinking something erotic, yet abstract. Not something that would offend future guests and family or confuse my daughter when she gets older."

Did she really say "*my* daughter" and not "*our* daughter," like I'm not even here?

Vance bounced his head in thought and said, "Something personal, perhaps. Something only you can appreciate."

Yes, something only *she* can appreciate. Never mind me.

Addelyn smiled and swayed, bumping her arm against his.

She said, "I can't stand it anymore. I want you inside me."

My ears received a different message. There's no way she said that. Not here. Not in everyone's presence. The glare I shot her came with a razor-sharp edge.

"What did you say?"

She paused a moment, wondering which words made me react.

"I said I can't stand it anymore. I'm excited to see what

134

he brings me."

I took a deep breath and slowly let it escape through my nose. Addelyn resumed her conversation, unaware or careless of my suspicions. She laughed when he told her a joke. It must have been the funniest damn joke anyone has ever told, judging from the way she laughed, the way she looked at him, the way she engaged his personal space, the way she placed her hand against his chest, even worse, how she didn't seem to mind his arm stretching in hopes of letting him wrap it around her.

Addelyn's head tilted to one side as she looked up at him, hanging on his every word. She hugged her knees to her chest, and I observed her bare feet and how she wiggled her toes, how she twisted and played with a strand of her hair like some nervous schoolgirl with a crush, how she pulled the rest aside and tossed it over her shoulder, unveiling her cleavage, and how she leaned in, casually.

Focusing my attention on Vance, I watched his eyes as they locked with Addelyn when he spoke. My gut churned, and I spoke to him with my thoughts. She's setting it up for you, dickhead. She's waiting to see if you'll sneak a peek. She is waiting for you to look down at her chest, even for a second. She's giving you permission; she wants to know if you'll follow through. She wants more of your attention.

An eerie drone, like the hum of electricity, clouded my hearing. Vance's lips moved in slow motion to whatever he was saying, but I saw him mouth the words, "Northwest corner. To the front. To the left. That's where you'll find it."

He must have said something else, something humorous because Addelyn giggled again and gently grabbed his wrist. An unconscious signal from her, blatantly obvious to anyone else. Vance raised his cup to his lips. I watched, waiting, and then it happened. As he took a drink, for a split second, his eyes dropped to her chest, so fast, it's questionable if Addelyn noticed the quick peek, the brief moment he used to check out the goods. Behind tight lips, my teeth nibbled the inside of my cheek, and my jaw clenched. My head swayed side to side with a slow-moving disappointment while I laughed internally at the satisfaction from being right all along. The pathetically predictable Vance had fallen for her trap. Yet, who is at fault? Who takes the blame? Who is worse, the person telling the joke or the person laughing at the punchline? The filmmaker who directs the movie or the audience who finds it entertaining?

The hum dissipated, and I returned my glare to the wall, hearing but not listening to Addelyn explain how she gave up art after college. She didn't pursue the hobby because she never had the time. When Vance said she should take it up again, she told him she was too busy taking care of a family, in a tone suggesting regret in her decision.

Next came an inaudible rumble of unclear words. My eyes closed, and my fists tightened on their own when I thought I heard Addelyn say, "Fuck me like my husband is watching."

My drink slipped. An array of ice, liquid, and glass shattered on the floor.

Shit.

I knelt down to clean the mess. Addelyn rose to her feet.

"Are you okay?"

"I'm fine."

I began scooping the ice and glass into a pile, incautious of injury.

"Calvin, let me get a broom. You don't want to cut yourself."

That's when I snapped.

"I said I'm fine! It's my mess! I'll clean it up myself!"

Addelyn and Lillian looked at each other. Paul lifted his head from the couch and looked at Vance. Gripping shards of glass, I carried them behind the bar. The sharp edges pierced my skin. Blood trickled from open wounds. Yet, I squeezed them tighter, basking in pain. To myself, I repeated, "It's my mess. I'll clean it up." I tossed the glass in the sink and ran my hands beneath gushing water.

Red-faced and shaking, I stared at my open palms, hearing Addelyn softly tell her sister, "I don't know what I did wrong. He's never snapped at me like that before."

Steam began to rise from the sink, from the faucet, from my hand.

You don't know because you haven't done it yet, but you will.

As fast as I turned off the water, my fury extinguished. A drunken Paul derailed my train of thought, but asking, "Calvin, buddy? You need a Band-Aid?"

Wrapping my hand in a towel, I replied, "No thanks, I'm fine."

"You don't need stitches, do you?"

"It's a tiny cut. The bleeding has stopped."

"You sure? I can run upstairs and get a meat cleaver from the kitchen. We can hack it off if need be."

"Funny," I chuckled, "Not necessary, but thank you."

The throbbing in my head vanished. The churning in my stomach withered away. Before returning to my wife, I tried to recall what made me so angry in the first place.

Apologizing, I said, "I'm sorry, everyone. I think I spaced out there for a minute. I didn't mean to cause a ruckus." I kissed Addelyn on the cheek, holding pressure on my hand, and said, "Sorry, sweetheart. I didn't mean to raise my voice."

With a bottle held close to his chest, Paul lifted his arm, swaying it back and forth as though conducting an orchestra of boring conversation.

"Here's a suggestion." He belched. "Is anyone up for a late-night swim?"

In the Swimming Pool...

Wayne stands at the patio door with his fingers on the handle, staring through the glass and into the backyard.

"So now we're making some headway."

Calvin is bewildered, stressed, and now his rage of recent memories has allowed him to feel the pressure of his blood pumping through his neck. He attempts to calm himself with slow breathing and pushing every thought from his mind until it's clear. He transitions from wondering about his wife and daughter to the questionable relationship between his wife and Vance. A short moment goes by, and Calvin checks his phone. No messages. No missed calls.

With a sigh, he says, "I don't understand. When I woke up this morning, I wasn't concerned if Addelyn was having an affair."

Wayne chews his gum and slides the door open.

Instead of responding to the statement, he says, "Watch your step."

The two step outside, and Wayne flips a switch to the patio light.

"It's too bad this house goes back to the bank. An in-ground swimming pool can add five to eight percent to a home's value. If you were selling, I'm sure I could make those numbers go up."

His eyes scan the gutters, noticing how his movements are not triggering the motion lights.

Calvin waves his arms and does a couple of jumping jacks, but the lights stay dim.

He says, "They worked fine before." Pausing briefly, he adds, "Listen. I'm through playing games. If you know something, you should come right out and say it."

Wayne writes on his clipboard. Aisu patio table, with six chairs. List price: $599.

He says, "I can't tell you about your past any more than I can tell you about the future."

"You told me I haven't seen the worst of it, which implies you know something I don't. So, cut the bullshit and tell me what the hell is going on!"

Wayne continues chewing his gum as though Calvin's anger has no effect on him.

He says, "What I meant was we haven't seen every room yet. I assume there's more and potentially worse destruction than what we've seen already. I'm all about full disclosure, and I have no reason to hide anything from you. Remembering what happened is up to you."

Calvin sighs again through his nose with his lips narrow and pinched together.

"Everything was fine this morning. All I know is I had an appointment. To be perfectly honest, I'm frightened to go on from here. When something bad pops into my head, it sucks the life right out of me, and if you are right and the worst is yet to come, I don't think I can handle it."

"Double-edged sword, isn't it?"

In a restless stance, Calvin tilts his head, and his brows pull together.

Wayne says, "Part of you fears what lies ahead, and the other insists on finding out." He blows a bubble. "Why don't you try to think of something pleasant? Search for happy memories and see what comes up."

Calvin tries this. Shaking his head, he shuts his eyes. He thinks hard but only hears sounds through the blackness. Laughter. Splashing. Addelyn moaning. Someone else is drowning, trying to scream through the water. The strange woman's voice says, "To the front. To the left. That's where you'll find it."

Calvin shouts, "Damn it," and pounds a fist against his temple. He guards his stomach and whimpers, "I can't do this."

Wayne removes his glasses and cleans the lenses with the base of his shirt.

"You don't have a choice, my friend. Think it through. What else? You said Paul suggested going for a swim. What happened next?"

Calvin refuses, swaying his head. The faint scent of chlorine fills his nose. He inhales, and before he can say another word, the details come flooding back.

———————————

Folded towels and scrunched up clothing sat on a cloudy blue and white glass Aisu patio table, surrounded by chairs. The motion lights mounted underneath from the gutters illuminated the backyard. The dim white lamp below the diving board made the water glow. I sat alone against the edge of the shallow end, watching Lillian, Paul, and Vance splash around. A dull pain ached inside my head, but I did my best to keep it from ruining the evening any further.

Addelyn came from inside, making her way toward the pool. She dropped her towel, exposing her tight body in the skimpiest *Venus* string bikini she owned. The top was neon green with spaghetti-thin straps tied around the neck and back, supporting two triangles that covered her breasts. The bottoms were black and also held together with knots at the hips. She passed by me like I wasn't there and sat on the edge, soaking her feet and sipping a glass of wine.

Toward the middle of the pool, a long rope hooked from one end to the other, a divider between the shallow and deep ends. Paul held Lillian face-to-face with their chins dripping above the surface. Her wet hair made it look black. Vance waded by himself, swaying his arms along the top of the water. His tight chest and pecs, his muscular biceps, all wet and shiny. To me, he looked like a model for a magazine cover and every woman's dream, a mysterious man with a respected career and impressive artistic hobby. I didn't care how much he made, and I needn't worry about losing Addelyn to someone else. She would never throw this life away to spend a few minutes in bed with a stranger. No way would she choose sex over family. Besides, we loved each other equally throughout our entire lives. If my feelings changed, hers would too.

Vance gazed toward my wife. A short glance, but in a split second, he had absorbed a still image of Addelyn's perfect body. A bit of jealousy raged through my blood. Over the next few minutes, my headache grew worse. It took me standing from my seat for her to notice me.

I said, "I'll be right back," and walked into the house, through the basement, upstairs to the half bathroom with my fingers pressed against my temple.

The bright light made me wince as I opened the medicine cabinet. My fingers flipped through bottles of over-the-counter medication, spinning their labels to the front, finally landing on a bottle of ibuprofen. I snagged it from the shelf, popped off the cap, and tossed two pills into my mouth. Then, I leaned forward, twisting the faucet, and cupped water to drink from my hand. Swallowing the medicine, I stared off into space, allowing my imagination to play disturbing visions of water beading between Addelyn's cleavage. The strings of her bikini came undone. The sounds of her moaning as her lips smash against Vance's mouth. Their tongues, twisting together. Him, lifting her in the pool, wrapping her legs around his waist. The water, rolling and rippling.

Is this happening in my absence? Paul and Lillian are there to chaperone unless, of course, they're letting them get away with it. No, no, no. It can't be. More than anything, I wanted to pour acid down my throat, wrap my head in a plastic bag, and drown in my own vomit and blood. I wanted to smack my palms on a heated stove, run naked through a storm, climb a utility pole, and beg for lightning to strike. If the heavens refused to end my suffering, I'd swing from the power lines and do it myself. A tear blinked down my cheek to my trembling lips. I felt weightless, empty. Speaking through clenched teeth, I said, "Stop torturing yourself." And after taking a few deep breaths, once I calmed myself, I returned the medicine bottle to its place, closed the cabinet, and headed back outside.

Have you ever felt invisible while surrounded by people you know? You want to sit back and hide, hoping for someone to realize you're not there. Sliding the patio door, I discovered the commotion had increased. Everyone was in the pool, including Addelyn. Curious, I observed her interactions with Vance, who was now bouncing up and down toward the middle, playfully splashing her as she laughed. Paul and Lillian were close by, only he would cackle and dunk his wife underwater.

When she resurfaced, she threw her head back and

jokingly shouted, "You're an asshole."

The party would have gone on with or without me. I figured this because no one noticed my return. I poured myself another glass of whiskey and sat on the concrete edge, folding my legs together and watching. Paul held his breath and submerged himself. Seconds later, he rose again with Lillian on his shoulders. She screamed before falling off and going under, and when she came back up, she shoved him and giggled. Without hesitation, Vance decided to do the same, but with Addelyn. He disappeared to a blurry figure below, swimming underneath her. She squealed when he lifted her on his shoulders. To intentionally inflict pain, I bit my lip. The sight of another man with my wife's thighs around his head made me grind my teeth so hard, I didn't care if they snapped.

Fearful of losing balance, Addelyn held onto the sides of Vance's face. From where I sat, I saw her caressing his cheeks. A moment later, Vance fell backward, allowing Addelyn to fall into the water. When she returned to the surface, she pushed her hair from her face and swam closer to him. With their faces inches apart, they shared a brief moment of silence. Had I been watching a movie, this would have been the anticipated moment where the two lovers were about to kiss. Part of me wanted to sneak back inside and watch through a window, curious of what would happen had I not been around, but all the same, it's like I wasn't even there.

The left strap of Addelyn's bikini fell off her shoulder, loosening her top and exposing more of her cleavage. She didn't know until Vance pulled it up. Strange enough, neither of them seemed embarrassed. Vance's fingers continued to drag down her shoulder and across the bare, wet skin of her chest. I witnessed his thumb peel a strand of wet hair from her arm. I expected Addelyn to pull away in this awkward moment, but instead, she grinned and leaned in closer to whisper something in his ear.

Rage swelled inside me, causing me to scrape my fists along the concrete. The fury burned inside my chest at a level I had not experienced before. I could taste blood on my tongue while casting a hateful glare at them as they continued to ignore my presence. I felt the rest of my body going numb. Then, Lillian rose to the surface beside me, lifting herself from the water. Her black bikini reflected the light. Her bare feet slapped the pavement, passing by me. Stretching a thin-lipped smirk across her face and batting her lashes, she retrieved a towel from the table. Paul swam toward the deep end, crawling out and stepping onto the diving board. Vance and Addelyn turned to watch him preparing to dive. Lillian returned and sat down beside me, scrubbing her hair with a towel. She reached for my glass, and before taking a sip, she said, "Northwest corner."

Whipping my head, I asked, "Do what?"

She shrugged like she didn't expect me to speak.

"I didn't say anything."

"Oh, sorry. I thought you did."

Paul walked to the edge of the diving board and clapped his hands together.

He shouted, "Three!"

I felt Lillian stare at me while drinking from my glass.

She asked, "Is something wrong? I know you're here, but it's like you're a million miles away."

Paul bounced once in the air. The tip of the diving board touched the water, and she shouted again, "Two!"

By now, I felt Lillian was the only person I could talk to.

Ever since Vance came over the first evening for dinner, she seemed to have my back, even though it wasn't clear to me why. I considered telling her the truth about what I saw and how I felt, but I feared my assumptions would make her think I was crazy.

Instead, I shook my head and told her, "I'm fine. There's a lot on my mind."

Paul leaped forward, and in mid-air, shouted, "One!"

A sharp pain shot through my head, through my brain. My ears rang. Water splashed from the pool, raining over the landscaping lights. They flickered, as did the submerged bulb beneath the diving board and the lights inside the house. Then everything went dark.

A brush of soft fingers slid through my hair and, what felt like soft lips, kissed the side of my forehead, followed by a whisper, "That's where you'll find it."

Find what? My eyes took a few seconds to adjust.

"What happened?"

Paul yelled from across the pool as he swam to the edge.

"I knew my dive was impressive, but I didn't expect it to knock out the power."

Standing and pointing toward the garage, I said, "It's not the power. It's the… thing… the…damn it, I can't remember what it's called."

Paul knew exactly what caused the outage.

Accompanying me to the garage, he used a flashlight to search the wall next to the fuse box and said, "The ground-fault circuit interrupter." His swimming trunks dripped puddles on the concrete floor. "Ah… here it is." He pointed to a small beige panel mounted next to the breaker. I stepped closer to observe, but not too close, as I feared a shock from the mixture of water and electricity.

Looking back in the direction of the swimming pool, I said, "The realtor was supposed to have the electricians set it properly before we moved in." I felt myself rocking back and forth, impatient. "Don't worry about it."

Reaching his damp fingers toward the contraption, Paul snickered.

"Yeah, well. In the real world, if you want something done, you've gotta do it yourself." He fumbled with the wires. "For the time being, I can disable it."

As more water splattered from his trunks, I stepped back even further. Tapping my fingers on my thigh, I looked toward the darkness again. This is taking too much time. Who knows what Vance and Addelyn are doing in the dark?

"It's a flood-light problem, isn't it? Maybe a short somewhere? Isn't the ground-fault thingamabob doing its job by killing the circuit?"

Paul plucked a connector from a circuit board.

"Ground-fault circuit interrupter, and yes, it could be, but that's the magic of troubleshooting. If it's a wiring problem with the lights, then what I'm doing should have no effect." He reset the breaker.

Turning back, we saw the backyard glowing once again and heard cheers from the others.

Paul grinned and said, "It's not your lights, but...hey, what's this?"

He leaned over to retrieve a lengthy green extension cord snaked in a loop on the floor, leading up over a rafter and into a hole in the ceiling.

Clearing my throat, I said, "Power for the security cameras. I haven't installed them yet."

"A do-it-yourself kinda guy. I'm surprised you don't pay someone to install them for you. In the meantime..." Paul ran off toward the pool with his feet smacking the pavement. He shouted, "Cannonball!" after turning the corner. Then came a splash.

I didn't notice at the time, but I stood there holding the green cord and in some kind of unguided, unintentional way, spacing out, watching my hands wrap the wire into a noose.

In the Backyard...

The mind is a joker, a prankster. When it has the opportunity, it likes to gag, throw you for a loop, and make its own versions of the story. Darkness sets the stage for deception, shadows reinforce illusion, and it's hard to decipher the difference between reality and the tricks the mind plays tricks on our naive and gullible selves.

The sky paints its final abstraction for the day. The sun is gone, and the cicadas begin their opus of villainous laughter. The fireflies dazzle the dusk with their intermittent mating calls with their lights warning others they're on the prowl. Wayne and Calvin cross the backyard through uncut grass, heading toward the house once again. It's a property, abandoned by care, left with ghostly memories. No longer a ground for joyful family life. Calvin watches the wind scatter dead leaves and hears them crunch beneath his shoes.

He asks, "When was the last time someone mowed the lawn?"

Wayne smacks the back of his neck and says, "I couldn't say. The bank will take care of landscaping before the property goes up for sale." He smacks his neck again. "Blood-sucking vampires."

"The bank?"

"No, the mosquitoes. Let's get inside."

They walk through the basement to the steps that lead up to the ground floor. Calvin takes a last glance around, trying to recall anything he may have missed, and there's a pang of nervousness in his stomach from the thought of what else lies ahead.

As they arrive at the top, Wayne asks, "Have you heard of something called the frequency illusion? It's defined as a cognitive bias. You notice something once, something your mind dwells upon, and then it seems to appear everywhere you look."

They make their way through the hallway, returning to the foyer, to the bottom of the half-spiral staircase.

Calvin stops and says, "Truly, you are a geyser of knowledge."

Wayne takes his first step and replies, "Old Faithful. You bet your ass. Knowledge is power, my friend."

He continues toward the second level.

Following behind, Calvin asks, "What are you saying? This affair between Addelyn and Vance is all in my head? If I saw one questionable interaction between them, then the idea manifested from there? It doesn't seem possible considering the details I recall."

"Ah, but did you though? A glance. A facial expression. The way his hand grazed her a certain way, their body language. These things can be misconstrued. You caught onto something; it raised your suspicions and sent everything spiraling out of control. True or not, it doesn't change your beliefs." Wayne continues at the top of the stairs, standing on the balcony. "It happens all the time. For some. It's hard to distinguish what's real and what's not."

Calvin tries calling Addelyn once more from his cellphone. The line goes straight to voicemail, and he sighs.

"It's late. Addelyn and Maddie should have been here by now."

Wayne turns to him with a sense of sympathy and asks, "Don't you think it's time to accept the facts?" As much as he doesn't want to say it outright, he can no longer keep up the charade. It's time for Calvin to hear it. "Addelyn and Maddie are not coming. Think about why that is."

First comes a beat of silence, then Calvin snickers, scoffs, shakes his head, and says, "They're running late."

Each passing second, Wayne retains a serious look on his face. He should apologize, but the best way to get the information to sink in is to allow time for its acceptance. Calvin looks down the stairs to the foyer, to the front door.

He says, "This is where we live," shaking his head even harder. "Eventually, they have to come home."

Wayne stops chewing his gum and says, "Think about why they are not here."

Before new memories resurface, the reason for his family's absence comes to light. Calvin's eyes well with tears.

"No. I don't believe it. I can't. I won't."

Wayne lowers his head and says, "Your wife and daughter are not coming home. They can't because..." He swallows to avoid choking on his words, "They can't because they're dead."

Addelyn slept on her side with her hair spread across the sheets, an arm stretched underneath her head, and a leg bent on top of a second pillow. A warm hand slid across her shoulder and down her arm, pulling the silk strap of her nightgown to her elbow. The hand traveled across her chest and cupped her breast. Soft lips kissed her neck. Waking with her eyes still shut, she smiled, pushed herself against a firm bare chest, and turned her head to kiss...Vance.

In a moment of panicked surprise, she pulled away.

He hushed her lips with a finger and said, "Shh. It's okay. Calvin is asleep downstairs."

She glanced at the doorway and whispered, "Are you sure ?"

"Of course. He'll never know."

A smirk shifted across Addelyn's face, like a woman about to taste forbidden fruit. "Good." She caressed Vance's chin and let him suck on her finger. Their audible kiss, smacking lips, heavy breaths and panting, could have easily been heard from outside the bedroom, but instant passion brushed aside all caution. She dragged her fingernails down his back once he lifted her gown.

Vance said, "Your body is perfect...symmetry."

She faced him, sat on his lap, wrapped her legs, and locked her ankles behind his hips. The bands of her lace thong quickly snapped apart, and Vance positioned himself to penetrate her, teasing her with his tip.

He spoke softly in her ear and said, "Tell me you want me, first."

She exhaled the words, "I want you."

He gripped her hair and pulled her head aside to lick her neck. The taste of her skin wet his appetite, causing an immense hunger to churn inside his gut.

Addelyn bit her bottom lip and whispered again, "I want you so bad."

She tried pulling him tight, to slide him inside her, but Vance wanted to tease her some more and take her to the very edge, to make her beg as if the world had nothing left for her to crave.

Vance whispered, "Tell me what you want."

She rocked her hips, each time pleading for him to succumb to her allure. He gripped her ass cheeks and smashed his face between her breasts, almost ready to end the foreplay and give her what she longed for, but not yet, not until she begged.

Addelyn snickered and grabbed his chin, staring into his eyes, she said, "Fuck me like my husband is watching."

When Vance slipped himself inside, she gasped and released a soft squeal.

My eyes sprung open so wide and fast, I thought my lids would fly off. Alone in the dark living room, my gut twisted with nausea, and any second I would puke all over the sofa and possibly choke. I sat up straight, wishing I had died in my sleep.

What time is it? Where's Addelyn? Where is that bastard, Vance?

I threw my feet to the floor, ready to charge up the stairway to my bedroom, ready to catch the two of them in action, ready to finally point a finger and bring my suspicions to an end, when I caught a glimpse of someone seated alone at the breakfast table in the kitchen. Addelyn gazed out the window to the backyard, sipping a cup of hot tea. I paced quietly, narrowing my eyes, and spoke with a sharp, flattened tone that startled her.

"Trouble sleeping?"

Addelyn jolted. She grabbed her chest and nearly spilled her tea.

"My God, Calvin, you scared me."

Treading toward her, I studied her surroundings and asked, "Why would you be afraid of your own husband?"

"I'm not. I was used to the silence."

A bar of moonlight shined through the window blinds and spread across my face. Addelyn wore the same nightgown I had dreamt of. Deep purple, almost black in the night, with the silk strap slid down to her elbow. I placed both hands on her shoulders and massaged her with my thumbs.

She tilted her head back and moaned, "Feels good."

"Does it?"

I barely blinked, scanning in all directions for anyone or anything that shouldn't be there. If I were sneaking in at night to fuck someone's wife, the first thing I'd do is take off my shoes, so I didn't make noise. I looked to the floor, to the laundry room leading to the garage. With nothing out of place, I figured Vance must have come in through the front door, through the foyer. Easily enough, it seemed, to avoid detection while I slept on the living room sofa. I sniffed the air, hunting the scent of cheap men's cologne, covered by hints of my wife's perfume. Lowering my head, I pulled her hair aside to rub her neck when I noticed a dark spot beneath her left ear.

What is this? A mark? A hickey or a shadow? I leaned closer to inspect, unknowingly increasing my grip.

She pulled forward and said, "Ouch. Calvin, you're hurting me."

How dare her assume I would do such a thing. Not intentionally. Not with malice. Vance, however, I would get my jollies off, clutching his neck, cutting off the blood supply to his head, watching him squirm within my grasp. I would love it if he saw me smiling while I crushed his throat and squeezed the last bit of life from his pathetic, worthless body. Amidst my fantasy, the movement of something dashing outside distracted me. The motion-activated lights should have come on, but they didn't.

Shit. The ground-fault circuit interrupter, remember?

I scuffled to the window and flipped the blinds wider. It

wasn't something, rather someone running across the lawn—a naked man covering his genitals with a bundle of clothes.

Vance, that prick.

Addelyn scooted her chair from the table.

"What's wrong?"

I bolted toward the front door, around the garage, down the winding sidewalk, to the backyard, and once there, I stopped in the center of the lawn, darting my attention in each direction and shouting, "You'd better run!"

"Who are you talking to?"

I whipped around, glaring at Addelyn standing on the back patio, shivering, with my arms widened.

"You know damn well."

"There's no one here. Get inside. It's freezing."

"I'm not."

Red-faced and sweating, I could have stood naked in a blizzard and likely melted snowbanks with the radiating heat of my boiling blood.

Addelyn asked, "What's wrong with you? You'll wake the neighbors."

Precisely what I need. An audience. A witness. Someone who can attest they saw the scumbag, Vance, breaking into my house, sneaking into my room, slipping himself between my sheets, and into my wife.

She said, "Come inside. Let's go to bed."

I surveyed the yard once more before following her inside. So pissed off, I don't recall going upstairs. So angry, I don't remember turning off the lights. So livid, I don't recollect climbing into bed. The next thing I knew, I was lying faced away with Addelyn curled against my back, trying to cuddle me, wrapping her arms around me, holding me from behind. There's no way I could face her. No way I could pretend things were fine. I laid there like a brick, still and hard. I sniffed the pillowcase, the sheets, hoping to find the hint of a man's scent other than mine. She grazed her fingers across my chest and kissed my shoulder, and said, "I love you."

I said nothing. Instead, I told myself, "I'll kill the slimy little prick."

In the Home Office...

Calvin stands on the balcony with his elbows on the rail, leaning over the foyer. What Wayne told him about his wife and daughter has yet to soak in. As of now, this information settles on the surface like greasy film on a sponge. With his cell phone out, he selects Addelyn's name beside a heart-shaped emoji. He presses the call button with his thumb, anticipating the sound of her voice (either answering or from a recording), but this time, the line plays a different message.

"The number you dialed has been disconnected."

Tempted to throw his phone and let it shatter against the wall, he refrains and squeezes it tight.

He turns to Wayne and says, "I'm not buying it."

Wayne says, "You can sell fabrication, but not facts.

"Stop." Calvin shakes his head and sighs. "Just...stop."

Chewing his gum, Wayne hangs back, leaning against the wall. He waits, examines his fingernails, rubs his thumb around the button on his ink pen. Meanwhile, the gears in Calvin's head are turning, moving like a machine, attempting to create any kind of reasonable explanation for his family's truancy and Addelyn's disconnected phone line.

We paid the bill. It comes out of our account automatically each month. They went out for dinner. The car broke down. What if they got into a wreck? Maybe I should call the hospital. They're not dead. No, no, no. They're not dead.

Inhaling an impatient breath of air, Wayne smacks his gum and says, "You're wasting time. You can't solve a puzzle when you don't have all the pieces."

Tight-lipped and trying to watch what he says, Calvin

looks over his shoulder.

"Addelyn and Maddie are not dead. Either you're misinformed or flat-out lying to me."

Dropping his arms to his sides, Wayne scoffs and asks, "For what benefit?"

"Then prove it." Calvin spins around and stomps forward. "Let's move on. I want to see how they died." Raising his voice, he smacks the wall. "I want to see how they *fucking* died!"

Wayne's gum-chewing slows to the pace of his swaying head. He says, "No, my friend. You don't."

Through clenched teeth, Calvin says, "Show me."

They approach a small room, a den used as an office, a place to work from home. Calvin peeks around the corner and sees the mess of scattered papers, ripped file folders, bills stamped with horrific red 'past due' ink. Cracked monitors hang from the desk by their cords. He leans over to examine a busted keyboard with missing letters, F, R, and O, and the broken keys, N, T, L, and E, lying nearby. A computer mouse lays unplugged from the tower, and it's been bashed into pieces.

Calvin waits by the doorway, hesitant to enter, regretting his demand for evidence.

Bad idea. You shouldn't have done this.

Wayne breezes by and says, "They didn't die in here."

"So, what happened?"

"Only you know."

Calvin inspects the room and says, "Nothing is salvageable."

"On the contrary, this desk is in good shape." Wayne slides a finger along the surface and examines the dust. "It needs a good cleaning and some minor touch-ups."

As Calvin leans against the wall, he says, "Tell me again why we need to sell this stuff. Last I checked, I have a pretty significant amount of money in the bank."

Wayne turns with an incredulous expression as though he's surprised Calvin doesn't know about this already.

"You're broke."

"The hell I am." Calvin opens a banking app on his cellphone. He tries to log in, but the screen says his account is closed. His gut sinks to his feet. Few things are worse than discovering everything you depend on to live is gone. "Where did my money go?"

Wayne smirks and says, "This may not be the opportune time to crack jokes, but I can see why traumatic memories fade; however, going bankrupt seems hard to forget. We're selling your remaining possessions to pay off your debts."

"What debts?"

Wayne pulls his glasses to the bridge of his nose and looks at Calvin over the frames.

"Answer me this. You walk into a room with a match. At your feet are a wooden log, a candle, and a stack of papers. Which do you light first?"

Calvin's not dumb. It doesn't take him long to come up with the answer.

"You light the match. What's your point?"

"Focus on the situation at hand before attempting to solve the next steps. You know why you're here. You know what you have to do."

"No, Wayne, I don't. And I fail to see the purpose in all this if I can't be with my family."

"Most issues promise a resolution no matter how desperate the circumstances may seem."

"This doesn't make sense. I saw them this morning,

when I woke up, before I left the house. They were alive, and this place wasn't such a hell-hole."

Calvin bends down on one knee and tugs a black cord plugged into the back of his computer. It stretches from behind a desk, into the hallway near the baseboards, and up to the ceiling through the attic door.

Wayne says, "You're missing hours, plenty of time for your life to flip."

"I don't believe you. I need to see their bodies."

The cable is snug, and he wonders where it leads. In a hopeless attempt, he pushes the button on the computer, but the machine won't turn on.

Half of Wayne's mouth rises with a sympathetic grin. His hands flounder as he raises the lid of a cardboard box and peeks inside.

"First thing's first." He writes on his clipboard: American oak veneer with grain finish—$3,330. "You can recall your childhood, your first kiss, your prom, your wedding, your parent's death, and everything up until today, but you can't remember the events of this afternoon. There's no doubt the answer is floating around somewhere inside your head."

Frustrated, Calvin grinds his teeth. His bottom lip trembles and he asks, "The least you can do is end the suspense and *tell* me how they died."

Wayne's mouth doesn't move for any reason other than chewing his gum.

Calvin shouts, "I deserve to know!"

"You're absolutely right, but unfortunately, the mind has enough room for only one version of the story. Sometimes it replaces the most troubling experiences with more convenient details. You know what happened. You've always known, but you chose to forget."

"Are you saying I can't account for my wife and daughter's death because I don't want to?"

"In a way. Disassociation is one of two explanations for your repressed memories, but you can't have it both ways."

Calvin's grimacing face transitions to confusion.

"What do you mean?"

"Like the basic complementary theory—two opposing colors, two sides of the same story. I told you before this doesn't work unless you pay attention. You need to focus. The other version is hiding within these walls. I'm here to help you, but I can't give you all the answers." Wayne pauses, takes off his glasses, and says, "You mentioned an appointment. Any idea what it was for?"

Calvin scours for a reply, but nothing comes to mind. He begins to sob, hugging himself, kneeling to connect with the floor.

"It doesn't matter. All I want to know is what happened to my family."

"You know already." Wayne clicks his ink pen and resumes chewing his gum. His chin falls to his chest, and he sighs, wishing for some way to alleviate Calvin's pain. He takes a knee, and for what it's worth, places a comforting hand on his shoulder. "You know because…" He swallows and says, "You know because you killed them."

In this day and age, cash is on the verge of extinction. Money is much easier to spend when it doesn't exist in physical form. When a currency is nothing more than numbers on a screen, it's easy to misinterpret the magnitude of its loss. The trick to making profits from the stock market is buying low and selling high. When a stock is green, it's at a higher price than before, and when it's red, the price has come down. Despite the framed diploma on my wall, my knowledge of business and finances, and everything my father taught me growing up, I stared endlessly at my computer screen, like some kind of robot with my finger clicking the mouse, investing large sums of money and burning through hundreds of thousands of dollars without a care in the world. Perhaps, because I simply wasn't paying attention. With my suspicions and insecurity, I had no choice but to make up some excuse to work from home. There's no way I could leave Addelyn alone in this house for hours on end, not with Vance on the loose, not without the ability to, at the very least, remotely keep an eye on things. He could persuade her, seduce her, and likely manipulate her into doing something she would later regret without me around. Then again, maybe the feelings were mutual. Who's to say she didn't want him as much as he wanted her?

I had ordered multiple video cameras and left them stacked in front of my desk in their original packaging. I had purchased them for the use of home security, but as it turns out, they served a different purpose. From my chair, still tired from losing sleep the night before, I watched Addelyn alone on her swing through the barely open window blinds. She was staring at her feet, pushing them against the dirt, swaying back and forth. From my view, she seemed lost, concerned over potential consequences, weighing pros and cons, worried about having to do or say something to someone. Obviously, she had a secret eating her alive from the inside. Her cell phone rang from her pocket, and I leaned closer and opened the window enough to eavesdrop. The subtle breeze carried her soft voice to my ears.

She said things like, "He's indifferent. It's as if he's not even there sometimes."—"He may already know, but I'm still afraid to tell him. I've tried to think of different ways to bring it up without getting him upset, but I can't."—"When can you come by?"

With no way of hearing the person on the other end, I assumed different topics of conversation. Either Addelyn was planning to leave me, or she was trying to find a way to confront me about her infidelity. At least, that's what I thought.

All kinds of ideas played through my head, all sorts of possibilities. I couldn't help but picture what would happen in my office had I not been home. Addelyn, holding Vance by the hand, giggling and pulling him to my desk, sliding her arm across the surface to knock papers and pens to the floor, spinning around, wrapping her ankles behind him, pulling him closer until they can kiss. His hand softly touches her face. Her smiling lips. The way her eyes close when he unbuttons her skirt. The way she groans when he drags his tongue down her chest, kissing her stomach, and stops when he plants his face between her thighs. The best feeling in the world for her, but for me, this agonizing scenario filled me with the urge to smash the window with my fist, climb out on the ledge and jump to my death. I wanted to land on the concrete so my head would split open like a pumpkin. If that didn't work, I could use shards of broken glass to cut myself open and rip out my own beating heart.

A warm trail of blood oozed from my nostril, down my lips, and stopped at the bottom of my chin. The computer screen displayed rows of green and red graphed charts with each button I mindlessly clicked. My sweaty palms clenched into fists, and like the hammer on a spring trap, I smashed the computer mouse into bits. As I pounded away on the keyboard, some buttons came loose, and others broke free. The graphs on the screen flickered and beeped, and eventually, the two monitors received a punch hard enough to shatter and fall off my desk.

It wasn't until her phone rang that I realized Addelyn had come back inside. I whipped my head toward the doorway where her voice carried upstairs.

She answered, "Hello?...Oh, hey. It's good to hear from you."

I crept into the hallway and, from the balcony, listened to her say things like, "The other night was crazy."—"No wonder we didn't get a chance to do it."—"I know, I was so excited."—"I hope we can get together sometime soon."

I fixed a twisted, evil glare at the wall, lowering my head, believing, once again, my suspicions were true, and a wave of pride washed over me. Each line from Addelyn's lips fueled my belief of her sneaking around behind my back. Even more when she lowered her voice and said, "Mm, I'm not sure."—"Sometimes he's home, and sometimes he goes to work."—"That's fine, but make sure you call first."

My fingernails scratched the walls as they came together in a fist. My entire body shook, but I continued to listen.

"Me too."—"Oh, I'm sure I'll love it."—"See you soon."—"Bye."

I'm gonna kill him. I'm gonna bash his face with my bare hands until his skull caves in. I'm gonna punch his chest until his ribs break, and I won't stop until the bones stab my knuckles. I'm gonna rip out his lungs and shove them down his throat.

Relax. Take a deep breath.

Rather than become enraged, I composed myself. Dropping each foot on a step, I came slowly down the stairs. When I entered the living room, my presence startled Addelyn.

She gasped and said, "Oh. Hi, sweetheart."

I kept a straight, empty face.

"Who was that on the phone?"

She hugged me and said, "Vance."

With her arms around me, I kept mine hanging at my sides while staring over her shoulder.

"Oh. Good ole' Vance. What did he want?"

Resting her face against my chest, she closed her eyes and smiled.

"He wanted to know when he could come by with his paintings."

A logical explanation and most likely the truth, but I had my mind made up, regardless of plausibility. Silently, in my thoughts, I questioned why Vance didn't bring the paintings with him the night we went to the club. Why did she give instructions to call first? Why did she say 'you too?' Was she saying, 'I love you, too?'

Addelyn dragged her fingers along my back, and I envisioned them as knives with sharp blades, slicing my skin apart, tearing into my muscles, chopping my veins and arteries so I could bleed to death. I wanted to cover my wounds with salt, cut off my limbs, scream until my head exploded.

Addelyn said, "I haven't been this tired in a long time." As I fought the urge to cry, my lips frowned, and my eyes tightened shut. It felt as if I was losing her forever when she pulled away.

She asked, "What are your plans for the rest of the day?"

Shaking my head, the first thought to rattle loose fell out of my mouth.

I replied, "Hooking up the Jacuzzi."

She examined my face, my stupid disgruntled face, and asked, "I thought the contractor was sending someone over to fix the pipes first?"

"I'm checking the circuitry. I need to find out what Paul did to our power the other night." These words came naturally and without foresight, but my thoughts raced with different dialogue.

Am I not good enough to fix a hot tub? Do you think I'm too dumb to figure it out? Do I need to rely on someone else to repair stuff around here?

Addelyn kissed my cheek, turned away, and said, "Be careful. I don't want something bad to happen to you."

With sweat forming on my brow, I said nothing.

In the Attic...

Calvin sifts through reasons for his family's death, other than what he's been told. Addelyn and Maddie died in a car wreck. They died in a fire, an earthquake, a terrorist attack, the blast of an atomic bomb, the carnage of a derailed train. They died by someone else's hand, by accident, by an unexplained phenomenon.

Swearing on his life, he shouts, "Not me! I did *not* kill them!"

He feels the thrum of his pulse in his neck. His mouth is dry, and his stomach hardens. Clasping one arm in a self-soothing gesture, Calvin holds his elbow tightly to his side. He sways and pouts, focusing on the closed door of his home office. Standing with Wayne in the second-floor hallway, his surroundings blur in a whirlwind of shock and denial.

"No. You lie. You're lying to me. You're a liar!"

Wayne tentatively places a hand on Calvin's shoulder to test if he can accept the truth.

"More than anything, I wish you were right."

Calvin's desire to flee, to run to who-knows-where, is abruptly dissolved by his mental fatigue. He sobs, quaking and trembling in his body, unleashing uncontrollable tears, pleading and begging for none of this to be real. His knees give way, and he collapses in the corner. He stares at the carpet with a flinty gaze, hugging himself and rocking.

"No," he cries, "How could I? Why can't I remember?"

Wayne lowers himself to the floor, sitting across from Calvin. He sets his clipboard beside him and waits for him to calm down before moving on. He refrains from blowing bubbles and chews his gum silently, watching as his client

167

falls apart.

Moments pass by. Blackness vanishes when light from below beams into the attic from the door and a wooden ladder slides down to the floor. Calvin's head rises through the opening, and he pulls a chain to a lightbulb fixture mounted on a wooden beam. Wayne clamps his bubble-gum between his teeth as he lifts himself into the attic, thumping his boots with each step.

Calvin is calmer now, but because he doesn't know in which room he allegedly murdered his wife and child, his stomach churns with fear of finding dead bodies. Shelves line the sides of the walls, and on those shelves are storage boxes of miscellanies. Wayne holds his clipboard, ready to jot down anything worth the ink in his pen. A thick sheet of plywood has been laid across the beams to keep anyone from stepping between them and falling through the ceiling. Calvin's confused gaze clouds and goes through cables and tools scattered across the surface like a secret, unfinished project next to an unplugged power drill. His ache returns, and he shakes his head.

He asks, "What is this?"

Wayne steps over to peek and says, "Looks like surveillance to me, equipment of distrust. You suspected your wife of cheating, but you had no proof. You tried to get it, though, didn't you?" With the toe of his boot, Wayne pushes a few strands of cut wires beside an open package for a security camera. "I can't get anything for the electronics. You're better off selling them at a pawn shop. I'll call my friend Monty and see if she can hook you up with a good deal. A few hundred bucks, if I had to guess. Want me to add this stuff to the list?"

Calvin catches a glimpse of a dust-covered shoebox

underneath a bottom shelf. He's distracted, so Wayne writes down 'Security cameras—estimated $500.' Calvin lifts the lid, and inside are unorganized memories in the form of photographs, pictures from the honeymoon.

He asks, "How did it come to this?" His fingers select an image of Addelyn in a red bikini, lying on a towel in the sand, soaking up the sun. Her skin is shiny from suntan lotion. Her hand holds a margarita with a pink umbrella. Heart-shaped sunglasses cover her eyes, but her smile shines brighter than the sky. "You said before I need to see both sides, how things were, and how different things could have been. You thought it would help if I questioned my past and allowed myself to consider the possibility of Vance and I switching places." Calvin fights with himself not to break down a cry. He adds, "God, how I wish it were true." He wipes his nose with his sleeve and goes on. "Addelyn and I drove to Myrtle Beach for our honeymoon. She had never seen the ocean before. I couldn't explain to her what it was like. I told her she had to see it for herself. The vast horizon revealed how much bigger the world is than what she imagined. That's what I promised her—the world. You should have seen the look on her face when she first saw the blue water. She just stared for a few minutes, as though she was trying to think of something else she wanted but couldn't because I'd given her everything. She wiped tears from her eyes as we watched the sun go down. She told me she'd never witnessed anything more majestic than the way the reflection of the orange and violet sky danced across the water. I told her I'd never seen her so beautiful. I kissed her tears away, and we made love right there on the beach. That's the night we conceived our daughter Maddie."

Calvin returns the memory to its place and whimpers, covering his eyes with his fists.

He says, "They don't deserve to be dead. I wouldn't kill Addelyn because she cheated, and it's no excuse to hurt my baby. All I've ever wanted was for them to live a happy life."

Wayne stops chewing his gum and says, "You are young, Calvin. I wish you had realized, ahead of time, that death is not necessarily a punishment. If people deserve to die, it wouldn't be something we all inevitably encounters. It's not death we fear. The true penalty lies in *how* and *when* it happens."

Sniffling, Calvin asks, "How did they die?"

"I don't think you're ready."

"I want to know."

"Trust me, in your case, amnesia can be a blessing." Wayne inspects a dime-sized hole in the attic floor and runs his fingertip around the rough edges. The room below is too poorly lit to identify, but it's on the second floor, and likely one they haven't been through yet. He assumes this because he failed to notice any holes in the ceilings before. "What if Addelyn's infidelity is not the reason?"

Calvin spaces out, attempting to trigger what caused his family's demise.

It's hard to say if crazy people know how crazy they are. If insanity is truly intellectual, one might think they would recognize the symptoms. A frail body, sunken eyes, the inability to sleep, and the clear voices in my head.

Addelyn was out for the day, running errands or

something. I swear she told me she had an appointment at the hair salon, but it didn't matter because I had no way of telling if it was true.

I had Maddie with me upstairs in the master bathroom while I messed around with the wiring to the Jacuzzi. After all this time, the repairmen had yet to come by. Each time I called the plumbing contractor to fix the water pipes, the recording said the number was no longer in service. Who needs them anyway? What kind of man would I be if I couldn't fix common household problems? I'll bet *Vance* knows how to fix a water leak.

I should have known from the silence that Maddie had crawled out of the room and into the hallway, and I didn't know she was heading through the balcony toward the staircase.

The problem was corrosion inside the fitting, which connected to the valve needed to run water into the tub. Puddles forming around two hundred and twenty volts of electricity would not make for a relaxing experience.

I heard the garage humming as it opened, and shortly after, the door to the laundry room and kitchen closed. I heard Addelyn announce she was home and call out, but I ignored her. Who knows where she'd been or who she'd been with? My mind wanted to give me scenarios, but I kept fighting them off, which also contributed to not knowing that Maddie was near the edge of the top step.

Fortunately, I was able to replace the valve and test it by filling the tub with water. The rush from the faucet clouded my hearing, and I barely heard Addelyn screaming from downstairs. At first, I thought she called my name to find me, but then came a shriek, followed by thumping on the staircase. Then, I heard Maddie cry, and I turned off the water. It worked. Now all I needed to do was reattach the wiring, and the rest would be cake. I could have waited for Paul to come over and do it for me, but I felt confident in my abilities to do a job without calling someone else to bail me out. My wrist continued to itch in the spot where the lobster pinched me, and I noticed a tiny red spot like I'd been poked with a needle. For some dumb reason, I figured by licking my thumb, I could wipe it off, but before I had a chance, Addelyn came storming into the room with Maddie in her arms.

"Calvin! Why was Maddie alone by the staircase?"

I turned around. Maddie seemed fine. She didn't fall down the steps; the thumping came from her mother running up to catch her before she did. No harm, no foul.

"Good to see you too. I'll have you know; I fixed the leaking water pipe. All that's left is to hook up the elec—"

"I don't give a shit about the Jacuzzi, Calvin! You left her unattended! She could have seriously been hurt!"

Maddie began crying, and I told her she was upset because of her mother's shouting. She could have been hurt, but was she? No.

"She's fine. At least she was until you started screaming at me."

Addelyn backed away with her mouth hanging open and tried to console Maddie.

"I can't believe you, Calvin. What the hell is the matter with you?"

What's the matter with me? Besides the obvious? Is she kidding? Here I am fixing a hot tub for my cheating wife while she's probably out banging her old high school flame. Now she's using our daughter against me, making me look incompetent so she can make herself look superior. Maybe

172

she's trying to find grounds for divorce, and you know what? No problem.

My muscles tightened. My knuckles turned pale. I nearly broke a tooth, clenching my jaw. That bitch.

Addelyn scoffed and took Maddie downstairs. I turned to the open panel of the hot tub where the disconnected cables stuck out.

"Screw this," I said to myself, reminded of the security cameras I needed to install. "I've got better things to do."

Shortly after, I was alone and at peace, crawling across the wooden boards of the attic floor with an electric drill in one hand, talking to myself and the strange woman's voice inside my head.

"I can understand if Maddie got hurt, but Jesus, she's fine."—"Are you sure?"—"No, this should be the guest bedroom right here."—"Trust me, it's not on the northwest side. No, it's not in the front and to the left. It's right here in the center."—"I'm positive. Clearly, you and I are looking for two different things."—"How can I take your word for it? You don't even exist. Or do I not exist?"—"One of us doesn't exist, so we should agree to disagree."

The guest bedroom had a ceiling lamp, and I located the wires coming from the fixture. That's how I knew I was in the right spot. I chose the best place to drill a hole while keeping it concealed. The small motor whirred, and the bit spun through the drywall. Then came the release of resistance, and when I retracted, a beam of light shined in my eye. Through the hole, I had a birds-eye view of the guest bedroom in its entirety. The perfect spot for a hidden camera, hardly detectable to anyone.

I continued talking to myself, "No one stays in the guest room, but you know Addelyn. She won't do it on our bed if

she is sleeping around. She's not *that* cold-hearted."—
"You're right. Anything is possible. We should put a camera over the master bedroom, too, just in case."

After splicing the wires together, I aligned the camera lens over the hole and reached for screws to secure the bracket into place. With my tongue out, my fingers pinched the bolts when a thud came from the ground floor. It startled me, and the screw slipped and fell into the insulation.

"Damn it."

I listened to the sounds of feet coming up the staircase. Addelyn called for me.

What did I do wrong now?

I shouted, "I'm in the attic. Be down in a sec."

Then her steps turned in the other direction and faded away. I came down the ladder, returned the door to the ceiling, and walked to the balcony. I paused when a brief moment of panic filled my chest. The spiral staircase is two stories high. Dear God, Maddie could have been hurt had she fallen down. What is wrong with me? Why wasn't I paying closer attention?

Truly, I felt like a horrible father. I loved Maddie more than I did myself. I would have done anything to protect her. It's likely the guilt of my neglect would have tortured me, but things could have been worse. If something happened to her, I would never forgive myself.

Downstairs, Addelyn waited on the sofa. I saw her first from around the corner of the living room. Standing by the wall, I stared for a moment before making my presence known. She looked beautiful. She always did. Then, I saw her rubbing her neck beneath her left ear, the same place I thought I saw a mark before. It reminded me of my distrust, and all I could do was wonder where she had truly been.

With a stern voice, I entered and asked, "What is it?"

She searched around for the television remote, not once looking in my direction.

"Come sit with me."

Seriously? I've got shit to do.

Frustrated, I agreed. "Fine. Where's Maddie?"

Addelyn found the remote stuck between the cushions. She told me, "I put her down for a nap."

I took my time strolling over to sit beside her, hands folded behind my back, suspicious. Standing above her, I spotted the top button of her shirt was loose, exposing more of her cleavage. I examined every inch of her, looking for clues. Freshly painted nails, lingering perfume, nothing out of the ordinary.

When I finally sat beside her, she leaned her head on my shoulder and said, "I'm sorry for freaking out on you earlier. I didn't mean to lose my temper."

I accepted her apology; at least I told her I did. We sat back together, holding hands. With her against me, I could get a better glimpse of her skin. I quietly sniffed strands of her hair, trying to catch the scent of fresh shampoo. Strange, I wondered, how it smelled exactly like the brand she uses at home and not something I would expect from a hair salon.

I secretly examined her cheek and lips as she focused on the television. A fresh coating of lipstick painted perfectly with rose red. No streaks. No smudges. Nothing to indicate a smearing match with someone else's mouth. My eyes floated down to her neck and widened at the sight of the mark beneath her earlobe. The coloring had faded, but it didn't take a genius-level education for me to identify it as a hickey.

My heart got angry, pounding itself against the walls of

175

my chest, thudding its pulsation in my ears. My stomach filled with pain, too heavy to stay in place, and sunk below my gut. My teeth clamped together, narrowly avoiding the edge of my tongue. If there was ever a sign, evidence, this was it. My mind raced inside my skull, gathering broken thoughts and putting them back together.

Should I say something? You know she'll lie. What happens if we start an argument? Will she leave and run to him? At the very least, she'll know I'm suspicious now and try even harder to hide it. She'll make sure to cover her tracks. You may never know if anything else happens. Shit. Stay calm. Take a deep breath.

Whether Addelyn was watching a soap opera, a game show, a movie, or a news broadcast, the only thing I could see on the television was my own horror. Brief static strobed like channels changing in a dark room. Clips of Vance sitting on our couch, Addelyn dropping her clothes to the floor and crawling between his knees. She unfastens his belt and unzips his pants. She's licking her lips and seductively smirking at him. The shot cuts to his face pressed against her shoulder and his lips sucking the left side of her neck. She's stroking him, rolling her eyes back in her head. Her lips, separating to exhale a euphoric breath.

Another flash, and the camera pans to those pretty painted fingernails as they drag down the skin of Vance's bare chest. Her mouth, whispering, "Don't leave any marks. We don't want Calvin to find out." The lines squiggle from signal interference, then clear to a shot of Vance grabbing her throat with one hand. They smash their mouths together. He grunts and replies, "I don't care if he does." The volume bar pops on the bottom of the screen, raising the sounds of Addelyn's laughter. She straddles him, pulls his head between her breasts, and says, "Fuck me like my husband is watching."

The picture scrambles like *Pay-Per-View* pornography, and the only way to see what happens next comes at what cost? I'll break the goddamn television. I'll shatter it with my head, swing my arms and knock it from the wall. I wished I had a bed of nails to lay on. I wanted to pound my face with my fists, bruise my skin until it cracked. I wanted hammers against my teeth, shards of bamboo beneath my toenails, cigarette lighters torching my skin. Anything else! Please! Anything else but this kind of pain!

As Addelyn combed her fingers through my sweaty hair, the picture faded to black. Then came a commercial break.

She lowered her face to me and asked, "Are you okay, sweetheart?"

I pulled away and sat up straight. I shoved my face in my hands and propped my elbows on my knees.

She asked, "Calvin? What's wrong?"

I massaged the growing ache in my temple and stared at the carpet.

"Just a headache."

"You've been getting a lot of those. Maybe you should see a doctor?"

Sure, I'll go see a doctor. That'll give you some free time to rendezvous with Vance. Maybe I should lie and tell you I scheduled a visit. Leave and park down the street. See if anyone shows up while I'm gone. When they do, I can come back home and catch you in the act—red-handed. Do I really want to see you with him, though? Not inside my head, but in the flesh? Could I handle it?

I replied with, "No. I'm fine."

The phone rang from the kitchen. Pausing, Addelyn let it ring once more.

Crossing my arms and tapping a finger against my elbow, I asked, "Are you going to answer it?"

Quickly, I apologized for sounding stern, like a grumpy boss to a vulnerable secretary. I blamed my sharp tone on my headache, and she bought it, not knowing I had reached my wit's end.

From the living room, I heard Addelyn answer the kitchen telephone. She said, "Lillian," and told her to calm down and take a deep breath. Apparently, her sister was sobbing and distraught. I listened to her ask stuff like, "Who told you this?"—"At the club?"

Later on, I learned Lillian's co-worker informed her that she saw Paul at the nightclub making out with another woman near the bar. At least, she thought she did. I recalled the night, thinking I witnessed the same, but I wasn't certain enough to mention it. Of course, Paul denied it. Why wouldn't he? Without proof, he could say whatever he wanted and get away with it. When Lillian confronted him, the friction of the back and forth conversation turned a simple accusation into a heated argument.

I listened more as Addelyn said, "He knows you've suspected him of cheating on you before."—"No, sis, you're not being paranoid."—"You should take a break. Spend some time away from each other and let things cool down."

It sounds like I'm not alone in this boat.

Then, Addelyn suggested, "You're welcome to stay here if you like. We have a guest bedroom."

I thought back to the evening we had dinner, to the sight of Lillian in her see-through dress, the way she touched me, the way she looked at me.

I recalled the night we went swimming and all her seductive gestures and expressions. My stomach filled with jittering butterflies at the opportunity for potential revenge.

In the Guest Bedroom…

The only squeaky door in the house leads inside a spare bedroom on the second floor. Wayne enters first and flips a light switch on the wall. Calvin stands in the doorway, both hands in his pockets, with his head hanging to his chest.

Wayne smacks his gum and asks, "Did you know the phrase 'red-handed' comes from centuries ago when someone was caught in the act of murder with blood on their hands?"

Calvin's not impressed. He says, "Anyone with half a brain could figure that out."

Shrugging, chewing, Wayne surveys the room.

"This seems nice and cozy. Have you had many guests stay in here?"

He jots down a Wayfair Audet wooden queen size bed frame with mattress—$1,800.

Calvin stares, lost in the carpet.

"We wanted to have more children. We hoped for a boy the second time around. We were planning to sell this furniture to buy new baby stuff for our second miracle." He pauses and thinks to himself. Don't dwell on that now. You'll start crying again. Out loud, he says, "So much for plans."

Wayne paces the room as he writes. Mid-century nine-drawer dresser with vanity mirror—$1,700.

"I have a son and daughter, you know? Girls are expensive. Boys, not so much. You get the best of both worlds, I guess. After a while, when they're old enough to start bickering with each other, it clouds the magic a bit. You know they love each other, they know they love each other, but once they reach high school, it's like living with cats and dogs. What's funny is—" He looks back and sees Calvin's long face. Wayne's smile fades. "Forgive me. I don't mean to boast."

Calvin shrugs his shoulders and says, "You can't miss what you don't have. This room has always been a spare for guests to stay in. If Addelyn's parents came in town for the holidays, or a friend was too drunk to drive home and needed a place to crash for the night, or if someone had a—"

"One night stand," says Wayne, scribbling on his clipboard.

Calvin darts his attention toward him and asks, "What?"

Tapping his clipboard, he says, "Carrington nightstand, list price: $150."

A sigh of relief comes from Calvin, but his ears perk up when Wayne asks, "What about a sister-in-law refugee in a lover's quarrel?"

He straightens his posture and removes his hands from his pockets.

"Lillian? She didn't stay here."

Wayne snickers.

"You sure? Last I heard you mention, she called upset, and Addelyn invited her to stay."

Calvin thinks back. Did she? He recalls faded memories of empty shoes, denim shorts, and a crop-top shirt hanging over the edge of an open suitcase, unmade bedding, blankets pushed to the foot of the mattress as if someone kicked them off in their sleep.

"No, Lillian didn't stay—"

"Then, why does your reminiscence say otherwise?"

Calvin's headache gradually returns. The growing pain blocks each moment he spends trying to recall. He takes out his cell phone, scrolls through contacts, and selects Lillian

Campton's name. He presses the call button, and the line goes straight to... "The number you dialed has been disconnected."

Try again. He scrolls until his thumb taps the name, Paul Campton. He presses the call button, and the line goes straight to... "The number you dial has been dis—"

"What the hell?"

Wayne covers Calvin's phone with his hand, pushing it downward. Their eyes meet, and he says, "You're wasting your time."

Calvin develops an overwhelming sense of dread. Oh, God. The unveiling truth falls on him like a loosened rock from a mountain. There's no need to ask, but he does anyway.

"Lillian and Paul? They're dead too?"

With a tightened frown, Wayne bounces his head. The phone plummets to the carpet. Calvin squats against the wall, covering his face with his palms, running his fingers through his hair.

"How? Why?"

Wayne towers above him, chewing his gum and holding his clipboard to his side.

"You did what you felt you had to do."

Squinting with tears and blurred vision, Calvin rises to his feet and steps forward.

"What I *had* to do?"

"They gave you no choice, so you murdered them."

"Why in God's name would I do something like that? I didn't quarrel with them. They were family. How could—"

Pausing, he thinks back and takes a look around the room. Automatically, like his head is programmed to do so, he looks up toward the ceiling and notices a small hole next to the light fixture.

The night Lillian came to stay, she brought a suitcase packed with enough clothes to last her a few days, not knowing when or if she would return home. Hoping the feud between her and Paul would soon resolve, she and Addelyn drowned her sorrows with a bottle of wine and chit-chatted with girl-talk on the living room sofa. They assumed I had left them alone to have their privacy, staying busy in my den. I was upstairs all right, once again in the attic. Suppose Addelyn questioned why I could give any excuse I wanted and likely get away with it. I would have told her I was busy checking the power lines for the hot tub. The actual reason was I had to finish installing the security camera over the guest bedroom.

Believe me, I intended to catch Addelyn in the act of adultery in case I had to leave home. I still had more cameras to place in other rooms, but obviously, the first installation had been interrupted. Knowing Lillian would be staying with us, I didn't want her to discover a strange cavity in the ceiling. At the very least, when I finished, I could disguise the hole with a white lens.

Their conversation didn't last as long as expected. Both women grew tired, and the wine had undoubtedly enhanced their fatigue. Crawling along the plywood floor, I made my way to the spot over the guest bedroom. I froze when I heard them coming up the staircase. Either Addelyn didn't notice my absence or didn't care since she went to bed alone. I heard the bedroom close. I waited, listening for her voice, but it never came. I snickered and continued my internal dialogue, saying stuff like, "Actions speak louder than words. I'm not surprised with all the adultery floating around in the air. You bitch. It's hard to wonder what your husband is up to when your head fills with fantasies of your secret lover." I said other things to myself, like, "I thought I knew you, Addelyn. I figured you would see your sister's pain and what it's like to have someone messing around behind your back. You should know how I would feel if I ever found out about you and Vance. Wait until I put a camera in the master bedroom so I can see what you're up to." I whispered, "Shut up, Calvin. She can't hear you."

The dusty air created a single beam from the hole in the ceiling when the guest bedroom light flicked on. I took extra caution not to make a sound. Someone was in the room, and to finish installing a camera would likely draw attention. I pushed my head forward, stretching my neck to see through the hole. Well hidden behind the light fixture, I watched Lillian close and lock the door. Several feet beneath me, she sat on the edge of the bed and removed her shoes. She unbuttoned her frayed denim shorts and slid them off from her ankles. She crossed her arms and lifted her crop-top shirt off over her head. She tossed the outfit to the floor, where they landed over the edge of an open suitcase. The sight of her smooth and tight body was as sexy as I had pictured, and more so. To see her in the flesh, her most intimate parts left to my imagination, covered with a black floral lace thong with a small burgundy ribbon in the front and a matching see-through bra, a rush of hormones overwhelmed me. My heart pounded in my chest. Beads of sweat formed on my brow, and my arms began to shake from supporting my weight.

Lillian lay in the bed on top of the covers. Her fingertips

trailed across her stomach, and her tongue wet her lips. She slid her hand across her chest and pushed the cups of her bra aside, exposing both breasts, pinching a puffy nipple. Despite being related to my wife, her bust was smaller but enough to grab and fill a single handful. Something different for a change. Something I was missing by staying loyal to my whore of a wife. Lillian propped a pillow behind her head to make herself more comfortable. Careless of sound, I did the same by scooting the rest of my body closer to get a better view without straining. I watched her other hand travel down along her stomach, to her waistline, to the tiny burgundy ribbon and underneath, as it slid between her thighs and her knuckles moved up and down beneath the lace. She made a whimpering sound and closed her eyes. I tried to mute my heavy breathing, afraid that she could hear me.

In my mind, Lillian pleasured herself to thoughts of me, imagining me inside of her. The thrill of getting caught by her sibling, my wife, in the neighboring bedroom excited me the most. She moaned and turned her head to muffle her squeals with the pillow. Her knees and legs trembled, seizing with a self-induced euphoria. Her feet pushed the covers to the foot of the mattress as though she'd kicked them off in her sleep.

Call me a hypocrite all you want, but until then, I believed I was the only person in this group who didn't have impure thoughts about someone else. I've always been faithful to my wife, even avoiding the thought of being with another woman. But with Lillian, it's not as if I followed through with it. It wasn't fair for Addelyn to act on her lustful impulses. It's not fair she's allowed to not only fantasize but actually sleep around with another man.

Lillian is a very attractive young woman, much like her sister. I've seen her before in the kitchen, at the pool, the way she winks at me and grazes me when she leans in close to tell me something. I didn't pursue her, though. All I did was picture myself between her open legs with her ankles locked around my waist. I did what she was doing to herself. *My* hand squeezed her breast. *My* fingers pinched her nipple. *My* tongue wet her lips. It was *me* inside her, thrusting until her body trembled from an immense climax, priding myself on giving her the most satisfying orgasm she'd ever experienced. And after everything settled, my senses returned, and I found myself still a height above her, hidden behind the ceiling.

Sweat glistened across Lillian's skin. She opened her eyes, gazing up toward the light. I like to believe she knew I was there. I like to think that what she did, she did with me in mind. She wanted to put on a show. If we couldn't have each other, at least we could pretend. The two of us had shared a fantasy together. Alas, my wishes came with the expense of head pain caused by staring through the light for so long, and my lust quickly dissipated.

In the Guest Bath...

Across the hall, Wayne enters the guest bathroom. With a flick of the switch, one bulb blows out. The carpet mat beside the bathtub has dried puddles of blue and white, gooey shampoo spilled from the empty bottles lying beside the toilet. Bloody handprints on the knobs of the sink's faucet. A mirror with cracks in all directions, centered at a point of impact.

Calvin peeks inside and says, "I'm having a hard time believing all of this. I'm not a monster, and the actions seem unjustified. Why would I kill anybody?"

Wayne chews his gum with his mouth closed, watching for a reaction, and says, "Give it a minute to come back to you."

Stepping inside, Calvin examines shredded pieces of ripped shower curtain stuck to broken rings.

"I don't want it to. Why should I have to relive the bad times when there were plenty of good memories too?"

"The past rushing back all at once is undoubtedly the worst part, I'm sure. The best thing to do is take them in one by one, each room at a time, which is why I've been holding back, rather than telling you everything I know in one sitting. Tell me about a good memory. Maybe it will alleviate some of the pain."

Calvin sits on the edge of the tub and says, "Maddie loved bath time. She loved playing in the bubbles. She would spend the longest time in the water until her fingers puckered. We called them 'moon fingers.' Before she got out, she stood up and slipped. She bumped her chin on the tub and busted her lip. The shampoo bottles spilled on the floor. I rushed her to the sink to stop the bleeding, which is why there's blood on the knobs."

Wayne tosses his gum around in his mouth and holds it in his cheek. He sighs. He knows something more, and it pains him to see his client so oblivious. Calvin examines the walls as he continues and says, "Once I calmed her down, I kissed her cheek. She pointed to her lip and said, 'Ouchie.'"

Wayne leans his back against the wall. With regret, he says, "Unfortunately, my friend. That's not what happened here."

Calvin follows the direction of his pointing finger toward the mirror. He notices the handprint on the corner. It's too big for an infant and too small for his own.

"Then why do I rem—?"

Wayne interrupts by saying, "Tragic memories sometimes get replaced."

"I'm not evil. I can understand why someone would be enraged if they discovered their spouse was sleeping around, but you don't sentence someone to death without proof of a crime."

"We're not in a courtroom."

"That's not the—" Calvin pauses. "Wait, wait, wait a second." He wipes the corners of his open mouth. "Why am I not in jail? If I murdered someone, then why am I not rotting away in a cell somewhere?"

Wayne leans his head back, eyeing the ceiling. He chews his gum as a means to delay the answer.

Sighing, he says, "The police haven't arrested you."

Scratching his chin, Calvin asks, "Do they know?"

"I would ask what you remember, but I guess you can't tell me if it hasn't happened yet."

Calvin is shaking.

Mildly frustrated, he rolls his eyes and says, "Don't play games. Are the police coming for me or not?"

"You would think so. After all, you are facing five counts of second-degree murder."

Calvin whips around.

"Five?"

Wayne heavily sighs again, looks over, and says, "Vance. He's dead too."

Blood drains from Calvin's face, and his shocked expression comes as no surprise.

Wayne adds, "C'mon, you had to have known that was coming. You've wanted him dead since he first came to your house."

"I *wanted* him dead, but that doesn't mean I would go through with it."

Shrugging, blowing a bubble, letting it pop, Wayne says, "It could be worse."

"How do you figure?"

"Jealous rage. Crime of passion. The law tends to sympathize with people in your position."

With each sway of his head, Calvin mumbles, "No, no, no, no..." He coughs as though choking on the news he's trying to swallow. Although he carries hatred toward Vance and has imagined the satisfaction of ending his life, he can't help but feel remorse. "This isn't right. It doesn't make any sense. You don't kill five people and simply go about your day."

Wayne says, "I told you before; this is not a joke, and you're not dreaming. This is all very real."

There's nothing else to say. Calvin follows Wayne from the guest bathroom, and before he turns off the light, he takes a final glance around.

He flips the switch, the room goes black, and recent memories come rushing in.

The telephone woke me up the following day. Despite the abrupt interruption of sleep, I found myself in a chipper mood for some reason. Perhaps from the private show I witnessed from Lillian the night before. Yawning, I stretched my arms and heard Addelyn's voice coming from downstairs, talking to her sister, trying to keep a low tone for fear of waking me. The high ceilings and spacious rooms played to my advantage. I could hear her saying things like, "Vance called again."—"I'm scared to tell Calvin what's going on."—"I know how he will react if he doesn't know already."

I decided to sneak down the stairs, through the foyer, and hide behind a wall to get a better listen. I wondered from her silence if she heard me coming, and by the time I reached the living room, Addelyn noticed me from her seat on the couch. She cleared her throat, wiped a tear from her cheek, and straightened her posture.

With a smirk, I said, "Don't let me interrupt you."

Lillian got up and told us she was going for a jog and getting some coffee. I couldn't help but wonder if her leaving had anything to do with our shared moment last night or she no longer wanted to take part in the awkwardness of the current moment.

After a light breakfast of nibbling a piece of toast, I got dressed for the day. Nothing fancy, but lying around for days with shorts and t-shirts made me feel icky and out of place. I decided to wear some khakis with a belt and a loose, buttoned shirt. Once I finished brushing my teeth, I felt this sensation like being kicked in the stomach by a shoe laced with anxiety. Through the window, I saw Addelyn in the backyard, on her swing, holding onto each rope, hanging her head.

I came outside with both hands in my pockets and strolled across the grass, walking barefoot. Judging from her expression, I could tell she had a deep, dark secret and no clue what to do with it.

"What are you doing?"

I didn't mean to startle her when I asked, "What are you doing?"

She whipped her head to me as if I had jumped out from behind the tree.

She relaxed and said, "Nothing. Clearing my head."

Her eyes returned to her legs, then across the yard, then to her toes.

I stood behind her, holding on to the ropes, and asked, "Anything I can do?"

"No, not really. A lot is going on with Lillian and Paul..."

Bullshit.

"I know I shouldn't stress over their issues, but I care about them both..."

There's more. I know there's more.

"And I hate picking sides..."

Whatever she said after that, I couldn't tell. The sight of Lillian jogging away from the house and down the street hijacked my attention. The back of her tan legs. Her tight ass, wrapped in shorts. The sunlight glistened against the sweat on the small of her back. The way the straps of her sports bra criss crossed over her elegant shoulders.

Her ponytail, swaying side-to-side. As she vanished around the corner, my lips curved into a smirk. I didn't notice at the time, but with my hands gripped so tight around the ropes, Addelyn's movements began burning my fingers.

I asked her, "Why don't you take the day to yourself?"

She said, "I am. I'm taking Maddie to my parents, and then I'm going shopping."

Dropping off the baby before shopping alone? Interesting. Bringing her sister along might be therapeutic for the both of them, unless, of course, Addelyn didn't want her around. Apparently, I wasn't good enough to watch my own daughter after the staircase incident, even though I assumed we had put it behind us. Before I could say anything, Addelyn rose from the swing and darted toward the house.

She didn't kiss me. She didn't hug me. She didn't say 'I love you.' She didn't say anything, for that matter. She simply left me by myself, knowing whatever secret she had buried inside was eating her alive. My eyes followed the ropes up to their tight knots around the thick branch above, and I tugged a couple of times to test their durability.

I finished hooking up the power supply to the Jacuzzi with the house all to myself. After a few tests, it worked like a charm, and although tempting to get in, I felt Addelyn should be the first and figured it would make for a pleasant surprise to lighten her mood when she came home.

The next project on my agenda was to finish installing the remaining security cameras. I planned on placing one above the master bedroom, the same way I did with the guest room. I would have to find sneaky places to hide for the others since I couldn't drill through the ceiling on the ground floor. The cameras were meant to be placed outside, in the backyard, the front yard, no different from the average family keeping tabs on their property. This would have been the case and much easier had Vance not come into our lives or if Addelyn had regained my trust. While thinking of convenient places to hide these devices, I decided to do a few chores. With a load of dirty laundry from the master bathroom, I came downstairs and dumped a few baby outfits from Maddie's hamper in the basket.

The tiny LED on the dryer indicated a previous load had finished and was ready for folding in the laundry room. After starting a new washing cycle, I opened the dryer door and removed a bundle of women's socks and lingerie. Lightly-lined Demi bras, lace panties, a silk pleated babydoll teddy, model-short pajamas with a low-cut collar, and a triangle top bikini with string-tied bottoms. None of which belonged to Addelyn.

From what I know, women only wear sexy lingerie to impress someone. Going through tough times with her husband, crashing for a few days at her sister's house, there was no one for Lillian to dazzle. Unless, of course, she had her hopes set on the only man in the house.

Lifting a thong from the pile, admiring the see-through material, I imagined what she looked like wearing them. I pictured her crawling into bed, curling her finger as an invitation to join her. I envisioned sliding this same thong over her knees and off her feet, then burying my face between her thighs, licking all the right spots, tasting a different flavor than the one I'm used to, and Lillian squeezing her legs together so tightly, my neck snaps and I'm killed instantly.

At least I died happily. At least I got the last laugh.

This fantasy came to an abrupt stop when I heard the

side door open. In a scuffle, my elbow knocked a bottle of liquid laundry detergent to the floor. The cap popped off, and some of it spilled. Lillian entered from the garage. I'm not sure if she saw me before I had a chance to throw her garments back into the dryer, but she didn't say anything. Instead, she smiled and squeezed by me, so close, I could hear the music playing from her earphones and see my distorted reflection on her tan chest, shining from sweat.

Did you know women's sweat contains behavior-changing chemicals called pheromones? Whatever biological magic was going on between us, it lured me in. I watched Lillian leave to go upstairs. She looked back at me, over her shoulder, and winked.

I thought, "Paul, you dumb shit. If I had this girl, I'd be smashing her ass day and night."

It wasn't until I heard the guest bathroom door close when I wandered up the staircase. Standing at the top, I listened to running water from the shower.

Walking across the balcony and through the hallway, I pictured Lillian's naked body, her smooth skin sleek with water. I saw myself washing her and rinsing the suds away before kissing every inch. Part of me wondered if the wink she gave meant something, and I had to ask, so I gently turned the doorknob and discovered she had left it unlocked. Before I could push it open, I heard the faucet squeak and the water shut off.

Take a deep breath.

I froze in silence, disrupted by the hum of a car outside, fading away as it drove down the street. At first, I thought it might be Addelyn, but she would be gone for however long it takes women to shop. What they say will be an hour may turn into several. Likely excuse—plenty of time for her to be with Vance and not have to rush back home.

Then came visions I didn't want to see. Recurring images of Addelyn and Vance. I didn't know what his home looked like, so my mind had nothing to reference. Instead, it set the stage with other places they could be, like a vacant road somewhere surrounded by trees, isolated from the city. Addelyn's car with an open passenger door. She's bent over the seat with her skirt pulled up. Vance stands behind her with his pants around his ankles. His hands on her hips, shoving himself against her, pushing her back and forth, using her like a piece of meat, like a two-dollar hooker, like she means nothing to him. Her hair hangs in her face and sways with each motion. Her wet lips, screaming so loud because she knows no one is around to hear. Shouting over his grunts and telling him how good he feels, so good. She begs him to go deeper, faster, harder, until she trembles. She doesn't mind being used. It turns her on to be treated like a whore. She tells him she's never been with a stud like him, and no one fucks her like he does. Vance suggests calling me so I can hear her repeat it. Addelyn laughs. Between panting breaths, she says, "I would, but Calvin's not worth the effort." She gets on her knees and faces him. Vance steps closer, using one hand to hold her head and the other to guide himself inside her gaping mouth.

Witnessing these things, I wanted to scream until my vocal cords ripped apart, run until my knees buckled, slam my fist against a brick wall, bust my fingers, break my bones, set myself on fire, anything to suffer less than this. Instead, I settled for another way to release my built-up aggression.

Bursting through the door with no shame or sense of embarrassment, I found Lillian standing in front of the mirror applying lipstick. She wore this sexy, violet skirt with a backless top and spaghetti straps, like a sundress. In fact, it wouldn't have surprised me if she had borrowed the outfit from her sister.

As though she'd been expecting my company, she snickered and asked, "Don't you knock?"

"Not in my own house. Besides, you've been waiting for me to come inside."

"Have I?"

"Of course. I'm very perceptive. It's no surprise; you want me as much as I want you. Why waste time playing games? Your husband is cheating on you. My wife is cheating on me. Why should we let them have all the fun?"

She smirked and spoke to my reflection, saying, "I wondered how long it would take before you came around."

I locked the door behind me and moved closer.

"Why didn't you say something?"

"It's not as if I can blatantly announce it. I was hoping you would get the hint. Where's Addelyn?"

Inhaling, I held my breath and let it out.

"If I had to guess, I'd say she's with Vance, and he's doing to her what I'm about to do to you."

Lillian giggled and capped her lipstick. She began feathering her lashes with mascara. She asked, "What do you think she would do if she found out?"

"Who gives a shit? She'll be devastated. She'll cry. Her heart will break. And all I would do is make her watch while laughing at her pathetic face. If you ask me, it sounds like an even trade." I moved closer, scanning up and down the back of Lillian's body. Smelling her wet hair and placing my hands on her hips, I softly said, "Who knows? She might kill us both."

Acting playfully, Lillian grinned, put her makeup away, and said, "What she doesn't know won't hurt her."

Reaching over her shoulder, I snatched her by the throat. Instantly, she turned on, gasping from the excitement.

I held her body against my chest, and with my lips hovering close to her ear, I whispered, "Now you can speak freely." With my tongue licking her neck, her eyes rolled back, and her fingers gripped the front of my thigh. I dragged my nails down her shoulders, sliding the straps of her dress to her elbows. I shoved my hands underneath her top, grabbing her chest. "Now, you can tell me how much you want me." I pulled the dress down to her stomach, exposing her perky breasts. Like I had imagined before, each one fit perfectly in my hands. My lips smothered her shoulder, and my teeth lightly dug into her skin. I told her to "Say it."

Despite our gushing hormones, Lillian and I both knew this was a horrible idea, but when she said, "I want you, Calvin," it became quite clear that neither of us cared too much.

After that, her words went unheard when I covered her mouth with my hand. I used my shoe to pull her skirt to the floor. I slipped my fingers beneath the bands of her lace g-string and ripped it off with a single, violent jerk. I kicked her legs apart and bent her over the sink. I teased her a bit, rubbing my tip between her thighs until she could no longer stand it. She reached her hand between them to guide me inside. She gasped again and released a soft squeal, the same I heard the night before from the attic. This kind of sex I'd been waiting for all my life, but soon, Lillian perceived it as the kind of sex that would bring about a lifetime of regret.

She said, "Okay, stop. We have to stop."

Grinding my teeth, fueled by anger and lust, unable to control myself, I smashed my hand over her face to silence her. I interpreted her moan as her canceling the request. Smacking my lap against her ass, I feared that they could hear what was going on if anyone passed by outside. Even though no one was home, I disguised the sounds by pulling the knob to the sink and releasing a roar of water from the faucet. Whoever may have heard would simply think someone was inside washing up.

I gripped a handful of Lillian's hair next to her scalp and yanked her head back. To catch herself from falling, she smacked a palm against the mirror.

She swung her head to break free from my clutch, panting the words, "Oh my God, Calvin. As much as I want this, we can't. We need to stop."

Time to up the ante. Ignoring her, I pushed her forward and shoved my fingers inside her mouth, tugging back on her cheeks like fishing hooks. Lillian tried to push me away, but I held onto her shoulders and flexed my muscles to keep her still. Sweat rolled down my face, dripping from my chin, and with my strength overpowering her, she wasn't going anywhere.

It wouldn't take much more, nor would it be much longer. I had in my mind to finish her off first. She would realize the sex she had with me was be the best she'd ever had once her body stopped convulsing from an overwhelming orgasm. Then she'll be glad I didn't listen to her, and who knows, maybe come back for more.

Lillian clawed at my skin while I choked her, tightening my fingers around her throat to the point she smacked my arm to let me know she might pass out, but in my heightened rage, I snubbed her disparity and squeezed harder. Seconds away from me finishing, I pulled her close and pressed my cheek against hers, pounding harder, faster. So many emotions, too many to name, began building inside my chest, rising in pressure, waiting to be unleashed. She broke free and elbowed my stomach, knocking the wind from me.

Coughing, she said, "This is not happening."

My reflection looked at her, confused, angry.

"What's your deal?"

Lillian tried to pick up her clothing, but I kept her pinned against the sink.

Again, she said, "I told you, this is not happening."

"I don't get it. You said you wanted me. All this time, we've shared a connection. We both knew what it felt like to be cheated and stabbed in the back. Why should we have to suffer alone?"

"You're making the situation worse than it is."

"So that's it? You're taking her side? Their side? I get to sit in the corner by myself while everyone around me fucks each other?"

She turned to face me, staring into my eyes. Once more, she said, "This is not happening."

"Stop saying that!"

Everything turned red. All I could hear was a single thud and the shattering of the glass and cracks splitting in all directions. When I could see again, Lillian had blacked out. She slid down the sink, plummeting to the floor. Her arms spread apart to her sides. Strands of wet hair stuck to her face. I took a step back when I noticed she was wrapped in a violet bath towel. No sundress in sight. No torn lace underwear. Glancing down, I discovered I still had my clothes on. My fastened pants. My snug belt. My buttoned shirt.

Didn't we have sex? Just now? Only a minute ago? Did I get dressed while my brain took a short vacation?

Finger-shaped bruises wrapped her throat. Her face was a lifeless pale, and her lips were a deadly shade of blue. I knelt beside her and checked her neck for a pulse. I'm not sure about her heart, but mine felt as though it stopped when I realized she wasn't wearing lipstick or mascara. Did any of this happen, or was it all in my head? This won't look good. A dead body in the guest bathroom. Even worse, my wife's dead sister.

Nibbling my fingernail, I panicked, spinning in circles, trying to think. Was this an accident? No. This was no accident.

I unlocked the door and checked the hallway. With a clear coast and an unclear conscience, I dragged Lillian's body by her feet to the balcony and down the spiral staircase. Her bleeding head thumped on each step, leaving a trail of maroon on the carpet.

At the bottom, I dragged her through the foyer, through the living room, all while repeatedly clarifying the situation to myself.

"You made a mess, but it's okay. You can clean it up. If anyone asks if we had sex, how can I give them an honest answer if I don't even know myself?" With sore legs and arms, I continued lugging her through the kitchen. "Addelyn can't get mad at me. She can speculate all she wants. This is all her fault, anyway. Her and Vance. She's been sleeping with him behind my back. It's only fair. I don't think she'll care when she finds out her sister is dead." I stop in the laundry room to take a short break and catch my breath. "Oh, shit. She is dead, isn't she? You can get away with this, Calvin. You know it. Think your way through. First thing's first. They're gonna do an autopsy. They're gonna find out she was strangled. If we did have sex before she died, they're gonna swab for my semen. They won't find it, though, will they? Not if we didn't do anything. What are you gonna tell them? Don't worry. You can get away with this. You know you can."

I opened the door and reached inside the garage to flip on the light, dragging her with short bursts of movement, over the threshold, and across the concrete floor.

In the Garage…

In the second-floor hallway outside the guest bathroom, Wayne picks a sticky string of gum from his bottom lip, returns it inside his mouth, and says, "Come with me." The master bedroom and master bath are the last remaining rooms on this level, but he tells Calvin they can wait. "We'll come back to them. First, I want to recall the events in chronological order. Now that you know how Lillian died, it's important to remember what you did next."

Calvin's not moving. He leans against the rails of the balcony and asks, "Why does it matter? She's dead! I practically raped my sister-in-law and then killed her." He falls to his knees, weeping in his hands. "Who gives a shit what I did afterward?"

Wayne releases a dreadful sigh, chews his gum, and says, "You told me the sex was consensual."

Calvin soaked up tears with his sleeve.

"At first."

"Then she told you to stop, but you kept going."

Sulking, Calvin nods, pinching his eyes closed with one hand.

Wayne kneels beside him and asks, "What else did she say?"

"That's it. She told me to stop, but I kept going."

"She didn't smack you. She didn't run away screaming. She didn't threaten you. She said something else, something she repeated.

"She told me, 'This isn't happening.'"

"And how many times did she say it?"

More tears flow as Calvin sobs.

He shrugs and tells him, "I don't know. A few times."

"Twice? Three times? How many?"

"I don't know. Three, maybe? Why?"

Wayne blows a bubble, sucks it back in, and asks, "Do you think maybe she was trying to tell you something else?"

Calvin lifts his wet face and says, "You can't be serious."

Smacking his gum, Wayne replies, "I wouldn't worry too much. You can't be charged with sexual assault if it never happened. At least not in this situation."

"Then why the hell do I remember? Where do all the details come from?" Calvin stands. "I feel like my head is about to fall apart. I can't tell what's real and what's not. You spend all this time pushing me to recall these suppressed memories, and now you're suggesting they might be fake? What is going on, Wayne?"

"I couldn't tell you. It's not my brain on the fritz." He waves his clipboard toward the staircase and says, "Come on."

"Give me one good reason why I should."

"Weren't you complaining about everything coming back all at once in a random sequence? Trust me, it's better this way."

"No, I mean, why should I keep following this craziness. Why shouldn't I leave right now?"

Wayne steps aside and holds out his arm, allowing him to leave.

Stomping down the staircase, Calvin sternly says, "To hell with this." When he reaches the front door, he jerks it open and adds, "To hell with you, too, Wayne," and slams it behind him.

Calvin breaths in the fresh air on the front porch and exhales with relief. Everything outside, the grass, the trees, the stars above, seem as real as he remembers. Mumbling to himself, he storms through the yard toward the driveway.

"I can't believe you would think I was stupid enough to fall for something like this."

He comes to a dead stop once he reaches the driveway. The reality he experienced only seconds ago instantly gets sucked away, leaving a vacuum of airless space and increasing the pull of gravity within his body.

His mouth falls open. He no longer blinks. He stands frozen for what seems to be timeless moments of bewilderment.

The garage door opens as its motor whirs, and a figure's shadow stretches across the concrete, shrinking in size until Wayne steps into the light. He leans against the wall, chewing his gum, clipboard in hand.

Calvin asks, "Where is my car?"

Popping a bubble, Wayne replies, "It should be here where you left it."

"Yes, it very well should be, but it's not!"

"Are you sure you drove it here today?"

Storming closer, Calvin says, "Of course, I'm sure! Someone must have stolen it. How else would I have—"

Oh, shit. No, no, no. Please, no, don't do this to me.

He spins, glancing around in all directions, growing dizzy as the lights from neighboring homes trail together in a swirling frenzy.

Wayne asks, watching and chewing his gum, "You don't remember how you got here, do you?"

Calvin points back toward the front yard, toward the porch.

"I...I showed up before you did, before you pulled your truck into the driveway. I...I was waiting for you on the..." Then, his fingers tap his lips. He's lost, desperate to recover missing time.

Wayne strolls and stops beside him.

He asks, "If the last thing you remember is leaving home this morning, then how did you get back?"

Calvin has no answers to produce, only the awareness of a need to admit to himself that he doesn't have a clue.

Wayne waits for this to absorb before he says, "Now you understand why it's so important we finish this." He checks his watch and turns to walk toward the open garage. "We can't stay out here all night."

If words could form on Calvin's tongue, he would likely swallow and choke on them. By now, not even *he* knows what to think. Wayne turns back and sighs. Through the garage and the open door to the laundry room, he spots a crusty, dried puddle beside a spilled bottle of detergent. Blowing another bubble, he catalogs items on his clipboard: LG Signature Turbo Front-loading Washer and Dryer Set. List price—$4,800.

He turns to see Calvin standing beneath the open garage door, hesitant to come any closer.

Wayne says, "You told me you dragged Lillian's body to the ground floor, through the house, the laundry room, and out here."

Though he fears what details are waiting to unravel, Calvin's curiosity is enough to keep him going. He nods, silently staring at the extension cord he last recalls holding the night Paul helped him with the floodlights and the ground-fault circuit interrupter.

Wayne's boots crumble through a small coat of kitty litter that spreads over an oily spot on the concrete floor. The garage is empty. No vehicles. No lawnmower. No tools. No boxes. The only thing in sight is the green cable, snaked in a circle beneath a storage beam.

Attempting to jog Calvin's memory, he asks, "You pulled Lillian in here, and then what happened?"

Lying, he replies, "I can't think of anything." This time, he notices Wayne rechecking his watch. He tilts his head and asks, "Are you in a hurry?"

Wayne wants to explain, but he can't.

Instead, he chews his gum and uses the excuse, "It's getting late, but there's no rush. Think it through."

With a hollow voice, Calvin says, "I can't."

"You can't or won't?"

"Both."

Keeping a calm demeanor, Wayne says, "It helps to think back, think hard, not only about the big things but the little things about the little things. The smallest details of the smallest details." He asks, "How did you clean the trail of blood from the carpet? What did you use to clean the blood off the sink in the guest bathroom?"

There's an empty spray bottle of hydrogen peroxide on the workbench beside a container of bleach. Calvin struggles to focus but draws a blank. Then, after a minute is up, individual memories come sneaking in.

"Cracking," he says, "like tires in the driveway. Something about a broom."

Wayne asks, "What did you use it for? Did you sweep something?"

An overwhelming sense of fear and desperation fills Calvin's chest, churning into his stomach.

Shaking his head, he says, "No. Someone wanted to open the garage door, the big one, from outside."

"Did you use the broom as a prop? So you could pretend to be working? To keep whoever visited from coming inside?"

Breathing heavily, nearing panic, Calvin nods, on the verge of tears.

Wayne pops his gum and places a hand on his shoulder.

"Take a deep breath. There's no reason to be nervous. Tell me what happened in this garage. Tell me who pulled into the driveway."

Calvin's lids squeeze the welling tears down his cheeks. His vision goes black like a theatre, and the feature film begins to play for the sole audience member.

I left Lillian's body lying next to a grease spot on the concrete floor. Tying the loop of an extension cord, I tossed the loose end over a storage beam and pulled the slack.

I told myself, "I can get away with this. I know I can. She's been depressed. She's been upset about Paul. Being cheated on, betrayed, it's unbearable. She killed herself. No one will suspect otherwise."

Wrapping the noose around her neck, I figured the strangulation marks would disguise the finger-shaped bruises on her throat. I secured the knot and pulled the cord to lift her until her feet dangled above the floor. The fixture crackled and popped with the weight. I tied the opposite end around the leg of my workbench, then moved a stepladder underneath Lillian's dangling feet and knocked it on its side.

Composing myself, I tried to forget what had happened.

I left her hanging, turned off the light, and went back inside.
What little blood smeared the carpet was easily cleaned with
a few sprays of peroxide. I knew I had to use the bleach to
wipe up the mess in the guest bathroom, the bloody
handprint on the mirror, and the dry stains on the edge of the
sink. Before I took my first step, my attention drew back to
the sounds of tires rolling into the driveway. I grabbed a
broom from the laundry room closet and hurried outside.

Around the corner of the garage, I found a familiar
vehicle. It belonged to Paul, who came to repair the ground-
fault circuit interrupter. He never said so, but it gave him an
excuse to come by and talk with Lillian and see if they could
patch things up. He didn't cheat on her. He didn't kiss
another girl at the club. He wasn't about to let their
relationship crash because of some false accusation. The
only reason he stayed away was to give her space to cool
down. Stepping from his car, he smiled and asked how
things were.

He said, "You look like shit. Are you losing weight? Are
you getting enough sleep?" He pointed at his own face and
added, "You've got bags under your eyes."

Without effort, the first words to fall from my lips were,
"I've been busy."

It's not a lie. I'm busy right now. Too busy for visitors.
Addelyn might be home any minute. What's gonna happen
when she finds her sister? What's she gonna say about the
mess in the guest bathroom?

Paul inquired about Lillian, asking, "Where is she? I
need to speak with her."

An array of excuses filled my mind, but nothing seemed
good enough to use.

"Oh, uh, well...You see, now's not a good time.

Lillian's not here. I mean, I haven't seen her all day."

Be careful, dipshit. You're muttering. It's a sure sign something is wrong.

Luckily Paul didn't catch on.

He said, "No problem. I can hang around until she gets back. Where's Addelyn and Maddie?"

"Addelyn went shopping. Maddie's asleep. That's why this isn't a good time. I don't want to wake her up. She gets fussy."

Paul chuckled. He walked over to pop the trunk of his car and produced a small contraption sealed in a plastic bag, a new ground-fault circuit interrupter.

"Unless she's asleep in the garage, she won't hear a thing. I thought I'd take a look at your fuse box, figure out what's going on with your floodlights."

Nervous, I bit my bottom lip. This isn't working. Think of something else.

"Really, it's not a big deal."

"Calvin. Buddy. Relax. It'll take a minute."

Take a deep breath.

I stood in one place as Paul passed by, heading toward the garage as if he knew he was imposing but didn't care. Placing the broom against the wall, I followed behind, and before his fingers touched the handle, I cleared my throat.

"Paul."

He stopped, turned around, and asked, "What's up, buddy?"

"Before you go in, there's something you should know."

He stepped toward me and said, "Sure."

"I...uh...I fixed the ground-fault thingy."

With a big smile on his face, he asked, "You did?"

"Well, not me, but I…uh…I had someone come out and take a look at it."

Paul hung his shoulders.

"Oh, buddy. Why'd you do that? I'll bet you paid an arm and a leg when I could have done it for free." He turned away to lift the garage door. It rumbled as it rolled to the ceiling. Before he noticed his dead wife hanging freely above the floor, Paul turned back to me and said, "The least I can do is make sure they did it right." Then, he continued to walk inside, unpacking the device. "Those things are import—"

The contraption fell to the ground along with the plastic bag. Swaying at eye level were Lillian's purple feet. Paul lifted his head, examining her body.

He spoke partial words with an open mouth, choking on their syllables, "Oh. Wha—? N…n…no. Lil…Lillian!"

Scuffling, he tried to think of what to do first so he could save her. Lift her so she wouldn't hang anymore, or untie the cord from the bench?

He shouted, "What did you do, Lillian?"

Falling to his knees, his head smacked the side of the workbench, and his hands fumbled to loosen the knot.

"Calvin! Help me! Call an ambulance!" Once more, he shouted, "Help!"

I did neither. Instead, I paced toward him with slow steps, watching him struggle to free the cable.

In a soft tone, I said, "Paul."

"Calvin, do something!"

In the same soft tone, I repeated, "Paul."

When he felt my hand on his shoulder, he gave up. He curled his head into folded arms, sobbing heavily.

I stood above him, knowing I caused his weakness but

acting as his strength.

I said, "She's gone. There's nothing we can do."

Sniffling, he raised his head.

"You…you didn't see her all day? Did she say anything to you before? Did she seem upset?"

Biting my bottom lip, I shook my head.

I told him, "No. I mean, I knew she was upset because of what happened between you two, but I never imagined it would come to this." Helping a whimpering Paul to his feet, I threw his arm over my shoulder, and the two of us walked outside. I added, "C'mon, you don't need to see this. It's not how you want to remember her."

I led the newly widowed husband around the house, down the sidewalk, and to the backyard near the swimming pool. Dead leaves from the changing seasons floated on the surface. Paul sat at the picnic table, bawling in his hands. As if there was nothing abnormal about the situation, I lifted the cleaning pole from the ground, and that's when I noticed the white rope dividing the shallow and deep sides had come loose on one end and sunk to the bottom. Looking into the water, I realized the pump had kicked on and was trying to suck the line through the holes of the drain cover. I could have yanked until it came free, but instead, I stood near the edge, watching as the waves and wobbles along the surface distorted my reflection. So hypnotic, I felt as though my mind had wandered off into a trance.

With a dead stare, I said, "You know, the last time I saw you and Lillian happy together was the night we went swimming."

This pool, *my* pool, is forever tainted by awful memories.

211

Without moving or changing my tone, I added, "I remember because it was also the night I discovered something."

Paul sniffled and asked, "What did you discover?"

I turned to him and answered, "Addelyn. That's the last time I saw her happy too."

He lowered his head again, and I held the pole behind my back as I continued. "It's a shame because it wasn't with me. I was there. The five of us. Me, as the fifth wheel. I can understand how Lillian must have felt, thinking you cheated on her. Betrayal is a sharp pain that starts burning in your chest and radiates into your stomach. It's nauseating. It makes you want to puke your guts out. You want to scream until your lungs hemorrhage, and you choke to death on the blood. You want to dig your fingers into your flesh and rip yourself apart, but the agony milks all your strength. And your brain…" I rubbed my temple. "Your brain won't stop fucking with you! It doesn't care how badly your heart is breaking. All it wants to do is laugh and show you what it must be like for the love of your life to be with somebody else. It wants to convince you the sex she is having with someone else is the best sex she's ever had. You start to wonder why she would do such a thing. Then, it dawns on you, the person she's with kisses better. His touch is softer. He feels closer to home than you ever did. And soon enough, another burdening idea comes along to fuel the flames. In comparison to her secret lover, you've become obsolete. You're no longer important because she found someone superior. In the end, the insufferable truth is that no matter how hard you tried, no matter what you've done, or how many times you promised them the world, you're simply not good enough anymore."

Paul swung his feet around to face me and provided his full attention.

"Are you referring to Addelyn?"

I said nothing, but I like to think my reddening face and clenched jaw gave him the answer to his question.

"Calvin, I—"

Interrupting him, I stepped closer with the pole gripped behind my back.

"You know the worst part? It's not the lies and the sneaking around..." I took another step. "It's not necessarily the cheating itself..." And another. "It's not the sensation of your heart tearing from your ribs and shoved down your throat..."

Paul rose to his feet and gently grabbed my shoulder, ducking his face to make eye contact.

"Buddy, what are you saying?"

My cheeks trembled from the tightness in my jaw. My eyes burned from the blood boiling behind them.

I finished by saying, "It's the betrayal of everyone else around who saw it, who knew about it, who helped keep it a secret, and continued to blatantly encourage it."

Paul's brows curved to the center of his forehead.

"Calvin, talk to me. Tell me what's going—"

His sentence ended abruptly with my fist pummeling his face. The next strike came with white knuckles, specifically targeting his left temple so he could share my pain, enough to send him down on his knees and temporarily disable any reaction. The ache swelled through his head, and he tried to shake it away. Before he could stand again, I used my foot to shove him facedown and dropped the cleaning pole on the ground.

Paul groaned and asked, "What the hell did I do?"

Through gnashing teeth and the devil's face, I answered, "You brought him back into her life."

"Who? Vance?"

I leaned over and bent Paul's arm behind him in unnatural ways. "When you know their sins and do nothing about it..." I jerked tighter until his arm snapped. "...You are just as guilty."

I'm not sure whether I broke his bones or simply dislocated his shoulder, but he screamed in agony. Using the collar of his jacket, I dragged him toward the pool.

"I shouldn't be the only one who has to suffer."

Paul begged, "Wait! I didn't know anything about Vance and Addelyn!"

Stomping along, I asked, "Why am I the one who has to clean up the mess?"

"Calvin, listen to me! We can talk about this! I didn't know anything, I swear to God! If I did, I would have told you!"

When his head reached the water, he struggled to keep his face hovering above. Before I moved another inch, I got down on one knee beside him.

I went for the cleaning pole and said, "Payback is only redeemable when it's equivalent to the initial damage. You need to feel everything I have felt. You need to experience what it's like to have your friends and family stab you in the back. You need to endure the betrayal."

"Calvin, don't do this. Please, I'm begging you."

I leaned closer and silenced Paul's pleading with a whisper in his ear.

"I railed your wife against my bathroom sink right before I hung her in my garage, and you know what, buddy?" I yanked his head back with a fistful of hair so he could feel my spit on his face when I said, "She loved every minute of both."

Paul tried screaming for help, but I quickly stood, kicked him in his gut, and shoved him in headfirst. I watched him sink and wondered how difficult it must be for him to try and swim with a busted arm. Then, I used the tip of the cleaning pole to push his body closer toward the floor until the drain sucked his body against the cover.

Did you know the average pressure of a standard swimming pool pump is nearly seven hundred pounds? Did you know suction entrapment is nearly impossible to escape?

I watched Paul's feet kick and his uninjured arm reach for me. I laughed at his pathetic attempts to break free. I tossed in the pole and watched bubbles rise from his screaming mouth to the surface.

And soon enough, when they stopped, I found myself at peace.

In the Nursery...

As Wayne chews his gum and leads back into the home, Calvin hunches on the floor and heaves, but nothing comes up. The sounds make Wayne gag, and he smiles as big as he can.

Calvin looks up and asks, "Is this funny to you?"

Showing all his pearly whites, Wayne says, "Not at all. Smiling suppresses the gag reflex."

Spitting on the floor, Calvin shakes his head. "I didn't know that."

He gets up and follows Wayne through the laundry room, the kitchen, the living room. He whimpers along the way, folds his arms across his stomach, and almost stumbles from weakness.

Paul was more than a brother-in-law, more than family; he was your friend. So was Lillian. How could you do such horrific things to them?

Calvin's thoughts pop like Wayne's bubblegum at the sight of the next room he's about to enter.

Stopping in the hallway, he sways his head and says, "Oh, God."

Wayne turns around. He flips to a blank page on his clipboard and asks, "What the problem? We need to check out Maddie's nursery."

The recent memories of Paul and Lillian's deaths, mixed with knowing baby Maddie died too, is too much for Calvin to handle. He hugs himself tighter and says, "No, I can't do it. I won't."

"You don't have a choice. You need to remember what happened."

Wayne blows another bubble and continues ahead. From around the corner, Calvin hears him say, "Nice brand." He slowly approaches an open door and listens to Wayne scribbling on his clipboard and saying, "White Roh crib."

List price—$2,099.

Calvin's legs fold beneath him. He lands on his hands and knees and vomits on the carpet. Wiping his chin with his sleeve, he says, "Not the crib. Not the nursery. Not Maddie. I can't bear it."

He refuses to look inside the place where his child, his infant daughter, once slept. He protests the sight of bright pink walls, toys, bibs, diaper bags, onesies, and outfits. More importantly, he refuses to face the truth, what he believes to be the worst part of any parent's nightmare.

Wayne peeks from the door and finds him whimpering, curled against the wall. He accepts that Calvin's distress and lack of memory are genuine.

Disappearing into the room, Wayne shouts, "It's not as bad as you think. I promise. We can clean the crib. I can take it home myself and give it a fresh paint job. Replace the mattress. Make it like new, if you want. Now, will you please come in here?"

Clean the crib? What's wrong with it?

The first thing his mind goes to is blood. Maddie's blood.

"Honestly, you can burn the house down for all I care."

"What do you plan to do for money?"

"I have a job. If I don't end up in jail, I can transfer to another city. I can start a new life."

"You mean, you *had* a job."

Calvin freezes. His eyes bulge.

With a loud, shaking voice, he says, "Bullshit."

"You were fired."

He pulls out his cellphone, scrolls through his contacts, finds 'Work' on the list, and presses the call button. The line clicks and buzzes with a busy signal. Hiding his face with his hands, Calvin slowly walks into the room, doing his best not to see anything more than his feet.

"Fired? For what?"

Wayne chews his gum, lifts the corner of a baby blanket with his pen, and says, "*The A Corporation* is a worldwide communications company. They couldn't risk the bad publicity."

"But I haven't been arrested. What happened to 'innocent until proven guilty?'"

"Look at it from the company's perspective. You're a liability. Keeping a suspected murderer on the payroll isn't something the stockholders find easy to swallow."

Calvin scoffs and says, "No one said a thing to me."

"When's the last time you went in?"

"Yesterday."

"It's Thursday. Why didn't you go to work today?"

"Because I had…an appointment." Then it dawns on him, Calvin will never return to his job. He says, "Guilty, regardless. Those greedy bastards. All they care about is money. Someone's life gets destroyed, and what do they do? They step on it and scrape it off the bottom of their two-thousand-dollar shoes. My father wouldn't stand for this. He would strangle those executives with their neckties, for sure."

"Unfortunately, he's not around to back you up." Wayne lowers Calvin's hand away, uncovering his terrified face. He says, "It's okay. I made a promise. This room is not as bad as you think. Whatever amount we can salvage should be enough to get you through."

Calvin's eyes well with tears.

"Money comes and goes, but Addelyn and Maddie are more valuable than anything to me."

Wayne sighs.

"I hate to keep correcting your grammar, but they *were* more valuable than anything to you."

Calvin groans. His cheeks flush with red, and he shouts, "Shut up! Stop rubbing it in my face!"

Smacking his gum, Wayne says, "The sooner you accept the fact they are dead, the sooner you can move on with your life."

"What life? According to you, I don't have a life anymore. I'd rather put a bullet through my head than live another day without them. I'd rather die than carry the guilt of what I've done."

Wayne taps a finger on his clipboard. Grinding his bubblegum between his teeth, he considers whether he should say anything, but the urge to do so is too much for him to contain.

"You did that already."

Calvin can't help himself. He explodes into a burst of sick laughter, throws his arms to each side, and says, "This is a gag. This is some kind of prank. You're standing there telling me I killed my family, and now what? I killed myself too?" He shouts. "I'm not falling for it! I am right here, alive, standing in front of you! I may not remember taking someone else's life, but I sure as hell would remember trying to take my own!"

Calmly, Wayne replies, "You didn't try. You succeeded."

"What are you saying? I'm dead? A ghost? You expect me to believe this is the afterlife?"

"Not at all."

"Then what is it?! Nothing you say makes any sense!"

Wayne adds another item to his notes: Gray Charlie dresser and topper.

List price: $1,000.

Calvin storms at him, shoving his chest and forcing him to take a step back.

"Listen to me, asshole! I've had enough of this shit! No more! Do you hear me? No more! Give me back my family!"

With a straight face and chewing his gum, Wayne nods his head to the side toward something sticking from the wall. Calvin turns to see a butcher's knife lodged in the surface. There's no body, but a large stain of blood that once kept someone's body alive surrounds the blade.

Wayne sighs and says, "You can't see it with the naked eye, but those are your fingerprints on the handle. You know it, and I know it, and I'm willing to bet a huge chunk of spare change the police know it too."

"But why is it still here?"

"Same reason as you."

Calvin hugs himself again as if he's cold. His mind is racing to find answers, anything that makes sense, while at the same time trying to keep his head clear to avoid recalling the horror.

"Whose blood is that?"

Wayne steps away, admiring the wall as though someone drenched it with a bucket of maroon paint.

"As a parent, I have to ask; why didn't you put the baby's room upstairs so she would be closer to yours?"

"I asked you a question. Whose blood is that?"

"And I asked you why you didn't put the baby's nursery upstairs. The difference is you already know the answer to your question. I, however, do not have an answer for mine."

Calvin thinks for a moment, desperately trying to put the pieces together.

When nothing clicks, he surrenders and says, "Addelyn and I took turns tending to Maddie in the middle of the night. We kept a baby monitor on the nightstand in our bedroom and decided to give her a room downstairs so whoever had to get up wouldn't disturb the other person. Plus, we planned to live in this house for a lifetime. Eventually, Maddie would grow up and want her privacy."

"As a teenager? They usually want their privacy for good reasons. Don't you worry she might sneak out to a party or something?"

Calvin looks at him with narrow eyes and says, "I guess I won't have to. Not anymore."

There's a brief moment of relief that washes over him. His memory rushes back, and he's able to bring forth the details of what took place in the nursery. This isn't where baby Maddie died. He knows this because she meant the world to him, and this blood, he recalls, belongs to someone worthless.

When I returned upstairs to the guest bathroom, I didn't bother cleaning my mess. In fact, I made it worse. I plugged an electric razor in the socket and as it buzzed, I spent the next several minutes, holding it in my hand, combing my fingers through my hair, staring at my shattered reflection in

221

a broken mirror, not thinking of anything specific. Not really thinking at all.

Addelyn came home, and as I suspected, Vance came with her. I wasn't there to see her reaction when she found her sister's body hanging in the garage. I wasn't close enough to hear her screams when she found Paul's dead body in the pool. I can, however, believe she assumed the worst, wondering if something bad happened to me too.

Hidden away, I remember Addelyn and Vance bursting into the house, calling my name. I heard them breathing heavily, desperate to find me, but their panting triggered visions of them kissing, tearing each other's clothes off, falling to the carpet, and making love in my absence.

Maybe they think I'm already dead. Maybe they believe they are finally free to be together. I considered these things from my place in the darkness until I heard Addelyn's feet running up the stairs.

Vance stayed on the ground floor, calling out as well. He checked the half bathroom, the kitchen, and the living room but found no sign of me. Making his way down the hall, he thought maybe he missed something in the garage or the backyard.

Maybe I was outside, but this late at night, doing what?

Vance followed a trail of shaved hair along the carpet, leading him into Maddie's nursery. He found the door ajar and entered with silent steps to avoid waking the baby.

He whispered, "Calvin?"

The room glowed from a subtle nightlight, revealing an empty rocking chair and the shadows of a spinning mobile above the crib as it softly chimed a nursery rhyme. When Vance turned to leave, he gasped. Behind him, as if I appeared out of thin air, I stood like a statue, glaring with an evil smirk on my face.

He put a hand to his chest to catch his breath and said, "There you are. You scared the crap out of me." Puzzled, he asked, "Why did you shave your—"

I silenced him by placing my finger to his lips.

"Shh, you'll wake the baby."

Confused, Vance looked over to the crib. It was empty except for a teddy bear and a crumpled blanket.

Then, he whispered, "But the baby's not here. Where is Maddie?"

In a low tone, I dismissed his inquiry and asked, "Do you know what I hate the most about you, Vance? Do you know what I loathe about your face? What I can't stand about you being in my home, much less alive on this planet?" His jaw fell open from the weight of my harsh words. "Walking around with your man-bun ponytail? Your cheap hipster cargo shorts and your flip-flops? Your ratty t-shirt?"

"I didn't know I—"

A flash of light blinded him for a second, a light from the reflection of a meat cleaver in my hand. Vance gulped and stepped back as I took a step forward.

"Do you know how sick I get when I hear someone mention your name? My stomach churns with acid. It boils into my throat and leaves behind a disgusting taste in my mouth."

"I'm sorry you feel that way, Calvin. Whatever I did, I'm—"

Sputtering my lips, I said, "Spoken like a true piece of shit. The only language you know is manipulation. You come into my house, spitting your 'beautiful symmetry' lines, dropping hints to my wife how much better things would be with you, sneaking around to stick a knife in my back while you smile at me with your stupid grin. The worst part is you think I'm too stupid to see it."

"Now wait a second. Whatever you think is going on between Addelyn and me, you're gravely mistaken. I would never intrude on your marriage. We're nothing more than friends. I came here tonight to deliver my paintings, the paintings I made for *your* home."

I stepped closer and asked, "*Gravely* mistaken? Nothing more than friends? How good of friends are you? Good enough to kiss her and shove your hands down her pants at the nightclub?"

"What? No."

I took another step.

"Good enough to sneak her into my bed? To make out with her in my pool? To fuck her in my sauna?"

The spinning mobile and its chiming lullaby began to slow, and when it stopped, Vance landed his back against the wall.

He begged, "Let's go find Addelyn so we can clear this up. We can sit down and talk about it. You'll see we have nothing to hide."

"Is that all you have to say? The two of you are good friends?"

"Nothing more. I swear."

I snickered, hung my chin, and swayed my head.

"Unfortunately, it's not the answer I'm looking for."

"What do you want me to say? What is it you want to—"

Lunging forward, I cut Vance's words short. Literally cut. With all my energy, strength, anger, and weight, I pushed the blade into his throat. He garbled and choked. His arms swung, desperately knocking over diaper bags and canisters of baby wipes. His hands smacked empty bottles to the floor. His eyes widened at the ceiling as though he could see death on its approach. I felt the knife cut through his vocal cords, his windpipe.

"I want to hear you say it."

The resistance broke free, allowing the blade to push farther back, slicing halfway through Vance's neck and resting against what I assumed to be his spine.

"Tell me what you said to her."

His legs loosened from underneath, but I kept his body pinned.

"I want to hear you repeat the line."

Each time his heart pounded, blood sprayed from his severed arteries, squirting across my skin and dripping from my fingers. Vance struggled to fight back, consumed by weakness with each passing second. My glare pierced his eyes. My breath heated his face.

"Tell Addelyn you want to fuck her like her husband is watching."

With a final push, a final thrust, a final jolt of power, the knife cut through Vance's spine and into the wall. His body fell limp, but his head, however, remained in place, on top of the meat cleaver like a trophy on a shelf.

I pushed myself to stand, scanning him once over.

"*Gravely* mistaken?" I turned to leave. "You're damn right about that."

Covered in blood, I headed down the hallway, trailing a path of footprints along the carpet, unaware the baby monitor had transmitted every word and sound of the incident upstairs to the master bedroom.

In the Master Bedroom...

The bedroom is arguably the most sacred room in anyone's home. It's where we make love. It's where we retire to rest. It's where we are at our most vulnerable while we sleep.

Calvin focuses on the back of Wayne's boots as each leg lifts to the next step on the spiral staircase. He listens to Wayne say, "There's the animal I was talking about. The animal, hiding deep inside you. Death goes hand in hand with life. It's human nature. Do what you can to keep your heritage alive, and when someone sticks their grubby dick in your Kool-Aid, you cut off their head."

When they reach the balcony, he guides the way toward the end of the hall.

Calvin wishes time would speed up so he can get through this hellish place he once called home. Slowing his pace, he comes to a stop outside the master bedroom.

Vanishing first into the room, Wayne calls out, "King-sized bed?" and scribbles on his clipboard.

Ophelia King, Monaco Cream—List value: $1,999.

Sticking his head through the doorway, Calvin pans the inside. He squints when he sees the walls, but the image remains behind his lids like the black and white photonegative.

Wayne touches the bed's footboard and bends down on one knee.

"Go big or go home." His hand grazes the wood finish, and he pushes the mattress a few times to observe its comfort. "You can get a pretty penny for a sleeper like this."

Bitter saliva floods Calvin's mouth. He might throw up

again but tries to control himself by swallowing and clearing his throat. He recalls Wayne's tip about smiling to suppress the gag reflex, but he can't imagine anything to smile about even for this purpose.

Wayne moves on to an oak chest of drawers. He slides the top drawer open, examining rows of rolled underwear and socks, then closes it again.

"I see you're a boxer-brief kinda guy." He opens the second drawer, and unfolded lingerie comes into view, most of it silk and lace, thin and delicate, see-through, and no doubt, expensive. "No wonder you were pissed."

Calvin twitches and rubs the back of his neck. His other arm wraps over his chest, and he stands there like a tight ball of apprehension.

"How so?"

Wayne apologizes and says, "I don't mean to sound like a creep. As you mentioned before, women wear sexy garments when they want to impress someone. My wife stopped wearing stuff like this after we got married. I guess she felt she no longer had to dazzle me with her sensual sleepwear." Panning the room, he continues by saying, "I've met a lot of married couples in my time. Some of them were close personal friends. Some of them divorced after learning their spouse had cheated. Do you know what they all had in common?"

Calvin shrugs, awaiting a response.

Wayne replies, "They all said the same thing; 'I should have known.' Before they truly had the heart to admit to themselves something was wrong, each one of them was able to tell me what first led them to believe their relationship was headed on a downward spiral. A husband, coming home late from work smelling like perfume. A wife, joining a Yoga class on the opposite side of town. Strange behavior. Polar-swinging moods. Secret phone calls. Hidden text messages. A sudden change in grooming habits. New clothes." He lifts a pair of Addelyn's thongs with his ink pen. "Flashy lingerie."

Calvin's hand presses against his chin, turning it red. Through his clenched teeth, he says, "It means nothing anymore. She has an expensive taste. As far as I'm concerned, Vance is dead, and with him out of the way, there's no one else for her to cheat with."

"There you go again, talking like she's still alive. Even if you don't believe she's dead, you are convinced she did, in fact, cheat on you? Am I right?"

"I didn't catch her in the act. I found no evidence."

"Except for the hickey on her neck."

As Wayne ends his response, he opens the third drawer. Underneath folded shirts and shorts, his hand touches something cold, something metal, something of interest. He whistles, impressed by the sight of what he removes—a Colt .45 revolver loaded with six hollow-point bullets.

Holding it by the grip, he examines the shiny chrome steel and says, "Now this is what I call a gun."

Calvin steps away to one side.

"It belonged to my father. I keep it around for self-defense."

"Well, I'd hate to be the dumbass who breaks into your house in the middle of the night. Do you know what a gun like this is capable of?"

Calvin refuses to imagine all the revarnished gore and bloodshed in his mind, but Wayne gives him an example anyway.

He says, "A hand grenade in a watermelon." Curious to

see if he's paying attention, he asks, "Are you sure you haven't used this weapon before?"

Calvin shakes his head and says, "Don't start with that suicide shit again. I didn't kill myself. It's not possible. I'm not dead, and you know what? I'm seriously starting to debate the possibility of killing anyone, for that matter. Besides, guns are not my thing."

Wayne tosses the weapon to him, asking, "It doesn't jog your memory?"

Calvin scuffles to catch it, and when it touches his skin, a terrifying moment freezes in his head and attempts to replay, but like a film-reel stuck on a projector's scalding lamp, the image burns and melts away. He drops the gun to the floor. Wayne senses Calvin's newfound denial. Of everything he's mentioned, the flashbacks, the suspicions, his self-torture, it appears now, by repeatedly glancing into the hallway, he's somehow convinced his wife and daughter will show up at any moment.

"You no longer believe you murdered Addelyn? You won't admit you killed Maddie?"

"Vance died in the nursery, not my daughter. I look back at what I did to the others, and I feel like a psychopath, but the man who killed them wasn't me. Deep inside, I know the love I have for my family is stronger than any deranged compulsion or crime of passion, or whatever you want to call it, and I would never in a million years do anything to hurt them."

Wayne tilts and shakes his head.

"Well, my friend, we're not quite finished. How can you be so sure without unlocking what remains of your past? Maybe your jealous rage took over, and you did, in fact, slaughter your wife. No one said you had to catch her and

Vance in the act, but the idea may have been so real to you at the time, it drove you crazy."

"Why keep pushing the issue?"

Wayne retrieves the revolver from the floor.

He says, "Because, no matter how harsh or disturbing, the truth is important. I understand today has been rough. I understand it's hard for you to face your demons. I understand why you're so afraid." He grabs Calvin's empty hand and lays the weapon on his palm. "But if you are willing to bet Addelyn and Maddie are still alive, then what harm can it do to retrace your steps?" He closes Calvin's fingers around the gun. "After this, there's only one room left."

Calvin's eyes close, and butterflies flutter to their death in the pit of his stomach.

I found Addelyn curled against the bedroom wall beside the nightstand, hugging her knees to her chest. Frightened. Confused. She had been listening to the sound of my footsteps getting louder as I walked up the staircase, and when I stepped inside, she dialed 9-1-1 with shaking fingers. I stood in the doorway with blood dripping from all over my body, staring, absorbing her fear from across the room. The bed was unmade. Addelyn made the bed every day. No one had been to sleep, which left another reason the sheets were wrinkled, and the blankets were left hanging off the side.

She froze at the sight of my bald head, as if I was an intruder coming to attack her. I heard the operator asking, "What's your emergency?" And I could see the terror squeezing Addelyn's throat to prevent her from speaking.

The steps my feet made seemed involuntary and guided as if someone else's brain controlled them. It made sense because my head was filled with all sorts of shit, leaving no room for anything else.

I grinned, took the phone from her hands, and told the woman on the other end, "Never mind. Everything is fine." I even apologized for making a mistake and strengthened my assurance by explaining how I had the phone in my pocket and didn't know it had accidentally called the emergency line. All of this, I said while Addelyn sat folded, speechless, and shivering.

I shattered the phone against the wall with a baseball player's pitch. She flinched as pieces of plastic landed nearby, and her trembling jaw rattled the question, "What did you do with Maddie?"

Licking the blood from my wrist, I snickered.

"You still think I'm a bad parent? Incompetent? I assure you, our daughter is in a safe place. She doesn't need to see this. She doesn't need to witness the consequences of your lies."

"What lies? I haven't lied to you."

Kneeling in front of her, I glared and asked, "You know you deserve this, don't you? If I were in your position, I'd be shitting my pants right about now. I would have screamed while the dispatcher was still on the phone. I'd be kicking and slapping me, or at least trying to run. Not you, though. You know what you've done, and you're willing to accept whatever punishment I throw your way."

She muttered, "I swear...I... don't know what I..."

I tossed a strand of her hair over her shoulder, exposing her neck and the faint mark below her ear.

"I didn't give you a hickey. Hell, you won't let me touch you anymore. Yet, Vance gets to suck on anything he wants."

Addelyn released a breath of relief, confident she could explain herself, and I would see this was all a big misunderstanding.

"No, sweetheart. It wasn't a big deal. I'm not—"

"You're a liar."

"No, baby. I swear! How can I prove it to you?"

"I have all the proof I need. I've been watching. I've seen everything. The way you spoke to each other at dinner. The two of you, together at the nightclub. Your playfulness in the pool and the way you flirted in the basement. The night I caught him running through the front yard after sneaking into bed with you."

She put her hands out in some measly attempt to get me to stop and said, "Running through the yard? Honey, that was—"

"I've heard your conversations with Lillian. I've eavesdropped on phone calls. You have a secret you're too chicken-shit to tell me because you're afraid of how I might react. You worried what I would do if I found out. You think I'm completely blind? I've seen street hookers who don't flaunt as much as you do when Vance is around."

I think the last part cut a little deep, judging by how quickly Addelyn began to cry. I didn't care. Seeing her sob did nothing for me. My words were razors, and each slice they made, she had earned.

Words came loose between her whimpers as she said, "The doctor, Calvin. The doctor called about your test results. I thought you may have known already and was too afraid to tell you if you didn't."

Wincing with questions, I asked, "What doctor? I haven't been to any doctor."

"We scheduled an appointment, remember? Please, I'm telling you the truth."

"Speaking the truth is an asset you don't possess. You've had the wool over my eyes since we moved in, and that prick started showing up. I can see through the fabric, and all I've done is pretend I don't know what you've been up to. Acting like I can't tell when you're sneaking around behind my back. Playing like I don't fall for your excuses. It's not hard. Discretion is not your strong suit." My voice raised to a shout. "I'm not stupid, Addelyn!"

"You're not stupid, but you are wrong! You are so lost. Please, Calvin, come back to me."

I reached over to open the third drawer, shoved my hands beneath my folded clothes, and removed my father's gun. The shimmer from the handle sent Addelyn into a panic, causing her tightness in her chest and rapidly taking shallow breaths. She couldn't speak, which was fine for me since she had nothing else to say that I wanted to hear. I put the tip of the barrel against the top of her head. She squinted, put her hands to her side, and froze stiffly.

I told her to "Stand up. Take off your clothes."

She panted through her words, "Oh...God...Please...Calvin... don't...kill...me."

With my jaw clenched, I repeated, "Get up and take off your clothes."

"Please, believe me, I love you...I haven't...done anything...to hurt you."

Not once in our lives have I seen Addelyn so petrified, so horror-stricken, and so frightened. She fought to keep it inside, but the fear seeped through her pores in a cold sweat.

Her entire body shook. Her teeth chattered. Even her tears seemed too terrified to flow, and those that got away trickled down her cheeks as if they were running for cover. When I pulled back on the hammer, the clicking sound made everything stop. She gasped and held her breath.

Glaring, I said, "You will *not* hear me tell you again. Get up and take off your goddamn clothes."

Weakened and barely able to stand, she did as instructed.

"Whatever you think I've done, I'm sorry."

I let her sit naked on the edge of the bed. With the gun aimed in her direction, I hustled to the master bathroom, keeping her in my sights. I turned the faucet on the Jacuzzi. The water roared and began filling the tub.

I told her, "I fixed it for you! See?"

Had she not shown appreciation for my accomplishment, Addelyn feared I might have become more enraged. She calmed her demeanor, sniffling, wiping her face, muttering, "It...it works now?"

Lowering the gun to my side, I said, "Sure does. Like brand new. I wanted you to be the first to try it out. Hop on in."

She rocked from the bedside, covering her chest with her arms like I hadn't seen her naked before.

She said, "You shaved off your hair." She asked why, but I didn't answer because I had forgotten the reason, if I had one at all. She asked again, "Where is Maddie?"

Storming toward her, I returned my aim at her head, ordering her to "Get in the fucking Jacuzzi."

If not for the weapon pointed at her face, Addelyn would have refused and likely started an argument. Instead, she stood on weak legs and took small steps toward the master bathroom.

Blood oozed from my nostrils. Pain shot through my temple.

Addelyn recalled happier times. When we met. When we first kissed. The times we danced and held each other. Our engagement. Our wedding. Our honeymoon. The birth of our daughter. The downtown apartment. The day we moved into this house. The times I made her laugh. I could see in her face; her heart was breaking, knowing things would never be the same. The husband she loved was forever gone. Like our hearts were once melded together, I also felt the pain of them separating. We shared the misery of the life we strived for as it neared its end.

Desperate for answers, she begged me to explain and asked, "Why, Calvin? What is so wrong in your life, you have to throw it away?"

For a second, I wanted to stop, to hug her and kiss her, to tell her I was sorry. Explain to her I need help; I'm out of my mind. She means more than anything to me. I thought these things and felt the tears building in my eyes. Lowering the gun, I reached my hand. Trying not to choke, with a soft voice, I said, "Addelyn?"

She took this as a moment of weakness. She tried to run, but I extended my arm as she passed, smacked a palm around her throat, stopping her dead in her tracks. Pushing against her, I made her walk backward, stomping my feet, saying, "You…"

Her hands gripped mine to relieve the pressure. She struggled to shout, "Don't!" She fought to cry my name, to beg for mercy. Entering the master bath, we stopped beside the Jacuzzi, and with my hands squeezing tight, I pulled her face close to mine and whispered, "…Every day, it's you."

In the Master Bath...

Calvin violently sways his head, slams both fists against the wall, and wails, "I didn't hurt my wife!"

The Jacuzzi, installed in the corner with an off-white terrazzo marble tile, is empty with blood-tinged watermarks circling the drain. On the ledge are melted stacks of candle wax in their tipped-over brass holders. Dried towel rolls.

Paying no mind to the ruckus, Wayne chews his gum and flips the light switch up and down a few times. The bulbs have burned out. He says, "I don't believe you meant to hurt anyone, especially your family. However, the truth remains; you had no choice."

On his knees, hunched over with his arms covering his head, Calvin asks, "Why not? Why didn't I have a choice?"

Wayne blows a bubble, pops it with his teeth, and jots down 'Jacuzzi' on his last sheet of paper—List value: $2,999. He clicks his pen and tucks it in his shirt pocket, removes his glasses, and lets them hang from the string around his neck. He holds the clipboard beneath his arm and reaches down to help Calvin stand again.

"Listen," he says, checking his watch, "We need to finish this tonight. There's no way we put this off before the bank takes the keys. Stay focused, man up, and let's get through this together."

Calvin buries his face against the wall. He feels rage threaten its return, knowing the worst parts of his past remain ahead. He spins and storms at Wayne, shoving him back against the wall. He swings his open palm, smacking the clipboard to the ground. The sheets of paper fly apart, and Calvin says, "I've had it with these games!" He grips

Wayne's shirt with his fists, spraying his face with spit as he shouts, "I'm done! Tell me the truth! What happened?!"

Wayne spreads his hands aside in defense and coughs, saying, "Whoa. Take it easy. This is not a conspiracy against you. I know nothing you don't."

Tears trickle down Calvin's chin. It's obvious Wayne refuses to give him what he wants, and there's only one way for him to find what he needs.

Through gnashing teeth, he says, "Damn you," shoving himself away.

Wayne adjusts his posture and brushes the wrinkles from his shirt. He bends down to shuffle the scattered papers together and reattach them to his clipboard.

Coughing again, he grabs this throat and says, "Ugh, you made me swallow my gum."

His silhouette stands in the doorway, watching his troubled client crawl against the side of the hot tub, unknowingly smearing wet, black soot on his chin. In the darkness, Calvin stares blankly at the floor. Soon, he fades away and begins to remember.

Falling backward into the tub, Addelyn's head submerged beneath a tsunami of cold water. Once the splashing settled, her feet rose above the surface, and I noticed her curling toes. Gasping for air, she sat up like she had fallen into the ocean and woken up in a Jacuzzi. I knelt beside her, outside the tub.

"Does it feel so good it makes your toes curl? Like Vance?"

Addelyn hugged her knees to her chest, shivering. The

water in the hot tub was anything but hot. Shaking, she said, "Even if it were true, I wouldn't tell you. I love you too much to hurt you."

Tightening my knuckles, I punched the floor, cracking a single tile and leaving behind the bloody shape of my fist.

"You don't want to admit it. You don't want anyone to know you're at fault."

"Nothing happened. I can't promise any more than I already have."

I put the gun to her temple, and she sealed her eyes. I listened to her plead, "Wait. Please, wait. Please…" So, I did. I waited for her to say, "Tell me what you did with Maddie."

Swaying my head, disappointed, I replied, "Shame on you. How dare you question my ability to look after my daughter. If you must know, she's downstairs in the kitchen."

Addelyn whimpered and asked, "You left her alone? What if she gets hurt?"

I snickered and answered her questions with a question of my own.

"What kind of father do you think I am?"

"Please, sweetheart," she said desperately, "Tell me where."

For nearly ten seconds, I drew a blank, trying to recall the whereabouts of my only child. Then it popped in my head, and I know now, looking back, had I been the man, the parent, the father I was before, it would have killed me to realize what I'd done. Take that back; It wouldn't have done it, to begin with. Not in a lifetime. Not ever. Not to Maddie, not to anyone. If someone had done the same, I would have rioted. I would have called for their execution. I would have demanded they be tortured, hung, and slaughtered. No parent, no human being, should have the capacity, the evil, the illness to do what I was about to confess to Addelyn. Yet, for some reason, some unexplainable rationale, I wasn't convinced I had done anything wrong. My actions seemed perfectly normal. Any mother or father would agree, our child was protected, safe in one place, out of harm's way. I knew she was okay because hours had passed since I heard her cry.

"Maddie is fine…" Sighing, I touched Addelyn's cheek and smiled. "…I put her in the freezer."

Addelyn's wretched screams came from shallow breaths. I don't know how many times she shouted God's name, how many times she bargained, "No!" I couldn't tell you how painful it was for her to imagine baby Maddie alone in the dark, shivering, suffering, afraid, and crying out for no one to hear. There's no way I could relate because I simply believed I did what I did in my daughter's best interest. She didn't need to witness her father dragging Lillian's dead body through the house. She didn't need to watch as I drowned Paul in the swimming pool. She wouldn't understand why I had to cut Vance's head off.

I doubted Addelyn's ability to handle herself, knowing what our little girl had to endure. The more I thought about it, the more I questioned if it was true. Did I really stash my baby girl in the icebox? Did I truly seal her and her fate inside? Was she dead when I put her in there, or could she still be alive?

It's not for me to say how Addelyn managed to calm down. If I had to, I would have guessed she disassociated from her emotions. Isn't that what people do when they face horrific tragedies? Don't they mindlessly push through? Set things aside to forget later? She sat like a statue in the tub with a blank expression on her face. She no longer shivered, as if her body didn't care if she froze to death right there. The water settled. Like it was yesterday, I recall the way she looked at me, the emptiness in her voice when she asked, "Calvin? Do you remember what you promised me?"

Addelyn waited for an answer while I thought about it. How could I forget my sacred vow, more binding than a written contract, more solid than any agreement? Her last few tears made ripples in the water, and her will to live evaporated. What she wanted now was to punish me by leaving me with an everlasting reminder of my broken promise. I've said it before; Addelyn knows me too well.

Softly, she said, "You promised you would never hurt me."

Nodding slowly, I set the gun on the floor. Oddly enough, I thought bathing her would somehow make her feel better. I reached for a container of Epsom salt and poured it in. The white powder dissolved and clouded the water.

I told her she was right, cupping handfuls of water to pour on her shoulders. "I did make a promise, and I'm sorry I made you think I had it in me to hurt you."

Leaning away, I took my arm off the edge of the tub. Hovering my hand above the weapon, I glided toward the open panel of the Jacuzzi where I had rewired the motorized pump. I removed the loose cover, exposing the small display of twisted cords spliced and taped together.

And then whispered, "Trust me, you won't feel a thing."

In the split-second of me reaching inside to flip the main power switch, Addelyn shouted, "Don't! I'm preg—"

The sole purpose of a ground-fault circuit interrupter is

to prevent injury or death from electric shock. I didn't replace the device, nor did I intend to do so. In less than a fraction of a fraction in time, the negative energy shot through the tub, through Addelyn's body, through the salt, rendering her unconscious before the electricity did its damage. Her awareness came to a halt before she knew what had happened. Raging heat burned through her internal organs, and her brain shut down before it fried inside her skull. Every muscle in her body stiffened so forcefully, they snapped the weaker bones of her arms and legs.

At the same time, there came this hair-raising, high-pitched, whirring sound, like a small drill grinding through rock, and it seemed to come from every direction, both inside and outside of the master bathroom. I couldn't figure it out. I thought some tiny motor in the base of the Jacuzzi was about to explode. The screeching nearly deafened me. I covered my ears, and once it faded away, it left the room with the eerie hum of electricity. Sparks burst like fireworks from the wall socket above the sink. They showered from the panel across the floor. The lights throughout the house flickered. Eventually, the surge of power became so intense, it blew multiple fuses in the garage, and the house went dark.

Shortly afterward, Addelyn Cope-Delacroix, loving wife, mother, and friend was gone. Like a prisoner in the electric chair, accused, convicted, and sentenced to death, her frail body submerged as her arms floated in the steaming water. Her hands bobbed like buoys in a river. Not until her face began rising to the surface did I grasp the entire concept of what I had done.

Everyone dies with the same lifeless expression. Addelyn wore the same mask as my mother when I found her dead from an overdose. That's all it took for me to realize, my wife, my best friend, my everything—she wasn't coming back.

At first, I sobbed, but the more my body shook, the more I felt my whimpering turn to a peal of uncontrollable laughter as if I'd been told the best joke with the funniest punchline. Guarding my cramping stomach with both arms, I rolled onto my back and continued laughing even harder and bawling, "'Til death...Ha! Ha! Ha! Ha!... 'til death do us part!"

Once my eyes adjusted to the darkness, I could barely see the glimmer of Addelyn's ankle bracelet as water spilled from the rim and splattered on the floor, lifting her ankle toward the edge.

Oh, Jesus! Oh, Christ! Oh, God! What have I done?

I was wrong. I'd never been so wrong in my life. She was telling the truth. Her reasons were authentic. And what was it? What did she say right before she died? Before I killed her? Was she trying to tell me she was pregnant? Is that what I heard? I didn't give her a chance to finish. Her sudden death ended her sentence too soon, and her punishment became mine. I wanted to die. I wanted to jump from the tallest building, from an airplane, and splatter the ground. I wanted to drown myself in mud, take a hammer to my knuckles, drill holes through my knee caps. Anything else, please, anything else.

My sobbing curdled into a sustained wail of anguish. My wheezing voice, like a forced whisper, said, "Wait, wait, wait." I pulled her body from the tub and gently laid her on the tile. "No, no, no, no, no."

With folded hands, I pushed down on her chest, begging for her heart to beat again. I sealed my lips to hers with a desperate kiss, breathing life into her lungs. My efforts were useless. I heaved above her, covering my face, crying so hard, I was incapable of producing a plea to the heavens, to the universe, without breaking apart. "Please come back! I'm sorry! I don't want you to go away!"

Some people can argue those who return from death do so because their spirit has a reason to fight for survival. However, knowing how I betrayed her, Addelyn's spirit refused. I laid with her on the floor, holding her, rocking her, trying to keep her warm. Combing my fingers through her hair, I repeatedly whispered, "I love you. I love you. I love you."

Over time, I started telling her stories, rehashing our childhood. I asked her if she remembered summer camp and how we broke away from capture the flag to share our first kiss. I asked if she remembered the song the counselors sang around the fire. Kissing her forehead, I wanted to know if she remembered when I asked her to be my girlfriend under the bleachers at the football game or recalled our dance at the prom and how we made love for the first time.

Sniffling and wiping my face, I asked her, "Remember? Remember how I promised you the Milky Way?"

Not once did she answer, and after a lengthy silence, I gave up, thinking she had forgotten.

My boxer shorts dripped water along the carpet, through the bedroom, the hallway, the balcony, and down the staircase. Stomping each step, I smacked myself in the face, punched myself in the side of my bald head. I raced through the foyer, the living room, tossing cushions from the sofa, slashing them with the meat cleaver. I yanked the television from the wall, threw a fist to the screen, and left it broken and dangling from the mounting brackets. I grabbed the paintings Vance had left, waiting to be hung, and kicked them full of holes. I ripped them apart, piercing my hands with splinters from their wooden frames. I knocked over Maddie's playpen, and her toys fell out. I took her teddy bear and ripped it in half up to its neck as its stuffing fell out. I couldn't leave anything behind. Nothing to remind me of the life my family once lived. Nothing to remind me of what I destroyed.

I carried on into the dining room, the kitchen, smashing dishes, wreaking havoc on everything in my path. Suddenly, my rage abated at the sight of the refrigerator. As much as I didn't want it to be true, I knew what I would find inside. As much as I didn't remember doing so, I thought I had done right by wrapping the door in duct tape to keep it from swinging open so she wouldn't fall out and get hurt. I tore away the tape and took a deep breath before opening the freezer. The clouds of steam rolled out like smoke, and when it finally cleared, I saw my baby, my firstborn child, stiff, blue, and lifeless. I observed the tiny handprints she left on the walls and the scratches she made in the frost. I broke down, sobbing, taking her into my arms, holding her to my chest. I grabbed a towel from the drawer and tried to warm her, to revive her, even though I knew my efforts were as worthless as I was. I brushed her soft hair with my fingers. Humming a lullaby, I rocked Maddie to sleep, to death, trying to find justifiable reasons for what I had done and why I should be allowed to live.

Take a Deep Breath…

Calvin lies on the tile beside the empty Jacuzzi in the same spot he last held his wife. He knows almost everything that happened, and the memories are as real to him as any other. He's relived the same emotions, the anger, the pain, the heartbreak, the betrayal, and now he sustains the feelings of worthlessness and shame. He's run a dreadful marathon and no longer has the energy to continue. He's been beaten to a pulp by his own demons, who robbed him of his will to move on.

Wayne's sympathy makes him sigh heavily before offering assistance to help him stand. He says, "We should go now."

Calvin doesn't move but asks, "Are we finished?"

With an affirming nod, Wayne helps him to his feet and receives an apology.

"I'm sorry I made you swallow your gum."

"It's no big deal. I have another piece left."

Wayne leads the way from the master bath to the balcony. Before Calvin knows it, he's standing in the foyer with no recollection of walking down the spiral staircase. It's no surprise. The body runs on autopilot when the mind focuses on something else. He's been flooding his thoughts with history and considering what future consequences he should face.

Unwrapping a new piece of bubblegum, Wayne tosses it in his mouth, flips through the pages of his clipboard, scanning the listed items, and says, "Give me a few minutes. I need to add all this up."

He continues mumbling something and walks away, heading toward the hallway, leaving Calvin alone for the moment. His inaudible words fade, either from a distance or because Calvin has replaced them with his own as he whispers to himself.

"It can't be true. Any minute now, you're going to step outside and find Addelyn and Maddie waiting for you in the car. Wayne said you killed yourself, but you didn't. You're still alive, so that must mean they are too." Calvin takes a look around and continues, "If these walls could talk, they'd speak the truth. Unfortunately, you're all alone, and there is no one else here to substantiate fact from…" He pauses, frozen. "…fiction." His eyes refuse to blink, and his ears listen for a strange sound.

Like a glitch, something flashes, white light, on and off, racing downward like passing streetlights from the backseat of a moving car or the static bars of a television without a signal. The motion is nauseating, and they soon slow to a stop when his vision floods with a blast of light and intense pressure in his brow. Like staring into the sun at its brightest, the pressure transitions to sharp pain, a migraine. He groans and covers his eyes with his arms to block the light, but it's no use. It's hard to breathe, and he's brought to his knees. Calvin vomits in his lap, and now, his pants are smeared with puke. He uses his shirt to wipe his chin and vomits again.

As the pain subsides, the light dims enough for him to see. He takes off his pants and pulls his shirt from over his head. Wearing nothing but boxer shorts, he notices feathers of dark hair floating to the ground. Wiping a hand over his scalp, his finger grazes along the soft, smooth surface. He calls for Wayne, but Wayne doesn't answer.

Calvin tries to think of logical explanations. It's the adrenaline. It's the brain's reaction to high amounts of stress. His shallow gasps collect enough air to call out again, "Wayne!"

In this room, this foyer, the brief silence ends when Wayne's voice startles him, saying, "Here we are."

Calvin grabs his chest and whips around to find Wayne leaning against the wall with his clipboard underneath his arm. He says, "Shit. You scared me."

Wayne blows a bubble and lets the pop echo through the room.

"When I told you your family was dead, you didn't believe me until you saw it for yourself. When I said you killed them, you didn't believe that either until you relived the experience." He looks at Calvin and adds, "I also said you took your own life, but you're not dead because you have yet to remember."

Calvin swallows the last of the spit from his dry mouth. He's about to say something, but a strange sound draws his attention to the window.

He whispers, "Someone's outside."

Wayne begins to pace the foyer in a circle around him, calmly chewing his gum.

He asks, "Are you listening to me, or the sound of boots scurrying through the dew-covered grass?"

Calvin returns his widened eyes to follow Wayne as he continues to stroll around him.

"Boots?"

"Not cowboy or fashion boots, we're talking about tactical boots, the tight-laced footwear of soldiers, or, in this case, the SWAT team—specially trained police officers hustling through the backyard of your home."

Calvin pauses, hearing the swishing of polyester uniforms and the soft clanking of bulky accessories as they hasten across the lawn. The reality of the police coming for him has finally sunk in.

Wayne smacks his gum and puts his hands in his pockets.

He adds, "They move quickly but undetected because the motion-activated floodlights mounted beneath the gutters of your house remain unlit."

Shit, that's right...the power is out.

Calvin asks, "Are they here for me?"

Bouncing his head, Wayne moves closer.

Within reach of Calvin, he stops and says, "They carry rifles loaded with deadly ammunition, and right now, they're taking their places behind tree trunks, bushes, and fences, anything they consider to be protective cover."

Silence falls, and Calvin listens carefully. Soon, he hears a woman's muffled voice from a radio, like someone covering a speaker with their hand to limit the volume.

She says, "Northwest corner. To the front and to the left."

Calvin hides against the door as vibrant red lights flash from outside, illuminating the curtains of the windows and sidelights. Then comes another vibrant blue. Over and over, the two colors repeat, getting brighter with each strobe.

He whips around, looks to Wayne, and asks, "What do you suggest we do?"

"We? They're here for you, my friend. But there's no reason to worry, right? You're safe inside this house, protected by layers of brick, wooden frames, and drywall. After all, the cops can't shoot what they can't see."

Wayne watches Calvin deciding if he should peek outside. He continues by saying, "Unfortunately, safety is an illusion. It always has been. It turns out you're only as safe as your weakest barricade. The last thing standing between you and an intruder is a door. Some people feel by merely keeping it locked, the rest of the world stays contained outside, but a deadbolt means nothing when it comes to the pounding of a battering ram or the swift kick from a cop's boot to bust it open. As for the windows, they're nothing more than thin sheets of glass shielding you from nature's elements and weather, and the softest tap can break them into pieces."

Calvin's curiosity compels him to peek through the blinds and see squad cars blocking the streets.

Wayne adds, "The surrounding residents have been evacuated, and there's a strategically placed sniper crouching behind the chimney on your neighbor's rooftop, waiting to catch a glimpse of your head through the crosshairs of his scope, confident he can bring this lengthy standoff to an end."

Never before in his life has Calvin been so confused.

"Lengthy? They just got here."

Wayne replies, "There's a storm brewing, and right now, is the calm beforehand. Those cops are becoming more impatient by the minute. They've been trying to get you to peacefully surrender for nearly five hours before they'll decide to use more invasive tactics."

"What do you mean, *five hours?*" Calvin points to the wall and says, "For the last five hours, we've been going…" He pauses and looks back. "…through the house."

He peeks around the curtains, outside his front door, and sees another cop fastening the straps of his respirator and preparing to launch a canister of tear gas through the window.

Wayne begins another lap and asks, "Did you know tear gas smells acidic, like vinegar? Did you know it's not so much a gas but more of an aerosolized fine powder, irritable to the skin and mucous membranes?" He says, "If it gets in here and fills this room, your eyes will flood like leaking faucets and burn as though you've doused them with mace. Your nose will gush like the busted levee of a seemingly endless reservoir of snot. Your lungs will burn, and you will choke and gasp for air like some form of asthmatic punishment."

Calvin is getting anxious, and Wayne tells him to take a moment to relax.

He says, "Take a deep breath and count backward from ten."

It's hard to do when he can barely control his own breaths. They're too rapid and shallow, too panicked. But Calvin's breathing stops altogether when he gasps at the frightening sound of the phone ringing from the kitchen, through the living room, hallway, and into his ears.

Wayne says, "That's the negotiator calling your telephone. He's trying to get in touch with you to see if he can accommodate your demands."

"But I don't have any demands. Everything I care about is gone, and there's nothing anyone can do to bring them back."

The phone rings again.

Wayne says, "The negotiator wants to talk you down and offer you a chance to get out of this intense situation unharmed and alive."

Calvin shouts, "What's the point? Why go on like this?"

The phone rings yet again.

Wayne says, "The main concern during any SWAT standoff is the safety of everyone involved, but sooner or later, whoever is in charge of this shit-show will lose patience and attempt to bring you down no matter what's at stake. Eventually, they'll send in everything they've got at their disposal so they can finally dispose of you."

The phone continues to ring.

Although he's slow and far enough away, the circumference of Wayne's path around Calvin is dizzying.

"Don't worry, though," he adds. "You're in control, remember? The army of police staged around your home doesn't have a leg up on you."

Calvin has come this far, evading capture. He feels somewhat immortal and somehow doubts their fancy toys will affect him. He's too smart to fall for their silly tricks. Then again, the more he thinks about it, the more he realizes the truth. The more he fears, after all, he may not have the upper hand.

Wayne seals this realization by telling him, "Those cops outside, they're not leaving until this situation gets resolved. They won't give up until you're in custody or worse…dead."

He blows a bubble, pops it with his tongue, and begins another lap as the phone rings again.

Each time, the harsh tones echo louder inside Calvin's head like an ascending alarm. An ache pulses in his temple. He covers his ears to deafen the shrill sound as it becomes more and more unbearable.

He shouts, "If only there were some way to make them understand I'm not a monster."

Bouncing his head, Wayne agrees.

He says, "You're right. Not all of this is your fault, not

exactly. You've made a few mistakes. You tried your best to handle your affairs but simply lost control." Blowing another bubble, he adds, "You let the worst get the best of you. With a bit of luck, people will empathize once they hear your side of the story." He shrugs, chewing his gum, and says, "You should probably do the right thing and surrender. Toss in the towel and throw your hands in the air. Otherwise, it's highly probable you will lose this battle with a small infantry of officers who've taken an oath to protect society from people like you. Maybe you shouldn't have done what you did in the first place. It's too bad you can't change the outcome now that your future is grim with the inevitable."

Calvin realizes this, and it's terrifying.

The phone rings again, and after, he says, "I want to go back!"

Wayne hangs his head, pacing.

"You can't, but in a short amount of time, the one place you will be going is to prison for the rest of your life. Once they have you in handcuffs, the police will eventually find the dead bodies on your property. They'll find Lillian in the garage, Paul at the bottom of the swimming pool. They'll find Vance (and his head) in the nursery, Maddie in the kitchen freezer, and Addelyn upstairs in the Jacuzzi. Later, a judge and jury will declare you guilty of second-degree murder, and, given the nature of your crimes plus the number of victims, there's no doubt the prosecutor will seek the death penalty." Wayne asks, "Did you know this state enforces lethal injection?"

Calvin scoffs, scrunches his face, and replies, "Capital punishment sounds like a blessing."

His mind begins to race, thinking the worst, and soon, there comes an idea of something more horrific than dying.

The phone rings again.

Bouncing his head, Wayne smacks his gum, begins another lap, and says, "You're not wrong about that, my friend. The same attorney who fails at getting you off with a plea of insanity will fight to keep the needle out of your arm with recurring appeals, but how many nights can you sleep with one eye open? How many years will you spend looking over your shoulder? How many corners will you hesitate to turn, fearful of who waits for you on the other side? Once your fellow prisoners find out what you did, oh boy...who knows what creative and torturous methods of sanction they'll come up with? From keeping you starved by knocking your meal tray to the dining hall floor to daily beat-downs and gang-rapes in the shower, make no mistake, those inmates will deliver the living hell you deserve. From the second the bars slam shut to the moment you find eternal peace, you will fully understand what it's like to be the victim."

Picturing this in his head, Calvin guards his stomach, ready to vomit again.

As the phone rings once more, and Wayne asks, "So, what do you plan to do about it? What's your next move?"

The ringing stops, and it should be easier for Calvin to think clearly, but he can't because the abrupt silence means he may have missed his opportunity, and the police might be getting ready for the next step.

He shakes his head and replies, "I don't know what to do. Should I sneak out the back and run away?"

Wayne clicks his teeth.

"The cops have your home surrounded. Even if you could escape, where would you go? How long will you survive on your own, off the grid, hiding your face from everyone who crosses your path? You know what you did. You understand the difference between right and wrong. More importantly, you know the past will eventually catch up with you. You can run from the law, but you can't hide from yourself."

Calvin crawls to the center of the foyer, out of ideas, hopelessly wanting to surrender but searching for an answer.

Wayne comes to a stop in the doorway to the hall and says, "There is one option you can choose to avoid spending the rest of your days in a concrete cell. There's one plan you can execute to prevent the life of suffering you face."

"Which is?"

He looks to Wayne, who nods toward Calvin's arm. Then, he looks down, and his eyes widen at the sight of a gun gripped in his hand.

Wayne says, "That's right...your father's Colt .45 caliber revolver loaded with six hollow-point bullets."

Calvin pulls back on the hammer and observes the cylinder rotate to the next loaded chamber. The clicking sound marks the split second he realizes this shit just got real.

Rising to his feet, the anxiety nipping inside his chest won't go away. In fact, it's getting worse. His hands feel clammy, and a thin layer of cold sweat glistens across his brow. Suddenly, he feels weightless but also heavy, like a criminal astronaut floating through the vacuum of space while, at the same time, getting sucked into a black hole.

He shoves the gun's barrel between his teeth, and the tip scrapes the roof of his mouth. The sharp pain makes his eyes water. His heart pounds in the bottom of his throat. He can't swallow, and he can't stop shaking. Soon enough, the rest of his body goes numb because, like everyone else, it no longer wants anything to do with him.

Wayne says, "Try to stay focused," and asks, "Have you ever tasted metal before? Do you recognize the sensation of hard steel on your tongue? Is the idea of ending your own life anything like you imagined? All those trivial issues you faced before, all those times you thought you might be better off dead, they're laughable in the presence of this nightmare."

Calvin wonders if this will hurt. The tip of his index finger rests on the trigger, and if he squeezes it back any further, all of this goes away, fast, so quick, he won't even feel it. The brain can no longer interpret pain once it's been splattered across the wall.

Wayne continues chewing and says, "Your actions will be justified, and people will say you paid the price. They'll say you've squared your account with society. You've shed the blood of others, so it serves you right to shed your own. What other choice do you have? One way or another, you are going down. You know it, the police know it, everyone knows it, and there's no doubt about it; you've earned yourself a one-way ticket to hell."

Calvin is on the verge of tears. He groans and wants to respond, but it's hard to speak with a gun between his teeth. Wayne senses his distress, his hopelessness of finding no other option.

He takes a step toward Calvin, and with his hand out, says, "But wait a second. Take a moment to think this through. Suicide is a permanent solution to a temporary problem. Most issues promise a resolution no matter how desperate the circumstances may seem. Then again, there's nothing temporary about the retribution those cops plan to give you, not after what you've done. There's nothing short-term about spending your remaining years on death row, begging for your final day to arrive so you can escape the torment you've set in place. I wish I knew what to tell you other than state the obvious: this may not be the best plan after all."

The grandfather clock near the wall begins to chime, letting the two men know the hour has arrived. Through blurry tears, Calvin sees the face, and both the long and short hands point to the Roman numeral for twelve—XII—midnight. It's the dawn of a new day. A clean slate, but not in his case. He knows he's not getting out that easily.

Wayne glances at his watch and says, "It's time to make a decision."

The longer Calvin waits, the more nervous he becomes. With tears streaming down each cheek as he gags on a thick rod of metal, he wishes someone had stopped him long before it came to this. He wishes somebody had talked some sense into him, to convince him that what he did was wrong and what he is doing now is a very, *very* bad idea.

Wayne asks, "What's left to say? There's no one else to blame for you landing yourself in this predicament. There's no one coming to the rescue. The people who loved you, who were there for you in stressful times, your friends and family, they're dead and gone. You know this because you killed them. You are the sole person responsible for their demise. I know you, Calvin. I know how much you want to go back in time and make different decisions, but guess what? We are way too late in the game for that."

As his surroundings become clear, Calvin anticipates the possibility that in a split second, the bullet will blast through his head and exit the back of his skull like a bloody, brainy bolt of electricity.

Wayne cautiously takes another step forward, slowly chewing his gum.

He says, "Your hands are shaking. Either you pull the trigger on purpose, or your trembling finger will accidentally do it for you. With sweaty palms, the gun might slip from your grasp, and then what? It might land on the floor hard enough to misfire and send a bullet whizzing through the ceiling. The cops might hear the shot and decide to move in. Then, you will have missed your chance to get out of this dire situation at your own will. The police will kick down the door and bust through the windows, and if you continue to pose a threat, they'll take you out faster than you can beg them not to."

Sobbing, Calvin pulls the gun from his mouth and lowers it to his side. Something crashes through the glass panel, the window by the door. Something he thinks is a rock at first, but it smashes into the wall and clunks when it hits the floor, landing beside a family photograph with a twisted frame. The object hisses as puffs of white dusky fog spray from inside and fill the foyer, creating a thick cloud. Calvin is blinded by the tear gas. A cop's voice, a woman's voice shouts an order from a megaphone outside.

"Calvin Delacroix. Your house is surrounded. Come out with your hands in the air."

The front door bangs and rattles from someone trying to get in. The deadbolt is locked, but the wooden frame splits more with each thud. Calvin looks down at his hand. He feels the gun but can't see it. Spinning around, with the home too engulfed in a haze of smoke, flashing red and blue strobing the fog, soon, he can't tell which direction he's facing. His eyes sting and water. He feels suffocated. His lungs burn. Mucus gushes from his nose.

In a desperate attempt to prevent what he fears will happen if he doesn't answer, he shouts, "I can't come out! I can't find the exit."

The woman's voice on the megaphone assists him, saying, "To the front, to the left. That's where you'll find it!"

A glow beams from the windows, forming a majestic pathway, like the sun shining through the clouds. Calvin stretches his hands, feels the wall, and finally touches the knob.

When he escapes to the porch, a deep voice shouts from the front lawn.

"Get on the ground! Show me your hands!"

Lines of red lasers stretch across the yard and end with bright dots on Calvin's chest.

The voice shouts again, "This is your final warning! You have ten seconds to get on your knees and show me your hands!"

Even though he can't be seen, Calvin believes Wayne is still inside, lost in the fog. From each direction comes a whirring sound, like a small electric saw burrowing through a hard surface. Calvin smells the strange scent of bone as though a dentist is drilling into his teeth.

He yells, "This can't be real!"

The police think he's yelling at them with a gun in his hand, and he's become more of a threat than before.

The cop shouts, "Ten!"

From somewhere behind him, Wayne says, "I told you before; this is your gig. It's your show. You paid for the props. You built the foundation to punish yourself, and now, your horrific thoughts are mixed up with wholesome memories. That's why I wanted you to tell me about your relationship with Addelyn, how it came to be. That's why I suggested Vance in all those memories instead of you. I had to get you to second-guess yourself. Like the Basic Complimentary Color Theory—two colors, opposing the other, like each conflicting side of a story. Unfortunately, you're so lost; you don't know what to believe…"

Calvin's life of means flashes before his eyes. He thinks back to his childhood, meeting Addelyn for the first time in the park, picking flowers, and the kiss she gave him on the cheek. He begins to sob.

The cop shouts, "Nine!"

Shadows and silhouettes of soldiers with rifles inch their way toward the front porch.

Wayne's voice returns, but with burning eyes and gas venting from the open door, Calvin can't see him.

"You paid for everything with your jealousy. All the furniture, purchased by your suspicions. The curtains, the accessories, covered by your irrational decisions…"

Calvin recalls the first time he kissed Addelyn at summer camp. The red team, the blue team. Running off together in the woods. The clear sky. The Milky Way. The first time their tongues touched, how they couldn't pull away, caressing her face, holding her hand while seated around the campfire. The pain is so great; he clutches his chest.

The police see the gun, and the officer shouts, "Eight!"

Wayne raises his voice and says, "You decorated the walls with negligence. The best toys you bought and paid for with your failure to pay attention…"

Calvin sees memories of Addelyn in her cheerleading uniform, pushing him back, kissing and holding him, accepting his invitation to be a part of a life that ultimately leads to this.

"Seven!"

Wayne says, "Your lack of control. Your deranged sexual fantasies..."

Calvin recalls his dance with Addelyn at their prom. The way she looked. Her dress. The hotel. The hot tub. Making love for the first time. He hears her say, "I love you," and replies, "I love you."

"Six!"

The officers continue their approach. Calvin's face is masked with dismay.

Wayne's voice says, "All you had to do was speak up. All you had to do was say something to someone, anyone. You became so obsessed with doing the right thing, with making the right moves, with trying to make everything around you perfect for your family. But remember what I said about perfection? It's a mirage. It's a rainbow in your backyard. The closer you get, the farther it moves away. It's something you can chase but not acquire. The pot of gold doesn't exist..."

Calvin recalls his college years. The time he thought Addelyn took a trip to Destin, Florida, only to show up on his doorstep with her suitcase at her side.

"Five!"

Wayne continues, "Which is why everything fell apart. A thread of elegant fabric came loose. Rather than acknowledge the flaw, you ignored it. You signed it off..."

Calvin recalls the wedding. The first dance. Flashing images of Addelyn walking down the aisle, approaching him at the altar, but here, in front of him, it's the police on their approach.

"Four!"

Wayne smacks his gum, saying, "Flaws don't vanish

simply because you ignore them. Eventually, they unravel. The damage gets worse until it's far beyond repair. Had you caught it earlier, all this, everything, your pain, your rage, your destruction, this moment, it could have been avoided…"

The officers move close enough for Calvin to see the tips of their rifles aimed at no one but him. If he doesn't comply with their demands, the last thing he will see is a parade of bullets charging through the air toward his head.

He yells, "There's no way I did this!"

He recalls the honeymoon at Myrtle Beach, making love to Addelyn, conceiving their daughter, Maddie. He falls to his knees, still holding the shiny revolver.

"Three!"

Wayne says, "Hell is what you create. It's as real as you make it…"

Calvin recalls the birth of his daughter. Her sweet face, her tiny hands, gripping his finger. His wife, his baby girl, the three of them. He can hear her giggle and cackle, then cry.

"Two!"

He recalls Paul and Lillian helping them move. The grandfather clock. Seeing Addelyn on the swing in their backyard. All of these good memories of the perfect life he'd been given, now torturing him because he knows this life is gone. The pain worsens.

The cops advance with their rifles aimed, and one shouts, "Get on the ground!"

Shaking his head, Calvin yells, "If I can't have my family back, I'd rather die!"

Wayne's voice calms and says, "Well, my friend. That's precisely what I am here to prevent."

Calvin turns the gun on himself and shoves the barrel in his mouth. The police refrain from coming any closer. The same female officer with the jet black ponytail and a sleeve of tattoos, the one he recalls seeing at the nightclub, spreads her hands apart and shouts, "Take a deep breath!"

Everything seems to move in slow motion, and volume descends to a sustained tone, like ringing in Calvin's ears. His eyes float to the woman's vest, to her name badge above her breast pocket—A. Mayfield.

He remembers Quincy, the CEO and founder of *The A Corporation*, and the mention of his daughter, a police officer.

In comparison to the life he had obtained, the obstacles he overcame, the respect he earned, and the love from his family, Calvin recognizes that his own attempts at this kind of success have entirely gone to shit.

Close your eyes. Clear your mind. Don't think of anything. Give up what you don't deserve. Let go of all you live for and squeeze the trigger.

From somewhere behind him, Wayne blows a bubble, and it pops.

The gun goes off.

The bang is deafening.

Calvin's vision goes black.

There's nothing, not anymore.

No concept of time. No cognizance. No perception.

He's dead, and he doesn't even know it.

...Count Backward

There's a man's soothing voice echoing through the blackness.

It says, "Relax. Take and deep breath and count backward from ten...nine...eight...seven..."

I've heard his voice before, but it's been a while. I can't place it.

"Six...Five...Four...Three...Two..."

We didn't make it, did we? We didn't reach *one*.

The voice fades away.

I'm aware of the blindness, deafness and strangely *un*aware of how long I've been like this.

Is this what it's like to be dead? If so, should I be able to ask? Maybe this is the afterlife I didn't believe in. Maybe I've been proven wrong. If this is hell, it's surprisingly peaceful and calm.

Come back to life.

I can feel myself lying on something soft and comfortable. I sense the weight of gravity and the warmth of a blanket. I can wiggle my toes and twitch my finger. The air smells like disinfectant with a fresh lemon scent. It's nothing too offensive, but I didn't expect hell to smell so clean. I thought purgatory was supposed to be painful, but the only pain I'm aware of is subtle irritation on the front left side of my forehead. It's not an ache like before, not a throbbing migraine, rather more superficial.

Something is different, better, relieving, but I can't put my finger on it, and I mean this literally. My arms are too weak to lift my hand to inspect this discomfort.

I notice I'm not in handcuffs. I'm not shackled to the rails.

Did I live through the standoff? Did I survive the self-inflicted gunshot?

My wrist itches in the same spot where the lobster bit me. Why, though? It's been long enough for the sore to heal.

My thoughts are clear, no longer distorted, but still, I wish I knew what was happening.

Don't worry. I'm as equally confused as you.

My lips feel chapped, and I can barely wet them with my tongue. There's a metallic taste coming from the back of my throat. Without thinking about it, and similar to how my mouth would speak if it were doing so involuntarily, I respond to the odd man's voice by asking, "Shouldn't we wait for my family?"

Oh, that's right; they're dead. I know this because I killed them. This *must* be hell because my heart fills with heavy guilt that makes my body feel like it's sinking into the mattress. It's like the sensation of being pulled toward the Earth's core, and any minute now, I expect to feel the heat from the flames. But you know what? I deserve it.

Who is speaking? I struggle to identify the voices. The deep voice comes from the same man who told me to relax, take a deep breath, and count backward.

He says, "Congratulations," but to someone else. Then, he says, "I'm glad you came to me. Isn't it amazing? Hours have passed, but he didn't miss a second."

Why is he talking about me like I'm not in the room?

He must be conversing with a woman who replies, "He went away mid-sentence and came back to finish where he left off without missing a beat."

This might not work if they can't hear me, but I mumble, "What are you saying?"

The man replies, "You were asking about your family before, and you're asking about them now."

I try not to cry, but I can't help it. My head rocks from side to side. I sniffle and frown. If I am alive, I sure as shit don't want to be. Why are they keeping me in this cozy environment? What are they waiting for? Go ahead and lock me away for eternity! Bind me in chains and throw me into a flaming pit.

A gentle hand rests on my shoulder, and the man says, "Relax. Take a deep breath."

My head continues to sway, and I feel liquid trickling down my cheeks. The tears soak into the pillow behind my ears. My abs ache with each whimper.

With a raspy voice, I say, "Damn it, Wayne. Stop telling me to relax." Why did you bring me back? Why didn't you let me stay dead?"

The man says, "Well, my friend. That is precisely what I am here to prevent." Then, he asks, "Who is Wayne?"

The woman's voice answers, "Wayne Graves. He's our realtor."

Did I hear what I think I heard? Did you?

My eyelids are crusty and sticky like they've been glued shut. Obviously, it's not the case because I'm able to slowly open them as though I'm seeing the world again for the first time. My vision becomes more clear with each blink. Through narrow slits, my eyes adjust to the brightness of a panel of fluorescent bulbs on a ceiling. The last drop of cold tears streams down my temple. Is this what hell looks like?

A silhouette stands above me. The only details I can

define are long hair and perfume that smells sweet, a fragrance of Nashi pear, lotus flower, and balsa wood—the same fragrance Addelyn used to wear before I...I don't want to say it. Of all the senses, smell has the least resistant path to memory, but all I want to do is forget. I cough and begin to choke.

Please let me do this. Let me suffocate on my own phlegm, drown in my own saliva, suffer from inhaling my last breath. Let me die again, and this time, let me stay that way.

A firm hand grips mine and pulls my arm to help me sit up. A pillow slides behind my back.

The man says, "Get him some water," and now, it's coming back to me. I'm starting to remember his voice.

The tip of a plastic straw touches my lips, and cool water trickles down my throat.

The woman's hand rubs my back, and she says, "You're fine. I'm right here."

You still don't know what's going on, do you?

Don't feel bad. Neither do I.

This water is refreshing, and I swallow it like I have a mouth full of cotton, but the metallic taste remains, and my throat begins to ache. I release a breath and focus on the hand holding the cup as it floats away. There's a wedding band on the left ring finger. Shiny manicured nails painted violet, like pansy blossoms. I lift my face to see who they belong to, and my heart skips a beat as it has done so many times before. There is only one woman I know who has this effect on me. Strands of curly, blonde hair tickle my cheeks as she plants a kiss on my forehead. Her touch feels like home.

No. There's no way. It can't be, but is it?

"Addelyn?"

Her perfect lips smile and say, "Hi, sweetheart."

This isn't happening. As much as I want it to be, it's not real. It's impossible. No one could survive what I put her through. Even after, I tried to revive her and failed.

Am I dreaming? Can you dream when you're dead?

Part of me wants to get excited; the other is hesitant to get my hopes up. Either way, I can't help myself. I hug her tight, and I don't want to let go. Not now, not ever. She feels so real. The warmth of her body. The softness of her skin. Is this her? Alive and in the flesh? I consider the possibility of being in Heaven, reunited with her spirit, but what kind of God would reward me like this after what I've done? I'm not sure what to think.

After a knock, the door opens to a young couple.

Paul? Lillian? She has a baby in her arms. Is that...Maddie?

Oh! My sweet baby, Maddie!

What is all this? There's no other explanation. I must have sentenced myself to an eternity of torment in the false presence of people I betrayed.

I say, "This must be hell," and I'm wondering if this is the hell I created for myself, decorated how I see fit.

Paul chuckles and says, "Far from it, buddy."

I try to get out of bed, to rush to them and hug them, to hold my daughter, but Paul says, "Whoa, take it easy. One thing at a time."

He doesn't understand; I need this, I need assurance. If nothing else, I need to apologize, to say I'm sorry, to get down on my knees and beg for forgiveness. I didn't mean them any harm.

The real me would never do anything to hurt them. I wasn't in my right mind. I let the worst get the best of me.

You know where I'm coming from, don't you? You were with me through all of it. Were you not the voice in my head?

No?

Of course not. Why would you be?

Like the sun peeking around the edge of a passing storm cloud, as my surroundings become clear, I can't recall a time when reality has been so lucid.

Lillian bounces Maddie in her arms and asks me how I feel.

I tell her I'm not sure.

Too many emotions collide, and it's hard for me to sort them out. My wrist itches again, and when I go to scratch it, I discover an IV taped to my skin. There's a bag of fluid hanging from a hook beside my bed, and the line runs down my arm to my left wrist, where I thought a lobster pinched me.

"Lobster's revenge," I say, out loud, but not meaning to.

Paul snickers and asks, "What are you talking about?"'

He should know, though, right? Didn't Addelyn tell him about it over dinner? Never mind.

I look across the room to another man flipping through pages on his clipboard, leaning back against a countertop. A white coat. Hair, pulled back in a man-bun. He sits on a stool and rolls to my bedside.

"Well," he says, and finally, I recognize his voice and put a face to the name. "It's about time," he adds. "It's good to see you're awake."

"Am I in the hospital? How did I get here?"

The doctor laughs and says, "I think you're a little fuzzy from the anesthetic. You came in for your appointment, remember?"

My stomach growls as if I've skipped breakfast and lunch, and he says, "You've been fasting all day. I'll have the cafeteria send something down for you to eat."

"Appointment? What appointment?"

I think back. I think hard, not only about the big things but the little things about the little things—the smallest details of the smallest details.

A digital alarm clock, blaring from the nightstand—8:00 A.M. Addelyn rolling over in bed. Maddie babbling infant talk through the baby monitor. Stomach growling. Warm shower. Hot shave. Ticking wrist watch—9:00 A.M. Comfortable clothing—Nordstrom cargo shorts and cotton Guess t-shirt. No breakfast. Good-bye kisses and I love yous—"Don't be late," before Addelyn's reply, "We'll meet you there."

The doctor says, "The surgery took about five hours, but you pulled through with flying colors. Let me show you the results."

Five hours? Do you mean the standoff with police, or…wait…surgery? Is that why I can't remember anything past noon?

He removes an ink pen from his shirt pocket and clicks the button with his thumb. Using the tip, he holds a negative image, a scan, like an x-ray of someone's head, likely mine, I assume. As he does this, I inspect the identification badge he has clipped to his scrubs—Dr. Vance Allen—Neurology.

You have *got* to be kidding me.

I don't know what to call him. The doctor? The neurologist? The brain specialist? The whatever?

As much as I despise him, I can think of a few other names, like—wait a minute.

Why am I filled with these angry emotions, and why are they dissipating so rapidly? I don't hate him. I have no reason to hold a grudge. Do I?

Vance uses his pen to point to an area of my brain and says, "This area here is called the frontal lobe. Any obstruction to this area can lead to changes in personality, sexual behaviors, socialization, memory, attention, as well as increased risk-taking. Fortunately for you, my friend, we caught it early."

"Caught what early?"

"The tumor. Don't worry; it's benign, but pressing against this portion of the brain can cause issues with your emotions, reasoning, motor skills, and cognition. Had we not removed it in time, things would have eventually taken a turn for the worst."

"A tumor? Like the one that killed my father?"

Vance appears confused, as if the tips of his eyebrows have come together for a meeting above his nose.

He skims through his records and says, "You didn't mention a family history of tumors when we had our consultation."

Consultation? Where is he going with this?

"My father died a year ago when Maddie was born."

Everyone looks at each other suspiciously. Clearly, they know something I don't.

Addelyn slides her hand on my shoulder and tells me, "Sweetheart, your father's not dead."

"Of course he is. You were there. He and my mother both died when—"

Wait a second. It's hard for me to admit, but it's like I've been talking in my sleep and waking up to realize what I'm saying may not be true.

Lillian says, "Calvin, your parents are in the waiting room. They're both fine. Last I saw, your father was talking to the registration clerk about paying your medical bill."

Medical bill? All of this comes at my father's expense? "How much?"

Vance tells me it's expensive, but I should feel blessed to have loving parents who are willing to pick up the tab.

He says, "Relax. This is likely from your brain in recovery. He produces another scan from his folder and says, "Let me show you." He uses his pen to point to the same spot as before. "Now, this is where we found it. Luckily, the removal was simple, and the voices should be gone."

"Voices? What voices?"

Strange, I remember hearing voices, I remember all the other symptoms, but now, I feel as if they never existed, like my head is clear.

"Damndest thing," says Vance with a chuckle. "I'm sorry, I didn't believe you before, but it's a good thing we're friends, and I can take you at your word." The muscles in my face scrunch together, forming a curious expression. Vance adds, "You came to my office, practically begging me to help you. Even though you didn't appear to be sick, you mentioned hearing voices telling you where to find a brain tumor—to the front, to the left." He says, "I was skeptical, but to put your mind at ease, I did the scan and found the tumor in the precise location. I called your home and gave Addelyn the results, and, at first, she worried how you would react had you not already known." He snickers and shakes his head. "I must admit, your case is one for the books."

I lean back on my pillow and touch my brow, where

there's a bandage from an incision. I run my fingers across my scalp, but my hair is gone.

"Why am I bald?"

Out of respect, I'll call him Doctor, and Dr. Allen stands and replies, "Don't worry. It will grow back. We needed to shave it before the surgery."

Addelyn grins and tells me she thinks my new look is sexy.

Paul gives me a thumbs up, winks, and says it looks good on me.

Lillian grimaces and tells me that she misses my hair.

Maddie points at me and giggles.

I'm feeling better, but more questions remain unanswered.

"Confusion is normal," says Dr. Allen. "It may take a while for the medicine to wear off."

I lick my lips and taste the lingering flavor in my mouth.

"Why do I taste metal? Is that from the gun?"

Addelyn leans to the side and asks, "Gun? What gun?"

Dr. Allen shakes his head, reassuring her that what I'm asking is normal.

He explains, "It's from the intubation. We use something called a laryngoscope. It has a dull blade that we insert into your throat to push aside the anatomy of your airway. Then, we place a plastic tube into your windpipe. This way, we are able to control your breathing with a ventilator while we perform the procedure. Have you ever tasted metal before? I doubt you recognize the sensation of having hard steel pressed against your tongue. It's not very pleasant, but it will go away."

This is too much information to sort through, but I'm beginning to comprehend. My family is here. They're safe.

Alive. And right when I think things can't get any better, Addelyn's face brightens, and she tells me she has some exciting news.

She says, "I'm—"

I interrupt, "Pregnant."

"How did you know? I didn't find out until this morning."

My attention draws to a mark on her neck, a hickey. My heart sinks into my stomach, and I want to puke. This may not be the happy ending I had hoped for. From the corner of my eye, I notice something on the wall. A painting, abstract artwork with orange-yellow and blue-violet—basic complimentary color theory—two colors opposing the other, like each side of a story. It's not erotic like the image I recall from my living room. This is more anatomic. In the bottom corner are two painted initials—VA.

Oh, no. What kind of drugs did he give me? Some kind of potion to wipe my memory? Is the baby mine or is it—no, I don't want to know. Heat seeps from beneath my skin, and I wish the pounding in my chest would stop so this time I really would die. Judging from the look on Vance's face, the guilt-ridden mask of embarrassment as though he's been caught, exposed, for doing something wrong. It's clear to me that five hours of my unconsciousness is the perfect opportunity for him to take advantage of my wife. Is he truly my surgeon, or was he alone somewhere, screwing Addelyn on a desk or a hospital bed? Is that why Lillian and Paul have been watching Maddie? Were they babysitting this whole time?

Vance's voice begins to muffle like I'm hearing him from underwater. I can't believe it. Should I be surprised if Addelyn's baby comes out with a man-bun and a tiny baby middle finger in my face? Will it be a smirking fetus whose biological father got the best of me? The idea makes me grind my teeth, my fists clench, it makes my sight seem like I'm stuck in a tunnel of distorted truth.

I can barely hear him asking, "You like it, huh?"

Is this what he asked Addelyn when they were together?

He says, "I do some painting in my spare time. My wife says it's important to keep a healthy balance between work and life."

Vance Allen, you slimy little—wife? Did he say his wife?

Shaking my head, my ill thoughts vanish. The room comes back to me. Everything is clear again. Focused.

"You're married?" I ask, feeling the color return to my face.

Vance chuckles and shows me a photograph from his wallet of him standing next to his beautiful wife in her swimsuit on a beach with an ocean backdrop.

He says, "Selina and I have been together since college. How could you forget?"

I think about it. Vance and Selina. Her brother Todd and his girlfriend. Addelyn and myself.

That's right. Of course.

"Spring break."

Vance nods and grins.

He says, "Yes. The six of us flew down to Destin, Florida."

Why did I think Selina and Todd were my parent's neighbors? How could I believe that Addelyn would cheat on me even for a moment? She's my best friend, the love of my life. Vance, he's my friend too, always has been. At least, since high school. What a silly and ridiculous idea.

Addelyn notices me glancing at her neck.

She touches it and asks, "What's the matter?" She says, "It's healing."

I tell her to remind me.

She does so by saying, "My stylist at the hair salon, she accidentally burned me with her curling iron."

I remember her saying something about it the night we had people over for dinner. While she stocked the refrigerator with groceries, I recall her telling me something about burn cream for her neck.

Boy, do I feel stupid. What is wrong with me? There's no reason I should question her. I trust Addelyn with my life. She's always been faithful to me, and I've always been faithful to her, I think.

Lillian is sitting in a chair, and I watch her bounce Maddie on her knee.

Did I make a mistake? Did I bang my sister-in-law in the guest bathroom? Don't get me wrong, she's attractive, but I couldn't do it if I had been in my right mind. She's like a sister to me, and besides, I love Addelyn way too much. I'm relying on this because Lillian is alive; I didn't kill her, and therefore, did nothing else to her.

It's all coming back to me now, and when I laugh, Addelyn asks, "What's so funny? We've been trying to have another baby for a while. I thought you'd be over the moon."

How silly of me. Addelyn and I make love all the time. In the guest bath, the swimming pool, the sauna, the hot tub. We tried to sneak in a quickie at the nightclub near the stage, but Lillian and Paul were too close to us. And speaking of which, Paul wasn't kissing some other girl. That night, he and Lillian couldn't keep their hands off each other.

I touch Addelyn's chin, smile, and say, "I *am* over the

moon. I can barely contain my excitement, but I'm still trying to recover from these crazy thoughts."

She wants to know what kind of crazy thoughts I'm having, and I give an example. "Remember the last time we made love in our master bedroom. Afterward, you went downstairs to the kitchen to fix a cup of tea. At first, I thought I saw Vance running naked across our backyard, but it must have been me, which is why you tried to get me to come inside out of the cold."

Addelyn looks to Vance with skepticism, and he shakes his head, dismissing what I just said.

He suggests I stay overnight for observation and says, "You can go home tomorrow."

Panic sets in, and I shoot straight up in bed.

"Home!"

Addelyn holds my hand and says, "Yes, baby. Home."

"Our house is a mess. Everything has been destroyed."

"Sweetheart, we haven't moved into our house, remember? Wayne said he's waiting on the contractors to fix a leaking water pipe and replace the wiring."

Confused, I ask, "Then where do we live?"

"In our apartment, downtown."

She cups my chin and wonders if I'm okay, but how am I to know?

Oh, this isn't good. How could we have made love in a house we don't live in? How could I have run naked through a backyard on a property I don't own yet?

I feel like Dorothy in Kansas, waking up to a bad version of a *Victor Fleming* movie.

I tell everyone, "You were there. Or maybe not. I must have had a nightmare during surgery and assigned everyone a role to play."

Dr. Allen scratches his chin and says, "Unfortunately, my friend, it's unlikely. When you dream, your brain enters a deep state. A REM cycle, they call it. However, sleep is required in order to reach this level. Trust me; you were chemically sedated throughout the procedure, so there's no way you could have experienced a nightmare."

I know what you're thinking because I'm thinking the same; this doesn't explain a thing.

There's no ex-machina to answer any of our questions. How is it possible for me to rehash memories inside a house I don't possess? If Addelyn and I haven't moved in yet, why am I certain of everything that happened in each room? The burn cream? The dinner? The lobster bite? The swimming pool, the sauna, the nightclub? Making love wherever we could? What, then? How am I supposed to understand?

Dr. Allen senses my dismay. He can tell I'm stressed. He takes a seat on the edge of the bed and gives me his two cents.

He says, "People believe they know the specifics of how an event occurred, and they become so convinced, they are willing to bet their lives on it. Recalling an event in precise detail is impossible. What you see comes from your impressions of hindsight, not from the original memory. There are many reasons for this, though none are specific. Some people see what they want to see. Some remember the story the way they wish it happened, and when minor attributes escape, the gaps are filled with distorted variety. In all..." He pats my knee and says, "...the brain is a big fat liar."

"I don't get it. How can I have memories of things if they didn't happen?"

Standing, Vance scratches his chin and replies, "Well, your experience is likely nothing more than some vivid hellscape your imagination came up with."

It shouldn't matter because I have my friends and family back, but I'm still not convinced. This can't be explained as simple delusions. I was there, and so were you. It was more real than anything else I've witnessed. I need to find the truth if there is such a thing.

Dr. Allen pauses before he leaves.

He turns back with a cocked head and says, "Out of curiosity, Calvin. What *do* you remember?"

For Sale by Owner…

Tragedy doesn't care how much money you have in your bank account. Misery pays no mind to your social status. Devastation thinks nothing of the clothes you wear or the car you drive. Tribulation doesn't give a shit how perfect you think your life has become. It's inevitable—bad things happen to everyone, and in the end, everyone dies with the same lifeless expression.

Between the two and three-story houses spread long yards of grass divided by borders of small tree lines and fences. At the naive age of twenty-six, Calvin Delacroix is uncertain whether he has everything figured out. Here at 2700 Ironsmith Court, he waits alone on his front porch for a guest to arrive. Even though this meeting is informal, Calvin strives to look his best with slim jeans, a loosely buttoned dress shirt, a bronze tan, and stylish, tawny-brown, regrown hair.

A middle-aged couple, Mr. and Mrs. Silver, push their baby grandson in a stroller along the sidewalk. At first, Calvin's too busy thinking of how he got here, but not in a directional sense. He's not retracing the routes he took or complaining about the traffic he waited through. He's focused on more significant questions. He thinks back, trying to recall what he's done throughout his life to achieve such success. He thinks hard about what events led to his victory. More importantly, he wonders where, oh, where did it all go *right?*

Mrs. Silver nudges her husband's arm and nods in Calvin's direction. With smiles on their faces, they wave.

Mr. Silver says, "You must be the new owner. We live

down the street."

Calvin shakes his hand and introduces himself.

Mrs. Silver says, "It's nice to see a new family moving in. This house has been empty for more than a year. The previous owner was a certified looney."

"So I've heard."

Stepping back so Calvin can see the infant in the stroller, Mrs. Silver says, "This is our baby grandson," and asks, "Do you have children?"

"My daughter is two years old, and my son is three months."

Mrs. Silver gasps and places a hand on her chest

She smiles and says, "Oh, children are such a blessing. We wish you the best in your new home. If you need anything, please don't hesitate to stop by."

The couple strolls away, and Calvin catches the man across the road filling his lawnmower with gasoline.

With a friendly wave, he shouts, "Welcome!"

Daylight arches above this neighborhood as the wheels of a navy-blue Ford F-150 pickup truck come rolling into the driveway and squeal to a halt. A decal with the company name—*Graves' Northside Realty & Appraisal*—and a slogan beneath in smaller text—*'Moving you forward'* is printed on the side of the vehicle.

Calvin waits for the driver to step out. Wayne's appointment at the Delacroix's house is his most important stop of the day. He approaches with a *Crest*-white smile with a single key in hand, and a clipboard tucked beneath his arm. Thick-framed reading glasses hang from a string around his neck. He slides them to the bridge of his nose and removes an ink pen from his breast pocket.

He checks his wristwatch, 11:59 A.M.

"It's about time. Are you ready? I'm sure you have a million things you'd rather be doing, but time is of the essence."

Smiling and glancing at a full view of the blue sky, the sunlight, the white clouds, and the surrounding neighborhood, Calvin shakes his head and says, "No rush. I've got all the time in the world."

Wayne peers over the top of his frames, across the street, and over two houses to where the neighbors, Mr. and Mrs. Hill, waving from their window.

Wayne says, "Good people," and both he and Calvin wave back. Wayne removes a packet of bubble gum from his pocket and tosses a piece in his mouth. He offers another to Calvin, who politely declines.

Wayne says, "Your surgery went well, I presume."

"How did you know about the—"

He taps the left side of his brow and explains, "Your father sent me a copy of the medical bill to show you had no outstanding debts. $69,286. That's a lot of money. I was afraid we might have to sell all your furniture." He laughs. "I'm joking, of course."

Calvin's eyes squint with curiosity.

What a strange thing to say.

Wayne asks, "How's the job at *The A Corporation?* I know people who would sacrifice essential parts of their anatomy for a career like that."

Calvin snickers and says, "It's great. I've been promoted."

Bouncing his head, Wayne replies, "Well deserved." He pauses a beat and says, "Let's get on with it, shall we?"

Stretching his neck to see down the road, Calvin asks, "Should we wait for my family?"

The tip of the house key barely makes it to the lock before Wayne pauses.

"Are they coming?"

"I told Addelyn to meet us here." Wayne doesn't notice him staring at the back of his head, waiting for him to turn around. When he does, he stops chewing his gum and freezes, as if he's been caught doing something wrong. Calvin says, "Before they get here, maybe we should check inside to make sure the house hasn't been vandalized."

If Wayne doesn't know what Calvin is talking about, he's doing a pretty good job at pretending. He asks, "Why would we need to do that?"

With both hands in his pockets and a whimsical smile on his face, Calvin nods toward the bushes and says, "These roses. They were red before. Now they're white."

Wayne chuckles and says, "They've always been white."

"C'mon, Wayne." Calvin makes sure the coast is clear in both directions. There's no one coming down the street. No one is around to eavesdrop on the conversation. "We have a few minutes to talk about it."

Wayne narrows his eyes and asks, "Something happened during your surgery, didn't it?"

Puzzled, Calvin takes a step back and asks, "How did you—?"

"It happens all the time, but not nearly enough for anyone to recognize it. I meet people who experience the same thing in my career, even though they can't explain it. Something happens to them, some sort of physical or emotional trauma. Before they recover, the universe shows them a glimpse of how things are and how they could be. We think we know ourselves, but it makes you wonder if we've become who we truly intended."

Wayne tilts his head toward the sidewalk. "Like Mr. and Mrs. Silver with their grandchild. Had it not been for their car accident, things could have gone in a different direction altogether. They might have forced their daughter to abort her pregnancy and lived the rest of their lives angry at the world." He points across the street to the neighbor mowing his lawn. "Mr. Lang suffered a stroke. Luckily he made a full recovery without any deficits; otherwise, he could be in jail right now for tax evasion without a penny to piss on."

Wayne turns Calvin's attention back toward Mr. and Mrs. Hill, who happily work together in their garden. The husband hands his wife a plant, she thanks him before placing it in the dirt, but not before he leans over to kiss her. Wayne says, "Last year, Mr. Hill had a seizure, one that nearly killed him. If not, who's to say he wouldn't be secretly meeting hookers in hotels and bringing home hepatitis to his wife?"

He turns back to face Calvin, stepping down off the front porch. He continues chewing his gum and says, "Not everyone your age is blessed with a beautiful family, a nice car, a big house. Not everyone inherits their wealth or has the world handed to them." He clicks his teeth. "Not without paying some kind of price." Wayne points to Calvin's scar, or where it would be if he could see it through his regrown hair. "The universe needed to make sure all of this didn't go to your head. A lot of people are so self-absorbed, blinded by superiority. This world was here way before we came along, and to reside in it, we enter an agreement in which it reserves the right to terminate at any time for any reason. In this contract, everyone must vacate eventually, some sooner than others. The problem with perfection is it doesn't exist, at least not for us. Only the universe is perfect by definition. It has the power to replace the damage from chaos with a remedy of order. Even though we hate to admit so, we have very little control. We spend decades working to earn currency to purchase luxury, but in the end, the things we obtain don't belong to us. They get taken away as easily as they've been given."

Scratching his chin, Calvin asks, "So, other people experienced the same things?"

Wayne shrugs and says, "For all I know, it happens to everyone at some point. I cross paths with men and women who have the potential to fulfill their dreams or destroy them. Sometimes they get lucky, and the universe allows them to choose based on their experience of something different. Even if a person is on the right path, some event happens, and they get pulled to the side, like hitting the pause button during a movie or video game. Whether it be an injury that renders them unconscious, they slip into a coma, or, like you, get chemically sedated. Whatever the case may be, you're given an option of how you want the rest of their life to turn out. You see the good and the bad, like the basic complementary color theory—two opposing colors, two sides of the same story. You make your choice, and when you come back, it's like waking from a dream you soon forget. The only difference with your situation, my friend, is that you remember everything. Why? I couldn't tell you."

Calvin sighs through his nose and takes a moment to let the lesson sink in.

"Truly, you are a geyser of knowledge."

Wayne returns to the porch and says, "Old Faithful. You bet your ass. Knowledge is power, my friend."

Calvin says, "One thing I don't understand. The timeline doesn't add up. If I went through a glimpse into the future, my parents would have died when Maddie was born. And Selina and Todd are friends from school, not my parent's neighbors."

Pausing once again at the front door, Wayne snickers, pops another bubble, and says, "I don't have all the answers. I assume the brain takes what it knows and assigns random people to play the part. When you're unconscious, there's no concept of time, no cognizance, no perception. It's like you're dead, and you don't even know it." Wayne points to the sky, wincing at the sunlight. He adds, "Maybe there's a reason for what happened to you. Maybe there's not. I wish I could give you answers, but all I can tell you is what I've learned from meeting new people and hearing their stories. There's nothing for you to worry about, my friend." He shakes Calvin's hand. "You're gonna be just fine."

"Are you sure about that?"

"Nope, not one bit. I'm just your ordinary, everyday realtor, putting the 'real' in 'real estate.' Nothing more, nothing less. But I know a humble person when I see one."

Calvin turns back to an empty street. He takes his cell phone from my pocket, scrolls through his contacts, and selects Addelyn's name beside a heart-shaped emoji. He presses the call button, but the line goes straight to voicemail. He hangs up, looks toward the horizon, and smiles when he sees Addelyn's car coming over the hilltop.

"There she is."

She parks in the street and opens the back door. She leans in and pulls Maddie, who's ecstatic to see her father. She's a toddler now, running on her own two feet. She shouts, "Daddy!" and Calvin's heart melts. He runs to her, lifts her up, hugs her, and swings her around. "How's my princess?"

Addelyn leans into the back seat and unfastens the straps of a car seat. She closes the door, holding a baby boy in her arms. She blows Calvin a kiss and waves hello to Wayne.

"Oh, is this your son? We haven't met."

Grinning, she tickles the baby's stomach and says, "This is Evan."

Calvin plants a kiss on his son's forehead, puts his arm around his wife, and squeezes Maddie close. Wayne reaches to shake Addelyn's hand.

She says, "We're so excited. I don't think we could put this off any longer."

"Violet Fane. Am I right?" He winks at Calvin, whose eyes go wide.

How did he know about—? You know what? Forget it.

He says, "Good things come to those who wait."

"Well, congratulations. Everything check out with the bank, the papers are signed, and this house is yours. I'm just here to do a walkthrough with you to each room and make sure there's no further damage."

"This can't be real," says Addelyn, pulling a strand of her hair from the clutches of her baby Evan. "It's like a dream come true."

Calvin grins and takes her hand.

"It's not a dream. It's the life I promised you, remember?"

Wayne stands behind, watching.

He says, "Everything has been remodeled. There's plenty of space for the kiddos. I need to fully disclose that the family who lived here died a year ago. It's a sad story.

The husband went insane and killed his wife, daughter, and three others before turning the gun on himself."

Addelyn puts a hand to her chest. "Oh my goodness, how terrible."

Calvin feels as though he's gone for a swim in an ocean of fear and has come ashore with a sense of relief. There's no way to know for sure, but to him, Wayne's version of his uncanny experience makes the most sense and provides the certainty he's been looking for. The future is bright, and Calvin can lift a confident chin, knowing whatever the future brings, good or bad, he's learned not to let the worst get the best of him.

He kisses his wife on the cheek and says, "Don't worry. It's in the past."

"That's right," says Wayne, slipping the key into the lock and twisting it to the left. "Time to move forward. You don't need to worry. You've got a good man taking care of you." He pats Calvin on the shoulder, steps over the threshold, holding the door open for the Delacroix family to enter, and asks…

"Are you ready?"

ABOUT THE AUTHOR

Bradley Carter is an award-winning independent author, born in Evansville, Indiana, and currently living in Indianapolis. He's been writing and self-publishing twisted thrillers and dark comedy fiction since 2017.

DID YOU KNOW?

-In the 1940s, a woman in Europe began hearing voices telling her where to locate her brain tumor despite showing other symptoms. She implored the staff at a London hospital to scan her brain, where they found the tumor in the precise location. After a successful treatment, the last thing the voices said to her was, *"We are pleased to have helped you. Goodbye."*

-A young man named *Charles Whitman* was twenty-five when he began experiencing severe headaches. In 1966, after killing thirteen people from a tower at the *University of Texas*, police found his suicide note requesting an autopsy. Specialists found a tumor pressing against the amygdala, a part of the brain that controls emotion, fear, and aggression. Some agree this tumor was the sole cause of turning a bright and talented young man into a mass murderer known as the *Texas Tower Sniper*.

-In the "Living Room" chapter, the titles of books on the shelf have significant meaning, and the first letter of each spell something important.

-The news on television are reports of events that take place in *"Bodhi Crocodile."*

-In a scene from *"Bodhi Crocodile Part 2: The Button,"* a character is distracted by a woman (Addelyn Delacroix) passing by a window as she heads toward the hair salon.

-The numerical address of the Delacroix residence, 2700,

is the word-count of the opening chapter. The street name, 'Ironsmith,' is an anagram for the book's title, *"In This Room..."* And finally, Court is part of the address for its definition of someone "being romantically involved."

-Although it's not named, Addelyn's perfume, *Bulgari Omnia*, was suggested by editor Jamie Thorn who also inspired Avery Mayfield, a character found in each of the author's books.

-World-renowned DJ and music producer *Bad Boy Bill* has a written cameo as the performer at the nightclub.

-Quincy Mayfield is the founder of *The A Corporation* (a fictional communications company) and the main character of the upcoming true-to-life thriller, *"From the Sky."* He is introduced in the "Sauna" chapter, and a brief synopsis of his story is described in his scene. Also, in this chapter, Calvin's line, *"Addelyn and I loved our daughter without even knowing her...loving the idea of her existence,"* is a replica of how Quincy describes his mother at the beginning of this forthcoming series.